NİGHT FALLS
ON DAMASCUS

NIGHT FALLS ON DAMASCUS

·

FREDERICK HIGHLAND

THOMAS DUNNE BOOKS

St. Martin's Minotaur

New York

This is a work of fiction. All of the characters, organizations, and events portrayed in this novel are either products of the author's imagination or are used fictitiously.

THOMAS DUNNE BOOKS.
An imprint of St. Martin's Press.

www.thomasdunnebooks.com

www.minotaurbooks.com

Map by Carolyn Chu
Illustration by Ana Maria Gallo
Design by Kathryn Parise

ISBN-13: 978-0-312-33789-6
ISBN-10: 0-312-33789-2

First Edition: December 2006

10   9   8   7   6   5   4   3   2   1

To Edward Clark

"Ah, but a man's reach should exceed his grasp,

Or what's a heaven for?"

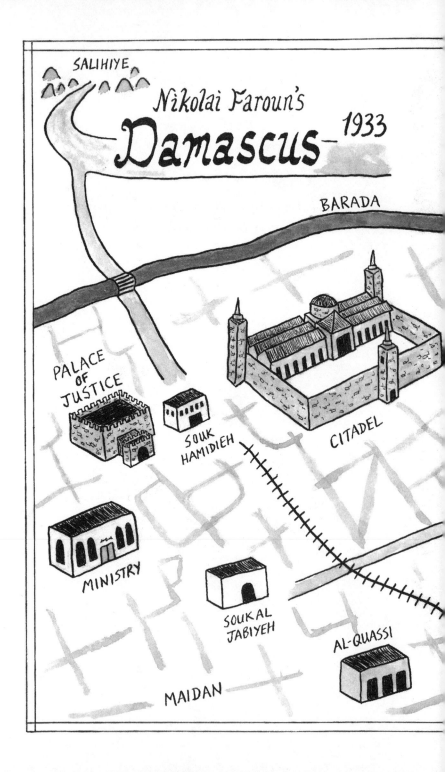

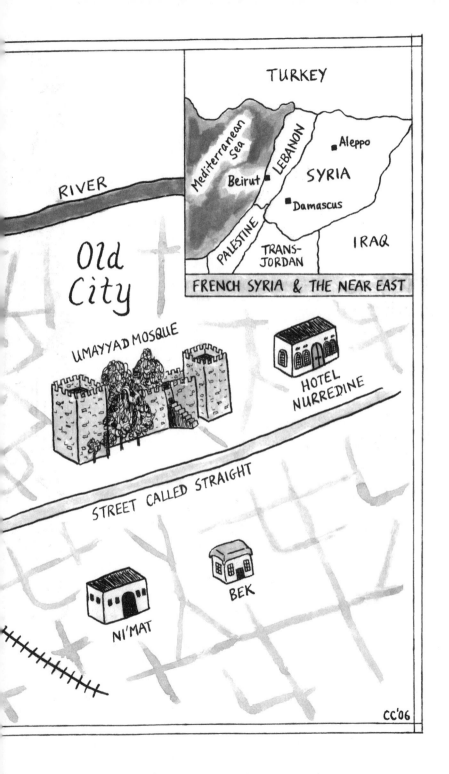

NİGHT FALLS
ON DAMASCUS

1

Even in the year 1903, caravans still traveled the Silk Road to Damascus, but they were no longer the great treasure trains of Arabian legend. Since the building of the Suez Canal, the ancient trade had dwindled. No more did one hear the shivering of bells on the harnesses of a thousand camels. The caravanners who stubbornly continued to ply their trade were as resigned as the brutes they cursed and coaxed out of the desert wastes. Times were hard. Even the bedouin bandits let them pass in peace. A score of half-laden camels were scarcely worth the fight. Western travelers were more likely to swoop down upon them in these days, cameras clicking. The drivers posed for piasters, but their smiles were worn and as bleak as their prospects. Then on they plodded to Damascus, travel-worn memorials to the passing of an age, knowing they would have little trouble finding a bed. The

Eight-Gated City with its soaring minarets still dominated the fertile Syrian plain, but now that steamships carried the riches of the Orient to Beirut, the inns of landlocked Damascus were silent and empty. Some compared the city to a once-pampered courtesan who had turned spiteful and hard.

Not that she had ever been even-tempered. Men had fought over her beguiling favors for centuries, and she had encouraged these attentions. Nor could she be trusted. Damascus was like a lover, wrote a Sufi poet, who lifted her veil while concealing a knife behind her back. Perhaps this history of deceit was on the mind of Tayeb Faroun as he spoke to his son, Nikolai, in the garden of their newly acquired villa overlooking the ancient city.

"A Turkish general was murdered here," said Tayeb Faroun. "Before this place became ours."

"Murdered, Father?"

"In his bath. By his body servant."

Young Nikolai turned his attention from a column of listless Turkish cavalry ambling through the Gate of Jupiter, or, as the Arabs called it, the Bab Al-Jabiyah, the Gate of Blessings. Sitting on the stone wall of the villa, he was practically eye to eye with the taciturn man in the business suit. He knew his father did not make up stories. His mother had been the storyteller. But his father kept much to himself and rarely said anything at all.

"Why did he kill the general, sir?"

"How old are you, Nikolai?"

"Ten, sir."

Tayeb Faroun took out an English cigarette and tapped it thoughtfully on a gold case before lighting up.

"The motive, it was rumored, was revenge. It seems the old general favored the company of young men and so the jealous body servant cut his throat while he was bathing. But I don't think that is what really happened. The true story is that the general had become very popular, and this offended the Sublime Porte."

"The Grand Door?" young Nikolai asked.

"That is the title—the honorific—by which the sultan in Istanbul is known."

"So the general offended the sultan?"

"Oh, yes. The body servant was merely carrying out the sultan's instructions. Sultans can be very jealous too." Tayeb Faroun released smoke in a long exhale and turned his attention to the city below. "Every house you see in the town below us, every room in every tenement of that city beyond," said Tayeb Faroun to his son, "has a thousand dark stories like that one, as far back as men remember."

"Why is that, Father?"

"Because Damascus is the oldest city in the world. Even older than Jericho in Palestine, I'm told."

"Older than Jericho?" the boy asked in disbelief.

Tayeb Faroun pointed to a hill in the distance. Nikolai stood on the garden wall to get a better look. "Abel is buried there."

"Cain slew him in envy," said the boy a bit self-consciously.

"Unfortunately, that murder wasn't the last. You might say the idea caught on," he chuckled, pleased at his grim joke.

"What happened to Cain, Papa?"

"God banished him to wander the earth."

"The police didn't put him in jail?"

"God was the police," said Tayeb Faroun. "And he was a lot tougher than the Turks."

Nikolai could not say for certain that this memory had been an omen, but now that he was chief of the Damascus Prefecture, he would often take his lunch to the promontory known as Abel's Tomb and look over the restive city whose peace he was assigned to keep. In the thirty years since young Nikolai had spoken with his father in the villa garden, great changes had overtaken Syria. The Turks had been defeated in the Great War and expelled from most of the Near East. For a brief moment of time, Prince Faisal al-Husseini, the grave and dignified warrior who had led the famed Arab Revolt against the Turks, had ruled the land. But in 1920, the French had driven the prince from Damascus and taken over Syria and Lebanon under a League of Nations mandate. The French were supposed to prepare their Arab wards for self-government, but everyone knew the occupiers intended to stay. So Arab resistance groups sprang up and the result was revolt, riot, and assassination. The French were heavy-handed, favoring artillery to diplomacy, a policy that fed the resistance.

By 1933, and six months after Nikolai Faroun had joined the Damascus civil police force known as the Prefecture, Syria verged on anarchy. The journey that had led Faroun to this post had begun when the young man had defied his father and signed up with a French Legionnaire unit during the Great War. It took many years for him to find his way home to Lebanon, but when he returned to Beirut, he learned that his father had died of heart failure in 1922. Gone were the fortune and his father's properties. The Maronite businessman from Lebanon had lost everything in speculation following the war. All that remained was the modest red-tiled villa in Mohajirene overlooking Damascus. The villa had been boarded up for years.

Faroun had been pleased to claim and renovate the property. He had hired some workmen. They had done a good job of restoring the roof and the façade. The interior of the house was still crammed with unpacked boxes, but Faroun was getting around to the task. The hours at the Prefecture were long, and some nights he didn't come home at all.

It was noon and one of Faroun's pleasures was to bring his lunch to Abel's Tomb. From this vantage point, the policeman could just discern the outline of the wall where he had once listened to father's story about the general and the sultan. He had just turned forty, a passage that seemed defined by his isolation. Long before his father died, his Russian mother had disappeared into the depths of her native land. An only child, he was the last of his father's line. A Lebanese working for the French occupiers, he was not a popular man. When his German girlfriend had thrown him over for a French officer a month ago, she had left behind a brindled cat. The cat had run away. Perhaps if he had been home once in a while and fed the thing, it would have stayed. Faroun folded the piece of wax paper that had held his egg sandwich and slipped it into his pocket. There was not much to mark the tomb of the Old Testament's first murder victim, an ancient stone cairn topped by a weathered iron crescent. Lunch over, he flipped up the kickstand of the Triumph motorbike and charged the air with the roar of the impatient engine. Down below, the crumbling honey-colored walls of Damascus were wonderfully picturesque. The oldest city in the world seemed in harmony with perfect creation, the navel of the earth, home of our first garden, the crossroads of ancient empire, and a place where all caravans found their end and their beginning. It looked picture-postcard sweet.

Abel's Tomb held a far deeper truth, as Nikolai Faroun's father had pointed out so long ago. Murder had begun here and it had caught on.

2

The streetlamp flickering at the end of Al Knisset Street gave only momentary substance to the shadows hurrying under the poplar trees. They carried their burden to the back of the black sedan, closed the trunk, and went around to the front. The motorcar started up and pulled away in a smear of blue exhaust.

This left only two men sitting in the remaining car, a sleek Rolls-Royce Phantom. They watched the sedan as it vanished into the night, and they were alone on the street.

"Where are they taking her?" Salim asked distractedly. He looked over at his brother Abdullah for an answer.

"That's not your worry now." Abdullah, a big man in a cashmere overcoat, nodded to the chauffeur in the front seat. The engine started up, a stealthy purr.

"I didn't do that to her," Salim protested as the touring car pulled away from the curb. "Do you think I would do that to her?"

"Did I say you killed her?" The other looked sourly out the window. "Head south, Hamid," he called to the driver. "Let's get out of the Christian Quarter. Go into the Maidan for a while."

"At this time of night, sir?"

"I didn't ask a question," Abdullah shot back. "Just make sure we aren't followed."

"As you say, sir."

"I loved her," said Salim, on the verge of tears.

"You see where that kind of love gets you." The big man settled his broad shoulders against the cushion. "You have a wife. What about your wife?"

"She is a donkey."

"You are the donkey!" fumed the other. "And it's because you act like a donkey that we're in this fix." He lowered his voice to a rumble. "You are lucky you even have a wife." Abdullah adjusted his tie, something he did when trying to control his temper. "Don't forget who picked that wife out for you."

The younger brother was silent, then blew his nose.

"All our lives, it has been one thing after another for you, Salim," the big man lamented. "Who picks up the messes? Me. I pick up the messes. But this business with that woman was the last straw. Not only a tramp, but a Christian tramp! She played you for the fool, Brother."

"What are they going to do with her?"

"She's not a person anymore. Don't worry about it. It's not your concern."

"She loved me!" Salim said defiantly. "She loved me like no other. When I find the animals that did this to her, I will kill them with my bare hands."

"You will do what I tell you," snarled the other. "Now, there's an end to it." A moment later Abdullah offered a fat Turkish cigar to Salim, but, petulantly, he pushed it away.

7

They drove around the darkened streets of the meanest district of Damascus for a while to cover their tracks. At one cross-street, Hamid rolled to a stop. Two gangs of toughs, Armenians and Alouite immigrants, had decided to settle scores beneath a streetlamp. They lit into each other with fists and clubs and knives and made a big commotion, more show than substance. The men in the Rolls-Royce were entertained for a few moments until Abdullah pulled out a large Parabellum revolver, rolled down the window, and fired twice into the air. The gangs froze, took one look at the car, and scattered in all directions. Abdullah and the chauffeur had a good laugh over this. Salim did not think it was funny.

"Why did you do that?" he asked fitfully.

"Twenty witnesses. We were here, not *there*."

"What if the police come after me?" Salim asked, once they were moving again.

"The police won't come after you. They won't find a thing."

Salim didn't look so sure.

"Cheer up," said Abdullah, patting his brother on the back. "Let's take a little drive into the country. We'll take a drive out to the Mozaffari mosque in the hill country and say our morning prayers." He lowered his voice, a man given to secrets. "We were nowhere near the Hotel Nurredine when all of this happened." Then he looked up and exclaimed, "Look over there!" The touring car pulled out of the back streets onto the wide Boulevard Farouk to the east of Damascus. "Look at the sunrise. God is giving us a glorious new day. We are going to say our prayers, Salim, and then you are going to go home and embrace your wife. And keep your mouth shut."

"They were animals," he said morosely. "I will make them pay for what they did."

Abdullah did not like the ominous tone. "Get it out of your head. You didn't see anything. And you didn't hear anything. And you don't say—anything! That's it, Brother. Just like the three wise monkeys."

3

Another wave of citizens, panic and fear distorting their features, broke around his police sedan and rushed on. Inspector Faroun's driver leaned on the horn, then threw up his hands. The policeman told him to wait it out as there seemed nothing else to do. Outside, a desperate man hiked up his robe and leaped on the hood of the car. He clattered over the roof, one leather sandal dangling from his foot. The bloodied foot left a smear on the windshield. Ahead, a frightened donkey was braying in the narrow street as it tried to drag a cart with a broken wheel. Debris and shattered glass from looted shops littered the sidewalks. Rounding the corner, a French armored car rolled into view, its gray turret turning from side to side like some beast of reckoning.

Faroun got out of the sedan to stretch his legs. He had received the call an hour before about the murder at the river. He had hoped the civil disturbance would not cross his path, but the black cats of revolt and riot were a common sight in the unruly city of Damascus, and this sighting had been entirely predictable. The Commodities Tax of 1933 was the tipping point, coming hard on the heels of other exactions the French administration had recently levied on its Syrian subjects. The merchants had turned out in droves, and the wholesalers, all the shopkeepers of Damascus, and the vendors from the neighborhoods and surrounding villages. This had been the perfect opportunity for Al Fatat nationalists and their comrades to organize a sympathy strike with the merchants. Faroun had watched them earlier that morning as they paraded down El Nasr Boulevard in their thousands, flags waving, drums booming, fists raised as they passed the government offices chanting black curses at the French occupiers of Syria and Lebanon. The response had been predictable too, for the French masters kept a grizzled tomcat for just such occasions. Colonel Bremond, the military commander in Damascus, had called out the troops for a little head-bashing. The soldiers had driven the marchers back into the old city. It was the perfect recipe for a riot and a little patriotic looting. Everything had played out according to the well-worn script. Now it was time to bind the wounds and mend the bones. And prepare for next time.

Though the mob had moved on, Nikolai Faroun's sedan was stalled at the outskirts of a square just off Midhat Pasha, one of the main thoroughfares in the old city. He had hoped to save some time by going through the Christian Quarter, but the disturbance had overtaken him. Just ahead, the armored car, the Tricolor blazoned on its doors, stood guard in the square, as helmeted gendarmes watched nervously at the street corners. To the west, a plume of smoke hung over the Al Kumeileh Souk like a malevolent jinni, and the inspector could hear the crackle of distant rifle fire. A path was made for a military hospital lorry, its tires crunching over rocks and shards of glass. There was nothing to do but wait for the all clear from the army before the inspector could proceed to the Barada River and examine his corpse.

Besides, the Peugeot 201 parked in front of Le Chat Rouge had caught his attention. Faroun crossed to the other side of the street, stepping over charred debris, until he stood before the automobile, a black box of a car that made him think of a hearse. The association was not unnatural. This was a good day for the "flying squads" of the political division, and the license plate confirmed his suspicion. Durac might be in the bar downstairs and Faroun didn't relish an encounter with the head of the Syrian Sûreté. Nevertheless, he felt a thirst coming on. Overhead, the neon cat on the bistro sign was blue, not red. The cat was dead, killed by a power failure. Faroun descended the stone stairs into the misnamed bar.

There was the slightest of breezes in the domed room, for the barman had propped open a rear door. Overhead, the long-bladed ceiling fans were silent, and a candle gleamed on the polished teak surface of the bar. It was an interesting piece of furniture, of Indian origin, its panels carved with ornate mazes. At the end of the labyrinth sat a swarthy Frenchman in a rumpled white linen suit and a bistro glass in his ragged hands. His scarred knuckles were red and rough as if he had just finished beating on some poor bastard, and perhaps he had. That was one of the many things not to like about Philomel Durac, the head of the French Sûreté in Damascus. When Faroun figured in the black shirt and the white necktie, Durac reminded him of a small-time pimp from Marseille.

"Get the inspector an arak," said the agent to the bartender in a gritty voice. "Or is it too early in the morning?" Dark, smirking eyes were set in a rough-and-tumble face, the most prominent feature being a craggy forehead, which receded to ash-colored stubble.

"It's never too early." Faroun slapped a couple of coins on the bar. "But I'll buy my own; thanks all the same." The barman, a diffident fellow with the thinnest of mustaches, slid hooded eyes in the direction of the agent and back to Faroun. He placed a jigger on the bar and poured, with a deft twist of the wrist, an exact amount of the anise-flavored wine.

"Suit yourself." Durac shrugged. "What brings you down here, anyway?"

"Seems there's a body in the river," said Faroun as he held up his glass of arak.

"Anybody I know?"

"Female. And that's all I know."

The agent grinned. "There's always a body in the river, or in some backstreet of this damned town." He turned on his seat to set his amused gaze on the other. "You've heard of an eye for an eye, haven't you, Faroun? Everybody always gets what's coming to them."

The sarcasm was not lost on the inspector. Relations between the two officers had soured at first sight. The antipathy stemmed from a planning session called by Delegate Montcalm, Faroun's boss, six months before. He had asked Faroun for a Prefecture review, and the newly appointed chief, armed with little information, had bumbled through an improvised speech. In his disarray, he had inadvertently slighted Sûreté agent Durac.

Following the meeting, the two men had some words on the broad marble staircase of the Palace of Justice. Durac demanded to know why the Prefecture chief had left out mention of a key post—that of liaison officer linking their two branches of law enforcement. Faroun tried to explain that his predecessor, removed from office by a terrorist's bomb, had not been around to inform him that such a post had been created.

Faroun had stumbled into a minefield. In the administrative maze the French had constructed to rule their League of Nations mandate, the two-tiered police system was wracked by internal strife. On the one side, Faroun's Prefecture dealt with civil crime; on the other, Durac's special agents had been created to handle, without much nicety about civil law, political opposition to

French rule. Where the cases fell into the gray, and there were many such cases, the two sides clashed.

Durac had been in the mood for a scrap that day and told Faroun that he knew his game, how Faroun was trying to gain power for the Prefecture at his expense. Faroun got a little testy and made a crack about Durac's black shirt. He might be on the best-dressed list in Italy, Faroun told him, but the last time he had checked, France was not yet a fascist state.

The sardonic man at the end of the bar may well have been recalling the same encounter. Faroun wouldn't have minded knocking the smirk off his face, but he decided to be conciliatory.

"The last time we talked, Durac, we had a misunderstanding," the inspector began. "No reason why we can't cooperate. We're on the same side, after all."

"Is that what you think?" Durac had dropped his guard, but his contempt had to do with something besides turf. It had everything to do with who Faroun was and what he represented. Faroun was surprised that he hadn't recognized the man's bigotry sooner.

"You have a body in the river," said the agent, pushing away his glass. "Me, I've got my hands full today." Durac returned to examining some papers he had laid out on the bar. Rumor had it that the agent carried around a list with the names of his political enemies on it. One by one, he crossed the names off the list as they found their careers gone up in smoke. Faroun figured he was high on the list.

The inspector downed his glass as he caught sight of his driver, Ihab, motioning for him to return. Apparently, the way ahead had been cleared.

Faroun's driver drove cautiously down Midhat Boulevard. The streets were now empty and forlorn, except for a canvas-topped troop lorry racing down the palm-lined thoroughfare in the opposite direction. The uniformed driver flicked away a cigarette butt as he flew by Faroun's car. When Ihab turned into El Dawamne, one of the main streets that cut through the Christian quarter of the old city, they were greeted by a solitary old Arab on an decrepit donkey clip-clopping down the street, bringing a load of charcoal into town.

"Since this is your first time out with me, Ihab, I'll tell you how things work," said Faroun, looking over at his new police sergeant. "This is a public crime scene. I don't like public crime scenes. The homicide has no dignity once it's out there for everybody to gawk at. Besides, a public crime scene gets muddled."

"Yes, sir." Ihab Kabir was a thin, fretful man in a slightly oversize uniform with his Sam Browne belt buckled so tightly it seemed wedged into his backbone. Given Ihab's sallow, humorless features and his monastic razor cut, Faroun wondered if he took any pleasure in life. He imagined Ihab sitting up all night listening to the radio and nursing an ulcer.

"What's wrong with Vice, by the way?"

"I was in Vice for two years, sir."

"So you were what—bored? Tired of busting street hustlers and pimps?"

Ihab looked over at Faroun cautiously. "I have to think of my career, sir."

"I don't know if working for me enhances anyone's career."

"Well, I think I can last longer than six weeks."

Faroun chuckled. "So you've been talking to Ali Feh, is that it?"

"He's not too happy being a traffic cop, sir."

"He gave you all the dirt, did he? I don't like someone who taunts me with the threat of an influential papa. That was his last mistake. The rest was sheer incompetence."

Ihab angled the car smoothly off Dawamne and onto Bab Your and jammed on the brakes to avoid hitting a white saluki that had darted across the street. The sleek hunting dog disappeared down an alley. "You won't find me incompetent, sir."

"No, I suppose I won't."

"Besides, I wanted to work with you, Inspector. You're one of us."

Faroun grimaced. "If you mean I'm an Arab, I don't know what that means. My father was a Maronite Christian from Beirut. Maronites are not popular in Syria, as I'm sure you know. Besides I'm an apostate, so that puts me in a minority of one. I belong to the Prefecture. That's my affiliation. Don't bring up this us business again."

"I didn't mean to offend, sir," the other said nervously.

"I got where I am because I worked at it, because I was dedicated. I didn't receive preferential treatment. I didn't kiss any asses, at least not any more than I had to."

Faroun looked over to see if the solemn assistant might show some trace of a grin. He didn't.

"Actually, I had to give long thought to bringing you on board, anyway, Sergeant. I've reviewed your service file. I don't much care for man who takes out his frustrations on his wife. A man with a short fuse is a liability."

"That was all a misunderstanding, sir. Besides, I separated from her."

"Then got back together with her again, then separated. What was that all about?"

"I can't leave her anymore," Ihab said tonelessly. "She's dead."

"Sorry to hear that."

"I sent her back to her mother in Aleppo. She died of consumption."

"It's your fortune or misfortune, Sergeant Kabir, that you were at the top of a very short list."

Ihab looked over at him, this time with something like a smile. "Four assistants in six months. Everyone is afraid to work for you, sir."

"I'll take that as a compliment, Sergeant." Faroun pointed ahead. "I want you to cross the old stone bridge and then stop at the other side. The only good thing about today's little riot is that this case of ours is merely a sideshow."

The sideshow had nevertheless attracted two dozen or so on-lookers, mostly the squatters who had built huts along the bank of the river, and Faroun set Ihab Kabir to dispersing the crowd. They had gathered at the top of the ancient Roman steps that led down to the reed-lined bank of the river. Legend had named the Barada as one of the four streams flowing out of paradise. This last river of Eden was now an oily, fetid stream that stank in summer and rolled turgidly on carrying the refuse of the city. Bodies turned up in it quite regularly too. Agent Durac was not far wrong in that. "By the Barada, they sat down and wept," Faroun said to himself as he descended the moss-grown steps. The punishment was not simply being locked out of the garden, he thought. It was not the loss of immortality and harmony among all of creation. The tragedy was that Adam and Eve had tarried outside the gate, as if they could not tear themselves away from the womb that had nurtured them and betrayed them. Here they had raised their offspring, both demon and human, and here they had begun the long, wearying life of scratching in the soil, the bitter taste of sweat on their lips, always in the shadow of the luxuriant garden, whose intoxicating fruits they would not taste again.

Here tarried one of their children, naked as she was born, curled in the fetal position in which she was found, freed from a burlap sack. Her long black hair was matted against her cheek, the drenched ringlets falling down her right shoulder and to her waist. They could not hide the red, raw, gaping wound at the neck. Two constables from the Prefecture stood guarding the body, relief on their faces at the sight of Faroun.

"Who found her?" Faroun asked.

One of the patrolmen pointed to a man with a cloth cap sitting stoically in a reed boat with a triangular sail. The inspector slowly circled the body. The black muck of the riverbank was slippery and clung to his shoes. He lowered one knee to the burlap as if he were about to say a prayer. Instead of praying, he pulled back the dense strands of hair from her cheek. With the face of the victim exposed, Faroun lowered his head, emitting a little sigh of recognition as he did so. Getting to his feet, he called for Ihab to get on the radiophone. He wanted Dr. Mansour's team out to the crime scene as soon as possible. And he wanted his secretary, Rebecca, to know he was going to break the news to Delegate Montcalm. He questioned the constables for a moment and then walked over to the fisherman. He stood up in the boat as the detective approached and pulled the cap from his shaven head. Yes, Your Eminence, she had come up with his fishing net, pointing to the place in the river. Yes, he had cut her out of the sack. He was so excited thinking he had found a wonderful treasure. . . .

4

Faroun had caught the delegate and Madame Montcalm at one of those rare quiet moments in their lives, a late Sunday breakfast of eggs and toast and coffee in the garden of their villa overlooking the city. It had turned into a brilliant spring morning, and the unaccustomed warmth had served as invitation to flocks of swallows to play in the cloudless blue of the sky. Most of the smoke from the disturbance had cleared from the horizon, leaving a clear and impressive vista of the ancient stone walls of Damascus. The graceful spires of the tomb of the Great Umayyad Mosque shone in the sun. The forbidding battlements of the nearby Citadel towered over the maze of quarters and districts and souks of the Old City. Surrounding the Old City, the wide boulevards built by the French Mandate authorities, like the spokes of a great wheel, radiated to the surrounding suburbs and villages. Montcalm's villa was located about five miles to the northwest of the hub, in an exclusive suburb on the hilly ridge of Mohajirene. The European rulers and their court had laid claim to the Mohajirene. Faroun's house was on the lower hills farther south, an exclusive enclave when his father had bought the property in 1903, but now a suburb for midlevel bureaucrats for the French colonial regime. To the west, Faroun could see the white ribbon of the new highway to Beirut that had been cut through the mountains passes of the Anti-Lebanon. It was a testament to the faith of the French that new roads would bring a blossoming of commerce and communication to ancient, backward Syria, although that had yet to happen, mostly because the new highways were frequently the scene of bedouin ambushes and terrorist sabotage. The roads to the northern suburbs closest to the old city had undergone a renaissance of construction, the roost of wealthy merchants and businessmen. To the south, past the restive district of immigrants known as Maidan, roads led around snowcapped Mount Hermon and broke for the coastal road that led to Tyre and Acre and British-controlled Palestine. The policeman could just discern the green fringe of the oasis known as the Ghofar to the east. Here the new French roads petered out, for this was the beginning of Great Syrian Desert.

The Montcalms, pale and beleaguered among the bone china and silverware that graced their breakfast table, regarded Nikolai Faroun with the wariness reserved for the messenger bearing bad news. The news the Prefecture chief bore was particularly bad.

"You're quite sure it was Vera Tamiri?" the delegate for French Syria asked, as if he might wish the fact away.

"We won't know for certain until there is a positive identification, but there's little doubt." Faroun had hoped to break the news to his boss in his study, away from the breakfast table, and out of earshot from Madame Montcalm. The delegate, however, was never one to wait when news was brought to him, good or bad. He insisted on knowing the worst, and often it was the worst, right away.

"Of course, you would recognize her," Montcalm mumbled. Madame Montcalm caught his napkin from falling as he jerked to his feet. He was disheveled, his tie missing, ash smudges discoloring his charcoal pinstripe. He had come from visiting the downtown battleground and hadn't bothered to change before enjoying a moment of peace with his wife amidst the profusion of clematis and morning glory and newborn crocuses. "I suppose I should be the one to tell her brother."

"I wouldn't do that just yet, sir."

"Oh?"

"I'd like Mansour to give the body a thorough examination."

"An autopsy?"

"Legally, I need permission from the next of kin."

"I doubt if you'd get that permission from her brother, Umar Tamiri."

"Except in the case of exigency, sir. You can make that exception."

"And you wish me to make that exception?"

"I would, sir."

"Why do I keep losing the best of them?" Montcalm said more to himself than to the inspector. Although taller than Faroun, he had slumped with his burden. He ran his hand through thinning red hair. His normally keen and inquisitive eyes were tired and distracted. "There was no woman in all of Syria like Vera Tamiri. She was generous and beautiful and kind and visionary. She was an inspiration to Arab women of a whole new generation. Her charities," he added, searching for words. "She worked tirelessly . . ."

"She was an inspiration," Faroun began, trying to recall some quote of Montcalm's.

"To all those who yearn to bring Syria into the modern world," Montcalm repeated. "For all who struggle against the tyranny of history." There came into his eye a moist gleam, as if he had found the theme for the eulogy he might be called on to make. "Thank you, Faroun. Please take some coffee." He took Faroun's hand in both of his and after giving a perfunctory shake, turned on his

gers through a bunch of yellow jonquils, as if they were the strings of a harp. "He has advisers, and one or two are even capable. Yet more of them are hangers-on and sycophants who, unlike you, shy away from bringing bad news. What he lacks is a friend. Besides, you have a unique view of the territory."

Faroun straightened his blue serge suit a little uncomfortably. "Of course, I will do whatever I can to help."

"I know you will, Inspector. Perhaps I can be a little help to you as well." They had come to a turn in the hilltop garden where there was a stone bench. She invited him to sit down. "Poor Vera." She looked down at her exquisite hands. Her wedding ring was a simple gold band. "Did she die horribly?"

"I think the murder was sudden and quickly done." Faroun could not mention the violence of the crime.

"She challenged the stereotypes of the Arab woman," sighed Madame Montcalm. "She had great courage. You met her, didn't you?"

"Once. You introduced us. At the charity concert three months ago." Faroun recalled the way Vera Tamiri's eyes had fixed on his in the crowded vestibule of the theater and the pleasurable tremor he had felt. The effect was like looking into the eyes of a former lover who had never left your thoughts. So there was warmth, and shared secrecy, and a touch of melancholy, for it seemed you had been in her thoughts as well. He scarce remembered what they spoke about, for it was over in a minute, before she moved on, champagne glass in hand, a slim, elegant woman in a black cocktail dress and pearls. Vera Tamiri had known his family name and mentioned something about how her father had been in business, briefly, with his father. . . .

"*Philanthropy* was Vera's middle name. Along with another word, I'm afraid—*indiscreet*." Something in Madame Montcalm's tone suggested that he should be as well. "I will not speak ill of the dead. And whatever Vera Tamiri's flaws, they were far outweighed by her qualities. I was not her confidante, but I know someone who was, Inspector Faroun. I would speak to her—quietly, of course. Her name is Eugenie Poquelin. She is the wife of Henri Poquelin. He directs the Sabine Corporation."

"I'm not familiar with the name."

"A new company here. Military contracts, I think." She broke into a smile as they spied the figure of the delegate hurrying down the garden path.

"I was just telling the inspector he has our full confidence," said the delegate's wife.

"And I've broken the news to Umar Tamiri, Faroun," he said a bit breathlessly. "I thought it better he hear it from me. He wants to meet with you tomorrow morning, Inspector. He insists that there be no publicity of his sister's death. Naturally, I agreed. I don't think that will hamper your investigation, but we need to keep him on our side."

Madame Montcalm took her husband's arm like a centurion, his last line of defense. The image of the doomed Bourbons once more came to mind. Montcalm looked like a man out of his depth, and to Faroun it seemed he might founder without this resolute woman by his side.

Faroun took his leave, wishing the delegate had not made that telephone call to Umar Tamiri and worrying about why he had.

5

Faroun put his hand under the elbow of Umar Tamiri and guided him down the stairs to the Prefecture courtyard. It was a grim place but not as grim as the morgue.

"I won't have her tampered with." Vera's brother had an angry tic beneath his left eye. "She's not a piece of meat for your butcher."

"I can assure you, Dr. Mansour is a skilled . . ." Faroun's mind raced ahead trying to reach beyond *surgeon*.

"Butcher!" cried Umar, his swarthy features livid. "I don't care what kind of pedigree you give him. I won't have my sister desecrated by that ghoul down there in the operating room. It is against my religion. It is against my principles." He paused to take a deep breath. "I loved my sister, Inspector, despite what you may think of her."

Faroun was caught off guard. "Why, I knew her only by reputation."

Tamiri turned on him, a short, stocky man with a pointed chin and bald patch running straight down the top of his head like a boulevard. "What kind of reputation is that? A spoiled run-about-town, a rich and decadent sybarite?" The handkerchief he kept squeezing in one hand was made of fine spun silk, and in addition to his tailored charcoal gray suit and broad red tie, he wore spats with brass buttons, a bit gaudy and out of fashion.

"No disrespect to your sister was intended," Faroun protested.

"You know what they say about her," Umar grumbled, rubbing the twitch below his eye.

"I knew of her through her charitable causes. And her work with the Women's Clinic."

"I supported her in these goals," Umar said. "Modern Syria needs educated men—and women. She just went too far."

"How do you mean?"

"Too far, too fast," he mumbled, cooling. "She was such a fool," said Tamiri, now a little uncertain on his feet, understand-able in a man who had just seen a loved one's face bordered by a white sheet. Out of respect, the coroner, Philippe Mansour, had exposed only the head and none of the carnage beneath. "I knew something like this would happen to her—I warned her."

Faroun looked up at the four gray walls that enclosed them—four stories of bleak windows, row upon row of paper shufflers who grudgingly nourished the flame of the civil ministry of French Damascus. Two stunted date palms stood on either side of the entrance to the morgue, their fronds drooping and yellow. There was a stone bench to the side of one of the palms and Faroun bid the brother of Vera Tamiri to have a seat, but Umar preferred to stand. "Do you know what it is to lose the last of your kin, Inspector?"

"I was an only child," Faroun said, unable to think of any consolation.

"Now I am an only child," said Umar. "But I will not have my only sister flayed like an animal."

"Your wishes will be honored, of course," Faroun said, trying to mask his disappointment. "You can help us in other ways, though."

"You want to know who I think would do—would do that to her."

"Enemies, perhaps. People who bore her a grudge."

"How about three-quarters of the city of Damascus?" Umar asked sardonically. "They all hated her. Had she not been a Tamiri, they would have hunted her down like a village tramp and stoned her!" He glared defiantly at Faroun and then lowered his eyes. "It came down to the same thing, didn't it?" He decided to take the seat and applied the handkerchief to his forehead, but not his eyes. "There were six of us, once. I had three brothers and two sisters, including Vera. The eldest, Anwar, died in a train crash. The other two brothers, David and Ormuz, rode with Faisal and died fighting the Turks. Even we Syrian Christians made our contribution to independence—for the short time we had it."

"You will forgive me for asking, monsieur. In her personal life, did she ever receive threats? Perhaps someone felt slighted. Jealous."

Umar shrugged. "I never met them. We never spoke of them. To speak of them . . . It only made for arguments."

"She would have confided in you if she felt in any danger."

"You must understand that Vera moved out of the house over two years ago. We didn't see much of each other, after that. She kept an apartment in the Kasaa district, off the Boulevard Baghdad. Then there was her clinic in the Old City, until the firebomb eight months ago."

"We know about the fire."

"Still unsolved," Umar said pointedly.

"We haven't given up."

"After that I begged her to come home. I told her I would do anything. I wouldn't judge her. I wouldn't criticize. I wouldn't try to run her life. She thought it was rather funny."

"About the fire?"

"About my promises." Umar was back on his feet, although he swayed slightly. "About the fact she was in danger." He pulled out a silver case decorated with black onyx. He selected a cigarette, but did not offer one to the policeman. The lighter illuminated a pitted complexion, a tiny waxed mustache, long, almost feminine eyelashes. "I don't want my sister to be an unsolved crime, Inspector."

"We will do everything we can, sir."

"The delegate made me a guarantee to find her murderer," said Umar Tamiri, exhaling a long trail of smoke. "I will hold him to it. I will hold you to it. Just keep that ghoul doctor away from her."

"You will send someone around for her then?"

"I will," said Tamiri, and took his leave, walking briskly across the courtyard as if relieved of a great burden.

"If that's the way Tamiri wants it," sighed Philippe Mansour, unhappy that he was being cheated out of an autopsy. "We might have learned a thing or two." He folded the sheet back to the dead woman's stomach. A pity, thought Faroun, that she had been so roughly handled. Vera Tamiri had, for a while, the favor of the gods, and though the animating breath was gone from her, beauty lingered. That beauty was a flowering of a city that had been the crossroads of East and West for thousands of years. The Egyptians had made her, and the Amorites, and the Assyrians, the Romans, Crusader and Turk, and the restless bedu of the desert. Some had envied that beauty and some admired—and one, at least, hated her enough to destroy it. "I didn't want to show this to you, not while her brother was here." Mansour pointed to the jagged cross-shaped wound carved on the woman's abdomen below the navel.

"I didn't see this when she was curled up on the riverbank. Postmortem?"

"I'd say so. She fought back. Two fingernails broken and skin under a third. The bruises on the face you can see. Then he pulled out his knife and went to work."

"Just to think of a religious motive for this crime invites a riot." Faroun took one last sad gaze at Vera Tamiri before Mansour covered her up again. "Let's keep this between us for the moment."

"Worship the wrong God, they kill you. Belong to the wrong party, they kill you. Get born into the wrong family, they kill you. Nice town, Damascus." The gangling coroner in the white surgical smock walked over to the steel sink and washed his hands. Hair close-cropped, owlish eyes with brows to match, Mansour observed the detective down the length of his long nose. "I keep my allegiances on wheels."

"Except for the little fact that you work for the French. They kill you for that too."

"Especially for that," Mansour chuckled. "I spit on the street every time a gendarme crosses my path."

The coroner's domain took up much of the basement of the west wing, a corridor of offices, labs, and an operating room. A camaraderie had developed between the coroner and the policeman in the months since Faroun had come to Damascus, for Mansour was another Lebanese who had found favor with the French administration. Mansour had studied in Paris and had adopted certain Parisian attitudes, an urbane and mordant humor, for one thing. A penchant for nihilism was another, and a passion for the avant-garde of the twenties, which meant he was a bit out of touch. He affected black velvet cravats. He took offense at the word *morgue*. His surgery was "Studio Bleu," an oblique allusion to the Picasso period of grieving women and grim acrobats on the beach. An autopsy was an "exhibition," and he liked to have visitors to the gallery. His surgery was, in fact, a gallery, hung with oils from obscure artists, mostly abstract or cubist, dripping in primary colors. For some reason the smeary blobs and polygons reminded Faroun of body parts, but that may have been reading too much into things.

"Did you know her?" Faroun asked.

"I met her once," said Mansour. "She even kissed me on the cheek. Most people won't even shake hands with me."

"Formaldehyde. They can smell what you do for a living."

"It's true," said Mansour, taking no offense. "I rarely get invited to parties." A wan smile played across his features. "I live for parties."

"This town is full of people who met Vera Tamiri once," said Faroun. "I'm also on that list. It's those on the more-than-once list I'm concerned with."

"All I know is that she got around—doing good deeds. Or making trouble. Depending on your point of view. Most saw her as making trouble. There are a lot of men in Syria who don't take it kindly when someone tells them their womenfolk need to be liberated from the veil, given a seat in the schoolroom, employed outside the home. They especially don't like to hear it from a female and an infidel at that. Her murder might be a warning."

"Infidel," Faroun repeated, as if he might tease something out of it. "Let me see the sack again."

They went over to a long steel table. Spread out before them, the bag in which Vera Tamiri's body had been tied. "Simple rice sack. Burlap. Nothing special about it." The coroner held up a leather strip. "Rawhide used to close the sack. Nothing special about that either."

"Twelve hours, you said earlier."

"At the most, I would think, before she was fished out of the Barada."

"Nothing else in the sack."

"Just the naked body. And this." He held up a black pearl earring. "Just the one."

"Any sign of sexual assault?"

"None. But sexual activity is tough to gauge after one has been floating in the Barada for a few hours."

"Why tie her up in a sack?" Faroun wondered. "Why not just dump the body? It makes sense if the body was weighted down. But there were no weights."

"Look here," said Mansour, holding up the bottom of the burlap. "The seam gave way."

"So the weights must have torn through."

"They were in a hurry."

"They?"

"Hard to imagine one man doing all of this."

Faroun started for the door, his hands dug deep in his pockets. "Let me know if you come up with anything else, Mansour."

"There is one other thing," said the coroner. "Perhaps useful." He took tweezers and lifted a tiny object from a black cloth on the table. He dropped the item into Faroun's palm.

"A bit of colored glass," said Faroun, holding it up to the overhead light.

"A piece of glazed tile," Mansour corrected. "The rose tint is interesting. Different. My assistant found it when she was combing out Vera's hair. There was a lump and a cut to the back of her head, as if she been struck or had fallen on a hard surface. Perhaps a souvenir of the struggle."

"Or picked up when she was laid out on the riverbank." Faroun squinted at the object. "Different, you said. Perhaps you can find something out about it for me. Perhaps you could put glazed tiles on the list of 'Little Studies' you ponder in your spare time."

"Ceramic is one of the studies," Mansour acknowledged with a tinge of pride. "Damascus is a good town to study mosaic if that's your thing. It's not a good town for a good time, however. Recall the old saying—'Travel to Damascus and you sleep alone.'" Mansour peered into the policeman's eyes with mock professional concern. "You look like you could do with a little sleeping around, Faroun. I recommend a weekend in the stews of Beirut. Just the thing for magnetizing the animal spirits."

"I didn't know you were exponent of Mesmer," said Faroun.

"Psychology is a fraud. Give me art, Faroun. Give me Dada." Mansour answered the phone and gave him a blank stare. "It's Rebecca. She can't live without you."

Faroun ambled back across the courtyard to his office in the east wing of the Ministry Building, which housed the Prefecture of Police. Two patrol cars were parked to the left of the entrance, several motorcycles in a neat row to the right. A solitary mechanic had popped open the casing of a Peugeot and was applying a wrench. He waved as Faroun went in.

When Faroun opened the door to his office on the second floor, Rebecca's desk in the reception room was empty, a bit of a surprise since she had telephoned him. He crossed over into the inner office, pulled off his suit coat, hung it on a coat-tree, stretched, and decided to tackle the stack of reports. He opened a file. Closed the file. His hands were sweaty. After the morgue, he felt the need to wash. He walked down the hall to the lavatory and threw water on his face. Droplets slipped down his smooth forehead, down the black eyebrows set wide apart. He rubbed his unshaven cheeks; they looked ashen and he slapped them to recall the blood. He rubbed his face clear of the water with a hand towel, then ran a finger down his nose. It was a well-formed nose, a Boyar nose, as his father had called it, alluding to his mother's ancestry. Unfortunately, it had been broken a couple of times; once in a Paris bistro during the war. On the other occasion, the lady had simply jumped to conclusions; he had been completely faithful to her, at the time. The hairline, also unfortunately, was receding, a worry considering he was barely over forty. He had compensated by combing his dark hair over his brow. This gave him an uncanny resemblance to the young Napoléon, the Napoléon of the First Consulship, before the hero of the republic became a plump despot plagued by hemorrhoids. He shared the same dimpled chin with the French hero too, and the swarthy complexion, for Napoléon was a Corsican. They might well have been related, at least Faroun liked to entertain the thought. Corsican pirates had been making off with Levantine women for centuries. Levantine pirates were known to pluck Corsican women from their beaches too. Somewhere in the mix had been a Faroun, he surmised. The eyes that looked back at him smiled at the thought, eyes as dark as onyx, but prone to melancholy, a humor that often troubled him when he thought of his past and his present purpose. The latter troubled him the most, because his job with the French occupation was fraught and problematic. Although Arab blood flowed in his veins, it was cut with that of Muscovy. Most of his countrymen held him in contempt, he well knew. He was a hireling and a traitor and his father had been a Christian. This dissatisfaction was mutual; Faroun despised the parochialism of the mob, their ignorance, their flair for fanaticism as a way of settling the score. He was among them but not of them. He often longed to be somewhere else.

His standing with the French was no less precarious. Even though Arab Christians were favored by the present rulers of Syria, his Levantine roots were always suspect, and the French were nothing if not masters of condescension. His post as Prefecture chief was complicated by the politically charged atmosphere in Damascus, where everyone, even Europeans, were subjects of interest to the Sûreté. He knew Durac was building a dossier on him, although it didn't cause him much loss of sleep. He had been appointed to his post by the high commissioner in Beirut, the chief administrator of the French Mandate. Durac's inquiries into his background would run up against impenetrable walls, and Faroun's true purpose for being in Damascus would go undetected.

The prematurely graying hair at his temples provided a hint of the travail that had brought him here. And his hands. Having dried them with a towel, he examined the thick calluses that would never go away and the scores on his palms. How did that old prison song go? "Oh, I have served Marianne, and first she broke my back. Oh, I have served Marianne and then she broke my heart."

He no longer broke stone, but it was part of the devil's bargain he had made. The telephone might ring at any time. So, like any man who realizes his freedom is but an illusion, he dreamed of escape.

His father had felt a similar sense of entrapment, although for very different reasons. Tayeb Faroun too dreamed of making a clean break from Levantine coils. South America . . . Nikolai's thoughts drifted to an imagination of Argentina, miles and miles of pampas, green mountains whose tops were lost in blue clouds, the shining shores of Buenos Aires. A slim hand rose out of the city and beckoned to him. Only the city was not Buenos Aires, but Kiev, and the slim hand was that of his mother. The hand sank back into a mound of bloodied snow. For many years, there had been no letters from Russia . . .

"She's in your office, waiting," said Rebecca as he entered the office door. "I went downstairs to escort her." His secretary put the finishing touch to a swatch of red she had applied to her lips and snapped closed a filigréed compact. She was a cute girl, Jewish, running a bit on the chunky side given her love of nougats and baklava. Anything sweet, actually. Faroun couldn't complain, for the sweetness at times went straight to her temperament. But not today. "Madame Poquelin?" she asked peevishly. Rebecca liked him to run on time, like a Swiss watch. The only problem was that the watchmaker who had put him together had cheated on the gears. "Young, blond, and rich," she warned in a lower voice.

"Thank you, Rebecca."

A curl of cigarette smoke hung over her yellow cloche as Faroun entered the office. Erect in her chair, her back to him, her long legs crossed, one of them swinging nervously. The shoes were back-slung heels, also yellow, Italian, expensive. Her left hand was adorned with a marquise diamond, set in white gold with a garland of smaller diamonds. She wore other rings too, fretful as they tapped out her impatience on the arm of the chair. Faroun bowed slightly as he swung behind his desk.

"I very much appreciate your taking the time to come down to the Prefecture, Madame Poquelin," he said smoothly. "I didn't want to inconvenience you. But I didn't want to come to your house either. I hope you can appreciate the need for discretion."

"As long as you catch whoever killed Vera, there is no inconvenience, Inspector Faroun." She was in her late twenties, Faroun figured, her blond pageboy complimenting the white gold of her necklace, round, doelike eyes a darker shade of Mediterranean blue, pert and impertinent, and set in a smooth, small-boned face. "Besides, I have a spare half hour. The children are walking with the nurse and Henri is away in Istanbul. My husband," she added. The accent was curious, slightly provincial, Avignon perhaps. Her nervousness suggested to Faroun that she pretended to more savoir faire than she actually possessed. "Do you have an ashtray?"

"Of course." Faroun rummaged in his desk for a tray and found a little dish with a Parisian showgirl painted on it. He hesitated before he set it down.

"You don't smoke, do you?" she said, amused at the tray and Faroun's blush.

"Rarely, madame."

"Eugenie Poquelin."

"I'll keep this as brief as possible." Faroun said curtly. "Madame Montcalm said you might have some information that could help us. Since my questions might be of a—sensitive nature—having to do with Vera Tamiri's personal life, I want to assure you that you can speak candidly. Everything is in confidence."

"You are prefect of the Damascus Police, are you not? I told her I would only speak to the man on the top." She smiled blandly. "At the top."

"I am Inspector Faroun."

"The title on the door says you are the prefect."

"I am both actually," said Faroun with good humor. "I prefer *inspector* because I like to keep in the field as much as I can."

"Well, I can see you don't like paperwork." Stacks of files were spilling out of their shelves behind his desk. "You are much younger than your predecessor, Inspector Benoit. I met him once. He was very bland. You are more interesting than bland."

"I regret to say that Monsieur Benoit was blown up by a terrorist car bomb some months ago. Blandness and all."

She lifted the corners of her mouth in amusement. "So you have a sense of humor too, I see. You are new at this prefecting business?"

Faroun thought about whether he would answer this. Perhaps she was trying to annoy him, even put him in his place. He decided the question was more piquant than rude. "I came to Damascus six months ago."

"So fortune has smiled on you. It must be difficult."

"Because I am an Arab?"

"You are—a cosmopolitan, it would appear."

"A tactful term, madame. My father was Lebanese." Faroun smiled to hide his exasperation. The interview seemed to be exceeding his grasp.

"So you are a Christian?"

"Born into a Maronite family."

"Named after a certain Saint Maro. The Crusaders persuaded the Maronite church to show allegiance to the pope. Probably at the point of a sword. Am I right?"

"So you have studied our history a little."

"You're peeved with me!" She lifted her head with amusement and blew a stream of smoke in the air. "Let's get down to business then." She stabbed out her cigarette on the showgirl's belly and leaned forward in earnest. A loose silk rose adorned her décolletage. Small boned but not small bosomed. Very piquant. Faroun eyes fell to the scramble of notes on his desk. "Vera Tamiri once told me that if one of her political enemies didn't kill her, one of

36

her lovers would. I cannot speak to her politics, Inspector, since I know nothing about them."

"Then tell me about the lovers. Who might have harbored jealous feelings, or been jilted?"

She took exception. "Do you expect me to give you a list?"

Faroun smiled. "Begin anywhere you like."

"You are all so ready to dismiss Vera Tamiri, aren't you?" she asked vexedly. "It's very easy to show contempt for a brave woman."

"I did not know her, Madame Poquelin."

"That is your loss, monsieur. There was no one like her in all of Syria. She alone stood up for that poor village girl who was about to be stoned for adultery—a crime for which she was innocent. She was the first one to bring such a case before a French court. And do you know what Vera earned for her courage? Death threats. Lots of them."

"I have heard of it, of course—the Al-Husri case. That was some months before I came here."

"The court demurred, for the judge was afraid of going up against local law and custom, so it was Vera who spirited the woman away—to save her life. It later came out the husband had fabricated the tale for spite. Just to get back at his wife's family." She shifted uncomfortably in her seat. "That's how it is in this benighted country."

"She made enemies, we know this. But in a murder investigation it's best to start with the known."

"Back to the lovers?" she asked impatiently. "I told you, Inspector, I don't know about them. Not much."

"Then perhaps you can tell me something about her state of mind. Recently, I mean. How did she behave? How did she appear?" She looked at him skeptically. "These are not leading questions, madame."

"Nervous. Excitable. Depressed. Elated. Confused. Quiet. Loud. She seemed to be becoming undone. I blame some of that tension on her brother Umar. He was trying to get her to come home. But she refused. She was moving at a pace in which no one could keep up with her. And she could be secretive. Especially about men."

"Perhaps she was afraid of something. Or someone."

"Vera Tamiri moved on a different plane, Inspector. If she was afraid—perhaps it was of herself. If she turned to men, it was because— She was searching for something. Who knows? She was filled with life. She was filled . . ." Suddenly Eugenie Poquelin lowered her head and tears coursed down her cheeks. She pulled a handkerchief from her purse and dabbed the corners of her eyes. "I miss her; I miss her terribly."

Faroun began to rise. "Perhaps I can offer some water. Or tea? Rebecca!" he called to the outer office. "Please bring Madame Po-quelin a cup of tea."

Eugenie waved him down with her handkerchief. "No, let's continue. But a glass of Vichy water would be fine." Rebecca, standing in the doorway, made an ironic curtsy behind her back. Faroun glared at her. "Vera was very discreet about her amours," Faroun's visitor went on. "Most of them. She usually did not let names drop. But she did talk about a Captain Martel. A Legion-naire. He got rough with her once or twice. She was angry about it and dropped him. That was about two months ago. And then re-cently she took up with someone new. She had a secret smile when she took on a new lover. I could tell."

"Did she speak of him? Was he a Frenchman, a Syrian?"

"I don't know. But she had a pet name for him. She called him Teddy. Perhaps after the stuffed bear, I don't know."

Rebecca brought in a glass of mineral water and offered a piece of baklava from a basket of treats wrapped in tissue paper of dif-ferent hues. Eugenie shook her head. "My figure," she said, glanc-ing at Rebecca's. The secretary gave her an evil little look and marched smartly back to the outer office. "She's in love with you,

I think." The young woman took a delicate sip of water. "Your secretary."

"I hardly think so."

"Then perhaps you are in love with someone else." Eugenie looked at him pointedly. "But I think not." She became solemn once more. "Forgive my flippancy. It comes and goes with me. Since I learned about Vera's death—I am beside myself. It is like I am reeling."

"Of course," Faroun sympathized. "About Captain Martel. You say he's a Legionnaire and a violent man. Did Vera ever say anything about him that would lead you to suspect he might be jealous?"

"I know that he didn't give up easily. He even stalked her for a while. But she got him to stop. I don't know how. Perhaps she told him who the Tamiri clan really is, and he backed off."

"Explain, please."

"Everyone knows about the Tamiri." Faroun took this to mean that anyone who was anybody knew about them. "They are one of the big families of Damascus—on this point Vera was very proud—but you would know about that."

Faroun got out of his chair and walked over to the tall, yellow-streaked window that overlooked the ministry courtyard. "So we have a jilted soldier and a boyfriend nicknamed Teddy."

"I wish I could be of more help." Eugenie snapped the handkerchief back in her purse and stood up, a poised and direct young woman with a touch of the demure. That shade of yellow became her too. "My children are waiting, Inspector."

"Thank you, madame. One more question before you leave. How did you come to know Vera Tamiri?"

"A year ago. It was a reception for my husband. He had just become the chief contracting officer for the Sabine Corporation in Damascus. I remember that reception well, and not only because of Henri. Vera was just coming out of mourning. We hit it off right away, Vera and I. Kindred spirits, you see. We did many things together. I contributed money to her charities. I even worked at the Women's Clinic downtown until Henri found out about it. He threw a fit. He thought of her as a dangerous woman. I think every man in this godforsaken town thought of her as a dangerous woman. And yet they came like moths to the flame."

"You said she was in mourning."

"Her husband. Fuad, I think. Dead before Vera and I met. She mourned but she got over it very quickly and she rarely spoke of him. Perhaps I have been some help?"

"You have. Rebecca will show you out."

"Thank you, Inspector, but I can find my own way. While I think of it . . ." She turned, more composed, although tears still welled at the corners of her eyes. "You might find it useful to talk to Madame Hallaf. She lives in the Amara district, I believe. She was the midwife and nurse at Vera's clinic."

"You will let me know if you think of anything else, Madame Poquelin?"

"I will." They shook hands. Hers was moist.

After she left, Faroun turned to his secretary, who was typing rather too furiously. "I'm sure she didn't mean to be rude, Rebecca."

Rebecca swung the carriage back with a vengeance. "A woman like that spends her life being rude."

"Take a walk in the park then. I find that always smooths things out."

"You never take a walk in the park. Besides, I'd just as soon smooth out these reports. The spelling errors." She lifted her eyes to the ceiling in a long-suffering look.

"Suit yourself," he replied, and went to the coat-tree for his raincoat and Basque beret. "If anyone asks—I'm taking Ihab and we're going around to Vera Tamiri's apartment in Kasaa."

"Then to Maxim's. Or is it Maxim's first?"

"Maxim's?" Faroun took a piece of nougat from her basket of sweets. "Never heard of the place."

6

Faroun looked in dismay at the ruin of the apartment in the Kasaa district off the Boulevard Baghdad. The thieves had been thorough, and the only consolation Faroun could draw was that there hadn't been much to ransack. For a woman of Vera Tamiri's wealth and social standing, the place was surprisingly bare and tawdry. Overturned in the center of the living room were a deal table and two cane chairs. An overstuffed divan with its innards torn out stood disconsolately in one corner beneath a reading lamp whose shade had been torn off and thrown across the room. Apparently, the thieves had been disappointed at the pickings and decided to take out their frustration on the furniture.

Faroun suspected more than thievery was at work, for the intruders had torn pages out of the stacks of pamphlets that had been piled in another corner, crumpled them, strewn them about. The policeman picked up one of the pamphlets and thumbed through it. Written in Arabic, it was an organizational manual for women's "action committees" at the village level. There were chapters on group solidarity, education, financial independence, even family planning. Curiously, they were composed in a dense, abstract prose, a style aimed at a lettered audience. The writer had overshot her mark. The manual was, in a word, useless, and rare the village woman who could read and comprehend. Rare the village woman who could read. Bold ideas nevertheless stir strong emotions, and the thieves had expressed their opinions by urinating on a pile of pamphlets in the center of the floor.

The policeman escaped the stench by going into the kitchen. The dingy apartment's one luxury was a Frigidaire, but there was no food in Vera Tamiri's icebox. There was, however, a half-empty bottle of gin, and gin of very fine quality. Faroun searched for a vessel amidst the broken crockery on the countertop and found a china measuring cup in a cupboard above the sink. He poured gin to the brim and, toasting the good fortune that occasionally accompanies chagrin, he emptied the cup. Carefully replacing the cap on the bottle, he returned it to the icebox and washed out the cup. There was no avoiding the flour and uncooked rice that had spilled onto the kitchen floor. Cracking grains of rice beneath his shoes, the policeman left a white trail of shoeprints as he went down the hallway, poking his head into the bare bathroom, before he passed into the bedroom. The disemboweled mattress had been dragged to the floor, exposing the bedsprings. A toy bear lay next to it, its stomach slit and the horsehair stuffing protruding. He set it on top of the bureau as a reminder to bring it with him. The bureau had been searched, the drawers pulled out and tossed into a corner. Except for a pair of silk underwear that looked as if it had been ground under a heel, no other clothing was in the room. He peeked in the walk-in closet. One of its doors had been torn away. A bathrobe lay crumpled on the floor, a silk housedress hung on a wire hanger, and a pair of sandals completed madam's wardrobe. Before he left, he got on his knees and looked behind the headboard. A shiny, round object caught his eye.

When Faroun returned to the living room, Ihab Kabir presented the concierge, an obese, agitated man who looked as if he had been stuffed into his white suit like a sausage. He was outraged, he was personally violated by what had happened to his apartment, particularly the coarse and disgusting pile of pamphlets in the living room.

Who was going to pay the damages? No, he insisted he had not seen any strangers in the building, and he resented any insinuation that he was not as alert as a fox. Only when he was threatened with being hauled down to the prefecture did the concierge remember he had let some painters into the apartment yesterday morning. He couldn't remember who they worked for or what they looked like. They wore caps with visors pulled down low, but he'd noticed they all had mustaches. As for Madame Tamiri, he hadn't seen her in days. She rarely came around anyway. The policeman praised the concierge for being a mine of useless information and told Ihab to get him out of his sight.

Irritated that someone had beaten him to Vera's apartment, he slammed the door to the police coupe. Ihab drove off. A wintry rain was blowing down from the chain of mountains known as the Anti-Lebanon, playing the fool with spring. He ran for the cover of the gold-tasseled awning of Maxim's on the Nile.

Maxim was at his post, shaking a martini, a bemused look on his face as he listened in on the magpies at the packed bar. He was a burly Ukrainian with a round, ruddy face, biceps the size of small kegs, and a mustache trimmed, curled, and waxed as if two scimitars curved at either side of his broad nose. Generally terrifying, he was touchy too, and this perhaps explained why there was little trouble at his club, although it featured the most uninhibited dancers east of Beirut and was frequently patronized by French colonial officers who drank themselves into private skirmishes.

To hear him tell the story, Maxim had been an Egyptophile ever since childhood when he had seen a picture book richly engraved with the images of death-defying mummies and crumbling pyramids. In 1917, he had surveyed his dirt farm outside of Kiev and knew it was Egypt now or never. So he left his wheat and his cows, his fifth wife, also, he had concluded, a cow, his thirteen unlucky children, and headed overland for Cairo.

He never made it. Maxim ran out of money in Damascus and turned to odd and itinerant ways of making a living, including some soldiering with Faisal during the Arab Revolt. Within five years, he had inexplicably acquired a nightclub in Damascus. He had not made it to Egypt, and so, with inspired energy, he set about transforming his cabaret into the land of his heart's desire.

Behind the thirty-foot-long bar, a mural of the river Nile greeted the eye, from the Valley of the Kings to Luxor, as it may have appeared in the time of the Ramessids. A royal procession bearing pharaoh in a golden litter traveled down the causeway that led to the Sphinx, while farmers, wearing red and white linen caps, planted grain in the rich alluvial mud of the river, the very body of the risen Osiris. In the distance, another procession, a funerary one, bearing the gilt coffin of a mummy, descended into a tomb, and at the far left a line of slaves tugged massive granite blocks up an inclined roadway to pharaoh's great monument at Abu Simbel. Graceful, square-rigged cargo vessels, one of them bringing a Hittite bride for pharaoh, navigated the bright blue water as a flock of waterfowl rose up from swaying stalks of papyrus.

A miniature of one of those graceful ships, the eye of Horus painted on its prow in cobalt blue and bearing a glass of fizzing champagne, docked in front of Nikolai Faroun. The inspector peered down the length of the bar where a half dozen such ships plied their trade, carrying their cargoes of drinks, along a little Nile that flowed right down the center of the bar.

"I am philosophic, Nikolai," said the Ukrainian, removing the glass from the ship and placing it on the bar. "I have come to realize two things. It is the Egypt of the pharaohs I really love, and since Egypt no longer has a pharaoh, I am bound to be disappointed. Secondly, even if I am fool enough to want to go to Cairo and spoil everything for myself, I still have time to do so. Drink up. On the house."

"I'll have a double arak on the side."

Maxim nodded sagely. "Woman trouble again. A new one this time or did Gertrude come back?"

"I only met this one once," said Faroun. "Twice."

"Then this is very serious," said Maxim. "Perhaps you should see a priest."

"Vera Tamiri," said the policeman.

Maxim clucked his tongue and set a full bottle of arak before the detective. "Then you do need a bartender."

"Why, does she like to drink?"

"She comes here with her group—the Dandies I call them, well-heeled married French dolls and their toads—lovers, gigolos, humorists, and gamblers. But I haven't seen Vera in a couple of weeks." He held up the bottle of arak and, eyeing Faroun under his bushy brows, had a drink himself.

"So Vera liked to carouse with gamblers?"

Faroun had pulled out an ivory disk and spun it on top of the bar. Maxim clapped a hairy paw over it and held it up to the ceiling.

"This casino chip is worth all of fifty francs. At the right club, that is. But you didn't hear it from me. Gambling is illegal in this town, and I respect the law."

"I could turn you in for worse things than that," said Faroun.

"That you could, *mon ami*." Maxim chortled. "If you did, though, I'd have to see you met with an accident." He smiled benignly.

"What's the right club?" Faroun said, taking back the token.

"You really don't know the ropes yet, do you? There are what—five?—six private clubs. All very discreet of course in order not to offend the pious—and in this town everybody is too damned pious! Well, you see the insignia of the knight in the center of the chip. Each club has its own symbol."

"Le Chevalier."

"A very charming and elegant hotel in the northern suburbs. The word is that you take the lift down to the basement, find the right door, say Pierre or Reynard or somebody sent you. *Et voilà*. The door opens to fortune. Or ruin. But you didn't hear that from me." Maxim leaned over the bar confidentially. "Where did you find this thing anyway?"

"Just by being a nosy cop." Nikolai turned on his stool as a howl of laughter went up from the dance stage. Shammara, Maxim's star performer, had enticed one of the patrons to the stage. A balding, bloated German in ill-fitting evening clothes began following the dancer around the footlights. The image that came to mind was of a bullfight, only in this case the matador was nearly the size of the bull. She led him on a merry farcical chase, graceful in spite of her girth, confounding the fellow at every turn, and plucking at his clothes, so that after each encounter he was in deeper disarray, his shirttails hanging out, bow tie plucked off, then the sleeve yanked off his coat.

Finally he stood in disheveled bafflement on center stage, a winded, sweating buffoon, until Shammara finished him off with a bump of her hip that sent him flying back into the audience. Shammara bowed to the applause, her oiled body gleaming in the spotlight. She then worked herself into the undulating climax of her dance, having slyly placed herself before a semicircle of tables containing a sodden troupe of French colonial officers who tossed banknotes beneath the dancer's nimble feet.

The lights went down, the stage went dark, the music stopped with a squeak, and when the spot snapped back on, a torch singer was onstage humming the opening bars to "Coquette."

"She is in fine form tonight, your Shammara," Faroun observed.

Maxim's taurine head rested gloomily in his hands. "You.see how she lives up to her name, my friend. She dances only for me, she says, but she sleeps with everybody else. She will probably even sleep with that pig of a German before the night is through. After the soldiers, that is."

"Maybe she's saving the best for last." After the policeman looked at the unsmiling face of Maxim, he tried another tack. "You certainly have no dearth of dancers."

"There is, unfortunately, only one Shammara," Maxim sighed with the grief of the unrequited. "One day she will drive me to murder. But I shouldn't be telling you that, should I, *mon ami?*"

7

Nikolai walked around the front room of the storefront office that had once been Vera Tamiri's Women's Clinic, kicking about pieces of blackened timber and stepping on shards of broken glass. Curiosity had led him here, not any vain hope that there might be some overlooked clue to a firebombing that had happened months ago. He picked up the charred pages of one of Vera Tamiri's noble pamphlets, this one on the importance of nutrition for pregnant mothers, written in the same stilted and elliptical style and illustrated with pictures of fruit and vegetables. The policeman went into the back, a long oblong room that had probably been used for meetings, to judge by the remaining odds and ends of table and chairs. A kitchen was in the rear, the basin and plumbing torn out by looters. Faroun wondered if Vera Tamiri had had any plans to reopen her office or whether, disheartened, she had just given up the project. Perhaps she had come to realize in the months before she was murdered how fearful this land was of change, how bitterly opposed people were to any idea that tried to alter the unalterable, whether it be tradition or the immutable commands of God. The Muslims were the most obdurate, yoked to the ancient wheel by the mullahs, but, if the truth be said, the Christians and the Jews and Druze of Syria were not more open to social change than their Muslim brothers. In any event, such change was not to be brought about by women, the lesser of God's benighted creatures. Faroun wondered if Vera Tamiri truly understood the forces arrayed against her or whether she was dabbling, the way a dilettante dabbles, and doing more harm than good by trying to do good works.

When Faroun returned to the front room, he was startled by an apparition dressed in a black chador, framed by the burnt doorframe and morning sunlight slanting over her back and falling in a thousand pieces on the glass-strewn floor below. The young woman moved out of the doorframe and took a hesitant step forward. She wore a head scarf close gathered about her face. Her dark eyes were alert and cautious. "You have seen her—the Madame Tamiri?"

"No, I have not seen her," said Faroun. "I'm a policeman." The woman's caution turned to fear. "No, please don't go," said Faroun as she turned away. "I am—a friend—of Madame Tamiri."

"Then you know where she is!"

"I have not seen her recently."

"I have not seen her—since the clinic was burned." Her Arabic was inflected with an Iraqi accent, a country girl from the Syrian frontier.

"You are a long way from home, little sister."

The young woman allowed the scarf to part, revealing a grim pockmarked face. "I traveled many miles from the Jazirah. With my two daughters."

"And why is that?"

"My husband threw us out. My family would not give us shelter. So we left."

"Why did you come to Damascus?"

"Everyone comes to Damascus, sir," said the girl as if this fact were known throughout the world. "When I got here, a woman told me about Madame Tamiri's clinic. So I came. My youngest, Yasmine, had a fever. The clinic doctor was very busy. When the doctor got around to her, my child was nearly dead."

"There was only one doctor?"

"She was a midwife actually, and she did her best, poor woman. So many mothers with their babies. But she helped my Yasmine." She pointed to a corner of the wall. "Madame Tamiri was here that morning and she gave me some piasters." Her face clouded. "I came back after that and sometimes Madame Tamiri or her assistant gave me piasters."

Faroun opened the singed copy of the pamphlet he had found. He held it out to her. "Do you know what this is?"

The woman took the booklet in her hands. "I cannot read, sir. There was some talk about reading classes, but I don't know. It was very confused here most of the time. I came for my piasters."

"Did many come for here for money?"

"Most came here for that." The young woman closed her head scarf and turned to leave. "We all miss her. Do you know when she will come back again?"

"I can't say," Faroun replied. "Before you go—was there any talk about who might have done this thing to the clinic?"

A look of fear stole back into the woman's eyes. With an abrupt shake of her head, she passed through the doorway, looking to the left and right carefully before scurrying away.

"They won't tell you anything," said the man who had replaced her in the doorframe. "Even if they knew, they wouldn't talk."

"Baramki," said Faroun, pleased to see his lead investigator. "I appreciate your coming down."

"They're all too scared," the detective added, as if he might not be too clear. Baramki was a good policeman, even if he sometimes belabored the obvious, a weathered-looking man, tall as a cedar, who walked as if he were always leaning into a wind. His family came from Damascus, and he had been educated in a French school. Like Faroun, he had fought on the Western Front in the Great War, but the two had been in different outfits. There was slight touch of rivalry, even a little injury, between them, for Faroun knew Baramki had been considered for the post of chief before Faroun had turned up, fresh and unheralded from Beirut. Baramki was part Druze, and these fierce enemies of France were not entirely trusted, even when they worked for the French Syrian state. Besides, Faroun had pull in the high commissioner's office, the door-opening kind of influence. As Baramki supposed.

"So your investigation turned up nothing. No suspects."

"It could have been any of a number of groups," said the other, running his eyes about the devastation. "High on the list was her brother Umar."

"They didn't get along."

"Once you get into air up there," he said, rolling his eyes to the top of his head, "the truth sort of thins out. They live in a different world, Chief. The old families of Damascus, I mean."

"Why did your investigation focus on Umar? He told me he approved of his sister's good works."

"Maybe he did," Baramki said a little uncertainly. "We think he might have been under pressure, perhaps from the other families, to trim her sails a little. In any event, we know one thing—he brought the investigation to a halt. That was the word from our chief."

Faroun could see he had touched a nerve. "Look I'm not accusing you or your previous chief of anything. I just need to know what you know."

"It was something I overheard. I passed by his office. He was arguing with someone. After that, he came over to my desk and said that we had more important things to do than look into fire-bombings. We get two or three of those a month anyway. He wasn't happy about calling things off. Later, I learned from the chief's secretary that Umar had leaned on somebody upstairs."

"There's only one man upstairs in Damascus. You mean the delegate."

"Your guess is as good as mine."

Faroun suspected that Baramki knew a little more than he wished to reveal. He would have to earn Baramki's confidence first. Meanwhile, it was a fine spring morning for a stroll into the heart of the Old City; besides, there was someone else he wanted to see.

Leaving behind the shell of Vera Tamiri's clinic, he wandered south of the Al Amara district along shop-filled lanes, past the Bab Al Faradisse or Gate of Mercury. Faroun made his way down winding streets well shaded from the sun, passing peasant and urbanite, the city men dressed in tarbooshes and lumpy gray suits, the country women wearing silk or cotton *ezars*, a string of gold coins across their forehead, as their men led the way in baggy pantaloons. Druze women in bright print dresses mingled with bedus covered head to foot in formless black haiks. Jews in black yarmulkes and sidelocks kept pace with Alawi men in the long shirts known as *qumbaz,* on their heads white kaffiyehs ringed with black agals. Here and there, black Senegalese colonial gendarmes stood at an intersection with rifles slung over their shoulders, nervous with keeping the peace in a hostile place far from home. This human bustle did not diminish the fact that Damascus was a metropolis of memory, of ancient gates and monuments, tombs and catacombs. The squalid tenements of the living crowded precariously against sumptuous memorials, vying with the dead for a little light and space. Some of these monuments were, like the Great Mosque, wonders built by a loftier race, spilling into ornate gardens, and others were merely foul cells at the end of a lane. The policeman passed the entrance to one of the tombs ascribed to Ananias, the man who had restored sight to Saint Paul after the apostle had been blinded by the truth on the road to Damascus. It was merely a hole in some rubble at the corner of a chapel, and a well-dressed French couple came stumbling out of the place, the woman coughing into a handkerchief, both of them followed by an Arab boy holding a candle high over his head. Among the living and the dead, children raced past Faroun in a furious game of hide-and-seek. At the head of the staircase that led into Bab Your, as the Christian sector was known, he paused to buy a sherbet from a man with a face like creased, polished leather, who juggled with acrobatic ease the copper urns and cups suspended in a wooden tray about his neck. Down another lane, just beyond an Umayyad arch, a little square caught the sunlight, where a fountain played and women drew water for their homes.

The staircase that opened onto El Dawamne Street was steep. Descending, Faroun found the neighborhood shops closed. He passed down streets where the houses were locked and bolted, the shutters drawn tight, the only sound of life the muffled cry of an infant, the high-pitched yelp of a dog. The tax riots had been put down, at least temporarily, but that had not settled the issue. A new set of rumors had already begun to drift down the streets of Damascus like vapors of contagion.

The Christians were in league with the French to impoverish the Muslim majority, went the whispers. They would seize Muslim homes and drive Muslims out of the city. Outside Damascus, Muslim villages near the desert were already being systematically razed and the villagers shot or sold into slavery to the emirs of the Persian Gulf. The French were building new villages and filling them with Christian Arabs and Jews. The French plan was to quietly exterminate the Muslim population of Syria. There was no end to the perfidy of the infidel.

Faroun knew the power of rumor in this ancient town. The silence and apprehension in the Christian quarter of the city was a testament to its insidious slide. The Christians of the Bab Your, though speakers of Arabic and as indigenous as their Muslim neighbors, knew from hard experience a pogrom could sweep over them. Faroun knew that the same fear extended into the Haret Al Yahoud, the nearby Jewish quarter, and to the Bab Charki to the east, with its Kurdish and Armenian populations. From some blocks away, Faroun could hear the rumble of army trucks filled with soldiers making the rounds. French soldiers had protected Christians in the Levant since the Crusades, but they were always too few and, as Delegate Montcalm liked to point out, always too late. For this reason, Christians barred the doors and kept weapons under the beds.

The house of the Al Fakri family proved elusive. The inspector had not visited Talifa since she had moved in with her grandniece. He knocked on several wrong doors before he arrived at an arched door-way, a terra-cotta angel bearing a crucifix set in its capstone. There was much whispering and consultation behind the stout timber door. Talifa was brought to the little square of the door window, but she was near-sighted and could not swear that it was her baby, Nikolai Faroun. Only after she had listened to him hum the little bedu lullaby she had sung to him as child did she shriek and break into a toothless grin.

The house was full of children, for Talifa's niece was as fertile as a she-goat; look at her stomach, will you, and the old woman crowed with coarse laughter. The big-bellied Marit, pregnant with number nine, smiled shyly and began to prepare a meal. Talifa led her visitor to little enclosed garden off the kitchen and made much of him, now that she had a little sunlight to see her former charge.

"More your mother's son that your father's," she said by way of compliment. The same fierce squint and hatchwork of lines scored her face, testament to years of hard desert life before she had come into the household of his father. "Mother Mary always guide her! You have heard from her, I think." Her eyes glittered, as if she were staring into the fierce light of the sun.

"Yes, and she sends you her blessings." For Talifa's sake, Faroun kept up the tale that his mother was alive and well in her native Russia, although he had not heard from her in many years.

"Do you think she still dances on the high wire? I always warned her that she would one day break her neck."

"She teaches now. In a gymnasium for girls."

Talifa nodded for him to take the wrought-iron chair across from her. His old nurse settled uneasily into her own chair, looking about as if the thing might collapse. She had never grown accustomed to city furniture, as she called it. "Then tell me what brings my son to me. Not to speak of old times, I think."

"A little information, grandmother. Marit used to do domestic work, didn't she?"

"And still, from time to time. To bring in a little extra money."

"The last time we talked like this, just after I had arrived in Damascus—"

"And a blessing it was to see you again, my little Nikolai! I thought perhaps you were dead." She reached over and squeezed his hand. "But then I saw you were alive."

"Fortunate the man who has two mothers," he said, squeezing her hand affectionately.

"Fortunate the child who has a good father." She shook an admonishing finger at him. "You should make children. Lots of them. Doctors make good money."

"Policemen make somewhat less, grandmother."

She looked at him with a shocked expression. "A policeman! That's a good way to lose your head. Especially in this town. And for not much money either."

"On that point we are agreed," said Faroun. "Now I wonder if I could speak with Marit."

The old woman called for her grandniece, who hurried in with a tray of Turkish coffee and sweetmeats. As she poured the thick brew into tiny cups, a gaggle of barefoot children, fingers in their mouths, stared shyly from the arched kitchen doorway. When Faroun asked her to join them, she shook her head, preferring to stand.

"You once worked in the house of Umar Tamiri, didn't you?" Marit shot an anxious look at Talifa, but the other just nodded at her. "I want you to tell me a little about that, Marit. How did Monsieur Tamiri get along with his sister Vera?"

"They were fine for the most part, sir. I mean they argued, but not that often, just as brothers and sisters will argue. Usually it was about Fuad."

"Vera's husband?"

"Yes, sir. They didn't get along. I mean the Madame Tamiri and her husband. He was not such a good man."

"In what way?"

"He was always making fun of her, called her ugly names, because she could never give him children. He was drunk a lot. Sometimes, when he was drunk . . ." Marit looked over nervously at Talifa again.

"He would hit her," Talifa said, sitting perfectly still on her chair. "He would beat her the way Al Alawi beat me, that old jackal, the one who abducted me from my birth tribe, the Beni Hassan. Those were the bad days. Bad, bad days."

It was almost as if Faroun could trace her thoughts, back to a time when Nikolai was barely two. His mother had found her in a hospice run by convent nuns. Talifa had been brought in from the desert, beaten so badly she could not walk. She mended under the care of the nuns and that of his mother, who, restless at home with an unaccustomed child, had taken up charity work. That Talifa had been sold into slavery was testified by the brand on her inner arm. Examinations showed several ribs and an arm to have been broken at different times. There were welts and scars all over her body. When she could speak again, she revealed that she had tried to escape from bondage several times. This time her bedouin owner had left her for dead.

"That was all so long ago," she sighed, putting down her cup. "And then your mother appeared to me like an angel of the Lord. And here I am." She smiled through missing teeth. "Now, Marit, you answer my Nikolai's questions. Surgeons need to know things."

Faroun offered an encouraging smile. "I want to know what happened to Madame Tamiri's husband. How did he die?"

"An automobile accident. On the road to Beirut."

"When was this?"

"Just before I left the Tamiri service."

"And how did Madame Tamiri react to her husband's death?"

"I can't say she was unhappy to lose her husband, sir. She didn't want to attend the funeral so there was a big argument with Monsieur Tamiri. He said she had to show some respect to the dead. Fuad was as good a husband as she deserved, he said to her. Monsieur Tamiri had picked out that husband for her himself. 'Better a devil from the pit than a husband like Fuad,' she said to him. They fought a lot after that. A few months later, she left the house for good."

"Was it about a man?"

"That—and other things."

"What other things, exactly?"

"There was the business about the clinic."

"Umar was against it."

"He said if she started up a clinic, he would burn it to the ground. I know, I was there when he said it."

A child's wail came out of the kitchen and Marit looked relieved. She hurried out of the room, but not before Faroun stopped her. "One last thing, Marit. Did Madame Tamiri like to gamble?"

"She gambled, she drank whiskey, she liked men." She drew herself up in matronly disapproval. "And then she left the house for good."

8

Monsieur Sezgin, the manager of the Casino Damasque in the Hotel Chevalier, was not pleased to see Prefecture Chief Faroun. The appearance of a state functionary only meant one thing to Monsieur Sezgin—the Squeeze. Some applied the Squeeze in a diplomatic way, as did Monsieur Fontenoy, an official with the devious title of "Collector of Illegal Taxes"; others, like the goon who worked for the Sûreté, were more direct and simply walked into his office with empty valises. Where the collector threatened fines and other unspecified sanctions, the latter threatened him with bodily harm. Naturally, Monsieur Sezgin, a responsible citizen of the French Syrian state, complied with these exactions and then went about applying the Squeeze to his own patrons to make up for the lost profits. The roulette wheel would be hard to beat for a while, and the faro and baccarat dealers were told to be especially sharp for a week or two. The Casino Damasque would then return to normal operations and everyone was happy again. After all, his clients realized how the game was played and adjusted their strategies accordingly.

The newcomer might prove overly zealous in his administration of the law and try to put the casino out of business. Monsieur Sezgin had a measure of security since the officials who came to dip their beaks would not be happy to see the Casino Damasque shut down. Then again this new functionary, vaguely resembling Napoléon at that, might be out to make a reputation for himself. More worrying to the casino manager, he might be a *cochon gros,* take the Squeeze to new heights and ruin the system, delicately balanced as it was. Monsieur Sezgin was just about to sound out his visitor on these points when his visitor began to sound out him.

"It's about Madame Tamiri," said Faroun, never one to turn down the offer of a particularly good brandy. "Vera Tamiri."

A diminutive man in an silk-bordered evening suit, the casino manager was immediately on his guard. "A remarkable woman. All Damascus sings her praises." He arched a heavily penciled eyebrow as if to admit he knew what all Damascus really thought of her.

"I did not come to the Casino Damasque to extol Madame Tamiri's virtues, Monsieur Sezgin. I want to know if she was a regular customer at the Casino Damasque."

"We have a policy, Inspector Maroon—"

"Faroun." The policeman followed the line of Folies-Bergère showgirls prancing across Monsieur Sezgin's office walls. The paintings had been inspired by Lautrec; only on closer inspection, the girls seemed to be boys. "Chief of the Prefecture Faroun."

"Of course, Prefecture Chief Faroun." Sezgin waved a handful of lacquered fingers in the air as if shooing away a fly. "I was about to say that our client list is confidential. We cannot operate without complete discretion. I'm sure you understand."

Sure of his ground, the manager rocked on his heels and rolled a brandy snifter with tiny hands, a wry smile on his rouged face. The snifter was crystal, its stem a nymph whose nakedness was partially covered by a swirling sheath of green-tinted seaweed. The desk between the men was a baroque monstrosity held up by a score of cherubs dripping in gold leaf. As an ormolu clock chimed ten of the evening, Faroun studied the bustle on the gambling floor through the picture window. Army men and ministry undersecretaries, some of whom Faroun vaguely recognized, moved about the tables, their women elegant or gaudy as suited the arm. Syrian nationals in evening dress and red tarbooshes mingled with Arabs in more exotic attire.

"This is your first time to visit the Casino Damasque, is it not, Chief Faroun?" Sezgin had produced a neat tray of gambling chips of different denominations. He slid the tray across his polished desk. "It is the time-honored custom of our casino to stake our initiates with a modest sum. If you are new to the tables, I can assign a German lady of some quality to escort you and show you the games."

"That's a delicate way of putting things, Monsieur Sezgin. I never thought of myself as an initiate."

"Be our guest," the manager said solicitously.

"And a German girl of some quality for an escort. Very game of you."

The manager regarded him doubtfully. "If a German girl doesn't suit, we have Odalisque. Straight from Paris. Reserved for only the most discriminating clients."

"Odalisque? She wouldn't be the tall redhead next to my detective at the roulette table? Or the blonde playing baccarat with Sergeant Kabir?"

Despite the rouge, the color drained from Monsieur Sezgin's cheeks. "Are you trying a shakedown, Inspector?"

"A *shakedown,* Monsieur Sezgin? That's a frightful term to use for a policeman who is just trying to do his duty."

"Now I see you are a real player," Sezgin said irritably. He pulled another tray of chips from his desk and slid it next to the other.

"Two bribes in the space of five minutes. That must be something of a record, monsieur. Even for you." Faroun set down the brandy glass and leaned across the ornate, polished desk.

"What is it you want from me?" the other cried in exasperation.

"I told you. A little information."

A sly look crept across Sezgin's pouting face. "Do you think I just pass out information?"

Faroun slid one of the trays of gambling chips back across the desk. "I always reward my informants."

"You are droll, Inspector . . ."

"Faroun," the policeman reminded him. "Yes, I am something of a humorist at that. But I am beginning to turn sour."

"You think you can just walk into my office and make demands?" The other gave him an arrogant stare. "You don't know who you're dealing with."

"This is how we are the playing the game, Monsieur Sezgin. I give my men the signal. The officer dressed in the Saudi *qumbaz* at the baccarat table will cry out how the games are an abomination against God, overturning some of the tables in the process. Meanwhile his cry will be echoed by several other of my men on the floor. They will chop up the roulette wheel with little axes. People will panic and there will be a terrible mess. And that is decidedly not good for business. Your clients, realizing your casino is not secure, might even start patronizing the Club Syrien over at the Rialto."

"The Club Syrien?" Sezgin cried. "You are insidious!"

"On the other hand, you can tell me what you know about Madame Tamiri's gambling habits and I can quickly regain my humor." Faroun slid the second tray across the table. "Now you have all the chips, Monsieur."

The manager nervously flipped the lid from the silver cigarette humidor on his desk. He lit up a cigarette with trembling hands and tossed a quick puff from the corner of his mouth. "All right—the Tamiri woman. She owes me."

"How much?"

"A great deal of money, I can tell you." Sezgin began pacing behind his desk, his cigarette making swirls in the air like a conductor's baton. "I carried her for a while and then I told her if she didn't pay some of it down, I would go straight to her brother. He's good for it, I know. That got to her. A week ago she paid some of it down."

"How much?"

"Three thousand francs."

"That's quite a sum. Where did she get it?"

"I don't ask questions," said the manager, dashing out his cigarette on a Turkish porcelain plate after only a few puffs. He reached for another cigarette and kept pacing. "Not from her brother—of that I'm sure."

"Tell me about the men. Who were her escorts?"

"Who can keep up with her escorts?" the other asked sarcastically. "I don't know . . . there was a French officer. Big, strapping fellow. A pretty boy, in a cruel way." A thin, jaded smile crossed Sezgin's lips. "Why all these questions about Vera?" He stopped pacing as a look of panic crossed his face. "Nothing has happened to her, has it? I haven't seen her since she made the payment."

"This is just a routine inquiry, Monsieur Sezgin, connected with another case. So there was this French officer. Anyone else who kept her company?"

Sezgin snickered. "Salim al Quassi—if you can call him an escort—he tagged after Vera like a lapdog. Otherwise he was a wolf."

"With the ladies, you mean."

"Handsome, yes. Leading-man looks. But mean like a wolf. Moody too. Quick to take offense, quick to temper. He nearly beat a man to death at the roulette table one night. I haven't seen him here in a while, though. Perhaps Vera dumped him or ran through all his money." He shook his head. "She could not master the tide."

"Luck, you mean."

"There are gamblers, Inspector, and there are losers. The latter become caught up in the vortex. They get swept up and around they go. There is no saving them when they get like that. They cannot save themselves. Utter ruin."

"But good for business," Faroun observed.

Monsieur Sezgin flapped his arms. Was that his fault?

The crates still had to be unpacked at the house of Nikolai Faroun. The policeman wandered from room to room, wrapped in his bathrobe, a glass of milky arak and soda in his hand. Since the move from Beirut six months ago, he had been seized by the urge, on several occasions, to get things out of boxes and turn his little villa into something other than a warehouse. His former girlfriend had put up curtains one afternoon, the kind of thing that had probably adorned statues of orgiastic deities like Dagon and Belial, pink and green pansies against a sun-yellow background. They hung in the kitchen, as tipsy as Gertrude had been when she put them up. Since they were the only decorations in the house, Faroun hadn't the heart to take them down even though Gert had moved on, leaving him with the cat. Now that the cat had moved on, there was just Faroun.

And his memories.

It was a snug little harbor though, bare walls and all, and Faroun was grateful his father had bought it and held on to it, even after he had lost everything else. Faroun had fond memories of the Villa Artemis, so named after a Greco-Roman bust unearthed by his father when he was planting an almond tree. Tayeb Faroun had set the weathered marble bust on a stand in the middle of the garden.

Nikolai threw open the French doors that led to the patio and walked into the starlit grove. The bust was still there, sightless and chill to the touch. The night was damp, the limbs of the budding fruit trees dripping with moisture from an evening rain. The stone wall was falling down in some places. He could recall the times he would visit the villa with his father; it was a male retreat and both father and son had liked that. His mother had rarely visited and stayed not long. Although she loved the desert, she pronounced Damascus a backward and provincial place. During those trips with his father, he would often sit on the wall with a book, swinging his legs, eating an orange, and turn his attention from time to time to the traffic traveling in and out of the ancient city, mostly French Crusader knights with high-prancing chargers and the silver-clad warriors of Saladin.

Those romantic figures of boyhood daydreams had long since vanished. When he looked down on the lights of Damascus now, he thought of other things. The ancient quarrels between East and West had never really stopped; they had turned into nasty little wars that reflected the character of the men who waged them. Occasionally, heroes like Prince Faisal or T. E. Lawrence would make their entrance on the stage, figures of high drama in an inscrutable play. The leading players were hidden too, for the most part, preferring to send their surrogates onstage. Surrogates like Nikolai Faroun.

The crates in the spare bedroom were still neglected. He pried open one of them with the claw of a hammer. Books with gilt binding were nestled between layers of straw. The first book he picked up was Burton's translation of the *Arabian Nights*. Faroun had always treasured the Burton edition, for he loved English, extolled by his father as a necessary language of commerce. Burton's style may have been overblown, but the stories were grand no matter who told them. He carried the volume back to the kitchen and replenished his glass. He recalled the tale of the beautiful and enterprising wife of a merchant who freed her lover from prison by hoodwinking various officials. The story led him down the path of association to Vera Tamiri.

In the real-life story of Vera Tamiri, the beautiful heroine looks to her lovers for release, but one of them turns out to be a murderer. But what had she been up to in the first place? Marit had filled in some of the gaps—an ambitious, crusading woman trapped in a loveless marriage, and a prisoner in her brother's house. At the moment of her liberation, at last free of the tyranny of her husband and brother Umar, with a cause and a plan, she had spun out of control, a descent that had brought her heavily into debt, a string of unhappy affairs, and at last to the bottom of the Barada River.

The manner of the crime hinted at a spurned or jealous lover, although complicated by the religious symbolism carved on her body. If so, then the murderer was likely someone with a reputation to lose. What was the ransacked apartment about? Perhaps there really was an incriminating list, although Eugenie Poquelin had scornfully denied it.

Then again, the killing might have been the work of an outraged brother. The evidentiary compass inclined that way— undoubtedly Umar was behind the firebombing of the clinic, despite his protestations of support for Vera's social causes. Why else had he stopped the investigation? It may have been his way of trying to bring her once more under his control. He could not bear her breaking away—not only had she become too independent but a scandal as well. Since she would not return to the fold . . .

Why, then, carve that bloody symbol on her body? Or was this to mark the fallen angel, a defiant and unrepentant sinner?

There was another problem with the Umar theory. Faroun had a difficult time picturing so fastidious and tidy a man being a cutthroat. Least of all to his own sister.

He came back to the lovers. He had tracked down Captain

Martel. He was assigned to an artillery unit on maneuvers in the Syrian Desert. The unit's bivouac was a couple of hours away, so he planned to question Martel later in the morning.

As for the other name that had emerged from his interview with Monsieur Sezgin at the Casino Damasque—Salim al Quassi—he was sweet on Vera. A man with money and a violent temper. Had be been bankrolling his beautiful gambling companion? Faroun thought he might set Sergeant Kabir the task of finding out something about him.

He returned his attention to the book. He knew every story of the *Arabian Nights* by heart, for it might be said that Scheherazade had not only saved her own life by telling tales but saved Faroun's as well. He had been in the military prison outside of Lyon for only a few days when he began to realize it would be his tomb. There had never been any formal trial; charges hadn't even been filed. He had just been deposited in a foul cell at the end of the world, beyond memory itself. He saw and heard no one for long hours, except for the heavy tread of the turnkey who wordlessly delivered his black bread and thin soup through a grate in the iron door. He looked forward to that tread once a day, and at first he tried to cajole the guard, but he could not extract even a curse from the man. After a few weeks, Faroun began talking and singing to himself, but as the weeks stretched into months, he realized he would need to find a task to stop himself from going mad. So he rummaged in his memory, going beyond the misery of the past two years, the endless slaughter in the trenches of the Western Front, past the awkward and unhappy days of his study at the academy in Beirut, reaching back into the lonely years of his childhood where he rediscovered Scheherazade and her wonderful trove of tales. So he had set himself the task of recalling the stories, repeating them in his head until he had reconstructed them and brought them to life as richly adorned as his imagination could make them. Tale after tale he recovered in this way and in the process recovered himself. Once he had stored them in memory, he then had a living book. He could delight again in the adventures of Sinbad and Aladdin and the Ebony Horse. At last, he found himself resigned to his buried life and even became a touch resentful when the door of his cell at last swung open and a French army officer ordered him to prepare to leave. What season is it? Faroun wanted to know. Autumn, said the officer. What month? October. But I came to this place in October, said Faroun, stroking his long, matted beard. Time has passed, said the officer. How much time? asked Faroun. It is 1924, the officer said. What happened to 1918? Gone, said the other. And is 1919 gone too? Yes, that year was gone too. And so were the others. Gone completely.

He looked out the study window now and saw that the dawn was not far away. The *Thousand and One Nights* lay open on the desk where, in his declining years, his father had loved to work on his stamp collection, traveling around the world in search of what, Nikolai never quite knew—a refuge, utopia, some brief release from loss and pain? A wave of fatigue swept over him. As he sought his bed for a few precious hours of sleep, the phone jangled like heavy chains.

The ringing of the telephone made him anxious at any hour, but early in the morning it made his stomach churn. His palms began to sweat and his throat went dry. Surely, it could not be time. He had been led to believe that there would be a respite, that they would give him a year; a year to know the territory, make the right contacts, and prepare. But now the phone was ringing and his heart was full of uncertainty and dread. He emptied his bitter glass, walked a little uncertainly to the foyer, and picked up the receiver.

There was no one on the line, just the crackle of static that might have come from anywhere in the world.

9

The night was not over for Salim al Quassi either as he stood in the garden of the family compound, for he could find no peace. He had experienced no peace or pleasure since the night he and his brother Abdullah had waited in the Rolls Phantom beneath the poplar trees while Abdullah's men had removed all evidence of the terrible thing that had happened in the Hotel Nurredine. They had taken away what was left of the woman he had loved and driven off. Now he was more alone than he had ever been. He could not bear it. Regardless of what his brother said, the thing was not finished. He could not leave this unsettled; his honor demanded it; Vera's soul cried out for it.

Vera's enchantment was on him and he had dreamed he had seen her silhouette in the face of the full moon until she had become the moon itself and swept down out of the sky to embrace him, her hair spread out behind her as a dark net for the stars. To Salim's mind, she had been lifted far above the squalid facts of her death. No, she had not died. She was not that wretched creature he had discovered in the hotel bathroom, the sight of which had brought him to his knees vomiting. That was not his Vera—that cut and broken thing dressed in bright red blood. That was not the Vera who had so loved her Salim, her little love, her *habibi*. No, someone had taken his Vera away, had kidnapped her, and substituted that awful thing in the bath. He had sent his bodyguard to find his brother, and the awful thing had been taken away by Abdullah. Then they had driven to the Mozaffari mosque in the hill country to say their prayers.

Salim al Quassi recognized his limitations even if he did not understand them, and for this reason he had looked to his big brother for everything. His brother had always been there to get him out of scrapes, to advise him, to guide him. "To tell me what to do," he said resentfully to himself as he walked the lime-tree bordered paths of the garden. His brother had seen to all his wants and needs, ever since he was toddler. Abdullah had found a comfortable job in the family trucking business for Salim, and so he did very little for a handsome salary. His brother had seen that he wanted for nothing—English-tailored clothes, a new Renault (although he wouldn't let Salim drive by himself anymore), money for everything, even, up to a point, his gambling debts. Abdullah had selected his wife and never ceased to chastise him for paying more attention to his hounds than to the woman he'd married. The truth be known, he despised the woman he'd married. He despised her because there was nothing to despise about her; she was a paragon, a perfect wife. She was respectful, indifferent to his indifference, patient, obedient, thoughtful, kind— she was too impossibly right. And because of these things, he knew she didn't really care for him at all. She knew his flaws and weaknesses and yet said nothing about them, ignored them as if they didn't exist. She went blithely on, saying nothing about his meanness, his mistresses, his drinking, his gambling, saying nothing about his refusal to visit her in the night and beget a son. He enjoyed denying her that pleasure; he enjoyed belittling her for only producing girls. She was a donkey and he told her so. She said nothing, she did not even cry when he insulted her. By ignoring his weaknesses, by pretending as if they didn't exist, she made them all the more glaring. He hated her for that. In one of his revenge fantasies, he dragged her out of her bed at night into the lime-tree garden and set the dogs on her. He watched and laughed and clapped his hands while the mastiffs did their grisly work. This was a just punishment for a deceitful donkey.

Vera had told him time and again to free himself of his burden, to leave his brother and his wife, to stand up for himself, to cast his own shadow in the sunlight. She had encouraged and exhorted him. She made him look at his true self in the mirror, and for this, among many things, he had loved her. Vera Tamiri made him think of himself as having potential, as becoming, as having élan, so she called it, the magical power to transform himself and begin anew. Because of her, he knew that his faults were really a symptom of his self-loathing. He had allowed Abdullah to bully him and dominate him and make him feel small. He knew that Abdullah did these things to make himself more important, to play the role of the indulgent father they had both lost when they were young. Vera told Salim that he must become his own father and bring himself to life as his own man. No one had ever spoken to him that way before, and it was more intoxicating than the champagne they both loved and drank in brimming glasses when they were alone in their "hideaway." They drank and sang and danced to the Victrola and laughed and made joyous love. With Vera, he was his own man, and nothing else mattered but the approval in her eyes . . . even when she was urging him to make painful changes. They both had the power to banish fear from their lives, she said; trust me! They were just one big win away from making this happen, from turning around the galling string of losses, from reversing the spiteful run of bad luck that had turned hearts and diamonds into bludgeons and spears. But she had a plan to change all of that, for the luck would be with them again, and he could help her do something about that, do something for them both, if he had the courage and would follow her plan. He would follow any plan she could devise, he told her. He was a different man now; he would go anywhere, do anything; he would follow her to the ends of the earth. It was a wonderful plan, she said, just what they needed to turn their luck around, and she had drawn him behind the crowd at the roulette table and kissed him wildly, brazenly. He had returned her kiss, hesitantly, then hungrily, not even looking around, and they had laughed and it didn't matter about the desperation in her eyes, the fear in her voice, for it seemed as if a brand-new sun were in the sky and all things were possible. . . .

"You can't get her out of your mind, can you?"

The sound of his brother's voice froze Salim's blood. It was as if Abdullah had a window into his thoughts, into his soul. "I couldn't sleep, that's all."

"Well, I couldn't sleep either. I'm excited. I'm excited for the both of us." Abdullah was wearing an evening robe, embroidered Turkish silk, with a tasseled, gold-braid belt. He pulled out two cigars from his breast pocket and offered one to his younger brother. Salim declined to join him.

"Why are we excited?" he asked suspiciously, familiar with his brother's snares.

"Al-Quassi Shipping is about to expand," the other said briskly. "We've done very well the past year, very well indeed. Not even a global depression can stop the Al-Quassi."

"I'm sure Papa would be proud," said Salim glumly.

"We have a fleet of fifty trucks now. Think of it—fifty! We are moving freight all over the region, Beirut, Sidon, even to Medina and Mecca. And I've just put in an order for twenty more. They are going to Aleppo."

"Why to Aleppo?"

"Because that is where we are going to expand, little brother. And guess what? There will be an important role for you there." Abdullah cut off the end of his cigar with a pocketknife and flicked the tip away.

"In Aleppo?"

"In Aleppo."

"I don't want to go to Aleppo."

Abdullah looked at the long roll of tobacco leaf in his hand as Salim prepared for his brother to explode. He didn't. "At least, hear me out, Salim."

"I'll hear you out."

"I know you have been frustrated with your job here; I know you want to assume a more important role in the company. So, I am providing you with that opportunity. You get to run the new Al-Quassi office in Aleppo."

"You want to get me out of Damascus."

Abdullah cleared his throat as a sign of his continuing patience. "I won't deny this is an element in my thinking. However, I am sincere about giving you a post of responsibility. This is the chance you've been waiting for. The moment has arrived."

"Let it arrive for someone else," the other said stubbornly. "I'm staying in Damascus."

"All right, then," Abdullah said in a modulated tone. "Why do you want to stay in Damascus?"

"I'm going to stay in Damascus and find her killer."

The big man dashed his cigar into the flowerbed. "I told you to get that business out of your head. It's over. It's finished. She's finished."

"It has been three days now, Abdullah. Don't you think it strange there hasn't been a word about her disappearance in the newspapers? There hasn't been an obituary, a funeral notice."

"That's because no one will find her."

"What did you do with her?"

"I will tell you," said the big man, stooping down to pick up the expensive cigar. He blew on the tip before he put it in his mouth. "Some men put her in the Barada."

"In the river?"

"In the stinking Barada."

Salim walked some steps down the garden path, shaking his head. Then came back. "They will find her. Nothing ever stays in the Barada. Everything that goes into the river comes out of it."

"They won't find this present to the river god. She's in a sack and there are stones in the sack. She will stay on the bottom."

"They put her in a sack like an animal!"

"What did you expect me to do, build a mausoleum?" Abdullah flicked open a lighter with a high yellow flame and drew deeply on the cigar. "Listen, I've told you what you wanted to know. Even if they do find her, who is going to link her to you or to me?" Abdullah sent a thick plume of smoke into the damp night air. "Nobody is going to talk."

"What about the woman at the hideaway. And her son? They know something."

"You think they are going to talk?" Abdullah said contemptuously.

"What about the men who—put her into the sack? They know something too."

"Do you think I am stupid, Salim? Do you think I would hire some idiot off the street for a job like this? I've done business with these guys before. They do things like this for a living." The big man took his brother by the arm. "You're going to be okay. Besides, you're going to be in Aleppo."

Salim shook himself free. "I'm not going to Aleppo." He would make himself free. He would stand up to Abdullah. He owed that to Vera.

Suddenly the big man was towering over him. "I tried to put this to you in a good way, Salim. But, no, you won't listen to reason. You are going to Aleppo in two days. You are going to tell your wife and your daughters to get ready, for they are going with you."

"I—won't go there," Salim said less certainly. He took a deep breath. "I am going to find her murderer."

"Do you think you can find the murderer of that woman on your own?" Abdullah chuckled sarcastically and then rounded on his younger brother, his words beating down like hammer blows. "You are hopeless! You can't do anything by yourself but run through money, lose at cards, and chase whores. Why do you think our mother died so early? Worrying about you. Sick to death of worry about little Salim, who was always getting things wrong. You are nothing but a screwup, Salim, and when I give you a chance to prove that you are not a screwup—what do you do?" Abdullah put a heavy hand on Salim's shoulder. "You will do what I tell you. You are going to Aleppo with your wife and daughters, and you will do what I say once you get there. And you will stay in Aleppo until I say you can come back to Damascus." He let Salim go and Salim lost his balance, stumbled, fell over a flowerbed, and was in the mud beneath a lime tree. His brother's dark shadow towered over him with the cigar glowing deep red in the darkness like a terrible cyclopean eye.

10

Faroun's Triumph rumbled past the venerable walls of the Old City just as Damascus was waking. The night before, an army column had been ambushed north of the city, and the pillar of smoke from burning vehicles dominated that part of the sky, but to the east, in the direction of Faroun's journey, the rays of the newly risen sun cast a golden patina on the dome and spires of the Grand Mosque and the hundred minarets of Seven-Gated City. Once outside the city limits, he accelerated the motorbike, easy with the machine's power as it tore down a dusty highway that had once been a Roman road. Before long the police inspector had left the suburbs behind and then even the solitary little villages scattered among dense orchards of plum and apricot, stopping only once at Sakba to draw water from the village well. The mayor, long a friend of the French, came up wringing his hands and asking Faroun for better security. Rebel gangs were in the hills, and they were scouting out the villages. Their neighbors in Jazrail had been raided two nights ago. Promising to pass on the information, Faroun mounted his Triumph and rode until the palm-lined fringe of the oasis of Ghofar appeared, grew like an exotic forest, then receded behind him. Five miles past Ghofar, the secondary road gave out and there was only a desert track to follow until it became lost in the parched and heat-splayed flats that marked the margin of the Great Syrian Desert.

Faroun remembered having made one or two trips to the edge of the desert when he was a boy in the company of his mother and his bedouin nurse, Talifa. His father, a city man born and bred, shunned such excursions, but his mother loved riding out on horseback to the desolate places, those austere gardens of sky and rock and sand. They cleared her mind of excess, she claimed. On one trip, they had caught sight of a distant caravan and his mother had become excited and hoisted him to her saddle to point it out. She said that if she had been born in a different place and age, she would have been a caravanner bringing rare spices and silks from Cathay to Beirut in exchange for Flemish brocade, Venetian glass, and Damascus steel.

The days of the great caravans were long gone; the romance of the desert, such as it was, a little less without them. When Faroun went into the desert these days, it wasn't for pleasure, either, but for business. The jurisdiction of the French Prefecture extended to the suburbs and environs, even to the old medieval fort known as Tel el Saladin, on the cusp of nowhere.

Long before he reached the Tel, Faroun heard the boom of artillery, French 75s, and when he rumbled up to the old fort on his Triumph, he was pleased to find the artillery brigade of Legionnaires unlimbered beside the ruins. The men in white-backed képis moved slowly and methodically as they loaded and fired their pieces, for though the morning was young, the sun was already a burning red wheel in the heavens.

The sergeant in charge of the cavalry patrol assigned to escort the artillery team cast an envious eye at the motorcycle. One of his ponies, tethered to a thornbush, neighed resentfully as Faroun got off the bike to slap the dust out of his suit.

"That's a beauty you've got there," said the sergeant admiringly as he came up to pat the fender of the motorbike. "New model, isn't it?"

"New as they're minted," said Faroun.

"A five hundred?" the Legionnaire asked, referring to the size of the engine.

"A five hundred." The Triumph had been a gift to the Prefecture from the British Constabulary in Palestine. When Faroun had first seen the gleaming new Model Six One, he'd lusted after it and had given orders that it be reserved for his personal use. On a cold day, as spring days often are in Damascus, he would bundle up in a trench coat and brown leather gloves, fix his Basque beret on his head, slip on aviator goggles, and roar down the boulevard, drawing attention, showing off. It was a small indulgence, he figured, a self-declaring cock crow from an anonymous servant of the state.

"Sad to hear you're police, Inspector," said the sergeant as they shook hands. "Had you been a mere civilian, I might have requisitioned that machine of yours for the good of the service." The grizzled veteran grinned broadly, the left edge of his mouth drawing up to the bullet crease that traveled across his lower cheek. Apparently, the rifle slug had finished its business by nipping off the bottom half of the sergeant's left ear. He was one step above a desert brigand, but the uniform made all the difference. The Foreign Legionnaire was a terror in this stricken land, but respected by his enemies.

"You'll offer me a cup of that swill you call coffee, instead," Faroun suggested.

"That I will," said the sergeant, motioning Faroun to the kettle hanging over the cook fire. One of his soldiers held out a mug.

"Recruits," said Faroun, nodding in the direction of the gun crew. He clicked mugs with the noncom and took a sip. Bitter regulation coffee augmented with grounds to make the coffee go further and laced with bitter regulation brandy to kill the taste of the coffee.

Faroun found himself looking over the rim of a tin cup at comrades he would never see again, scared young men waiting in a dugout near a bend in the Meuse, young men making light of their fear as they waited for the artillery barrage to stop and the attack whistle to blow.

"Aye, recruits," grumbled the sergeant as the artillerymen lobbed another round into the desert. "All they're good for is churning up sand and scaring the vultures."

"Captain Martel's men?"

The sergeant spat out a wad of tobacco. "I'll take you to him." The veteran led the way around the north of the medieval fort. The main gate had long since collapsed, the huge lintel tilting crazily, one end on the ground and surrounded by rubble. The fort had been built in the twelfth century by the Knights Hospitaller to protect Christian pilgrims to the Holy Land. Less a fortress than an outpost, the wall and keep had mostly crumbled. What the weather had not worn down, the outlying villagers had scavenged.

Straddling a pile of rubble, binoculars glued to his eyes, the tall, broad-shouldered Captain Martel assessed the artillery barrage. He fired an elaborate string of curses at the fumbling soldiers, then turned his displeasure in the direction of the waiting policeman. He examined Faroun with fierce, quick blue eyes. The policeman felt as if he were being sized up for a brawl.

"Vera Tamiri," said Faroun.

"What now?" the captain asked with a bitter laugh, the sharp angles of his face scored by saber scars. "She file another complaint? The woman's crazy."

"Is that why you were stalking her? Because she was crazy?"

"Look—I followed her around for a while. But to scare her a little! She wouldn't give up. She filed a complaint against me to get revenge."

"Or maybe because you liked to rough her up now and then?" asked Faroun.

"Maybe she liked to rough me up now and then. Maybe we both enjoyed it."

Though the captain wore his brutishness like a campaign ribbon, Faroun recognized the officer had something to gain by making Vera a willing accomplice in their pleasures. Vera's confidante, Eugenie Poquelin, had hinted that there was a sordid element in Vera Tamiri's dealings with her lovers. The question was how far had Vera and Martel had taken their whimsies and when? Where had Martel been a week ago, on the night Vera had died?

The soldier regarded Faroun with a shrewd slant. "Something has happened to her, hasn't it? She's got herself in some trouble, hasn't she?"

"It would help me to know where you were last Tuesday and Wednesday nights."

Martel pointed to the rocky wastes where the artillery shells were falling in sandy blooms. "Out there. On patrol."

"Then tell me something, Captain Martel. While you were following Vera Tamiri around, to scare her off as you say, perhaps you saw her with other men. Tell me about those."

"Tell me what this is about first," the soldier retorted. Then he looked beyond Faroun and the expression on his face changed from arrogance to worry.

The policeman turned to follow the soldier's line of sight. Two black Peugeot sedans had just pulled up to the bivouac in clouds of dust. The doors swung open and a squad of Sûreté men came bounding out, two of them armed with machine guns. Philomel Durac was the last to step onto the rocky soil and, after a quick exchange with the grizzled sergeant, headed for Faroun. Durac made a sweeping motion with his hand, and his men spread out. The agent practically pitched forward, on the run, trench coat flying behind him, fedora low on his forehead, a dashing figure gone ridiculous.

Martel was already backing up and preparing to take off when he tripped over a chunk of masonry. By the time he regained his balance, two of Durac's men were on him. A powerful man, he threw off one of the agents as if he were a terrier, but Durac himself was right behind his men and brought the butt of his pistol down on the back of Martel's skull. The soldier dropped to all fours as if poleaxed, and then an agent was straddling him, pulling out handcuffs.

"What the hell is this about, Durac?"

Durac, oddly enough, seemed pleased to see Faroun. At least he was wearing his best crooked smile. "Glad you were here, Inspector." He stood up, breathing heavily, and drew a paper from his coat.

Faroun scanned the arrest warrant and shook his head. "There are no charges specified."

Durac pretended disappointment, grinning all the while. "For reasons of state security, you understand."

"No, *you* don't seem to understand," Faroun said heatedly. "Captain Martel is a suspect in a murder investigation. I was just questioning him."

Durac tapped his forehead as if he had forgotten something. "Ah, that murder investigation! The Tamiri case, you mean." Durac lowered his voice. "Although I wouldn't just go shouting it about if I were you. You see, that's another matter of state security." Now the expression on Durac's pockmarked face was gloating, his little black eyes fixed on Faroun with the look of some portentous triumph.

"You mean a matter for the Prefecture."

"No, I mean a former matter for the Prefecture. The case is now under my jurisdiction."

"By whose authority?"

Durac shrugged as he turned away. "Why don't you ask your boss about that?"

Faroun stood amidst the rubble of the medieval wall and looked on speechlessly. The guns had fallen silent too as the artillery squad watched their dazed officer being dragged away.

Durac's hearses drove off at high speed. The grizzled sergeant came over to Faroun. "Never liked those bastards," he said, spitting on the dry earth. "They have the stink of death about them."

11

The two men bending over the table map of Syria in the delegate's office took each other's measure before resuming their disagreement. The recent riot in the Old City had given them much to disagree about, mostly concerning the level of military response to the current political crisis, or the ongoing political crisis, seeing as trouble had been a fellow traveler since the French first shot their way into Damascus some fifteen years before. Then again, Colonel Bremond, the French military commander of the Damascus district, and Delegate Montcalm found little common ground on policy matters. Their relationship, on and off the official stage, had become a fencing match, a game of thrust and parry, in which the style of the opponent was so well-known there was little in the way of surprise. Nevertheless, Colonel Bremond had adopted a long-term strategy of wearing down his op-

ponent, for he knew that, for the distracted Montcalm, it was just a matter of time.

"You can't be serious," said the colonel disapprovingly, as if the delegate were proposing an adolescent prank. "It sends entirely the wrong message."

"I mean to meet with the resistance leaders, Colonel," said Montcalm, relighting his meerschaum. "As long as there is some hope of dialogue."

Montcalm thought Colonel Bremond's policy of reprisal created only more insurgents. Bremond held Montcalm's policy of appeasement to be dangerously naïve. Privately, the colonel considered the delegate to be a deluded dreamer and schemed relentlessly to have him removed from office. As the high commissioner's delegate in Damascus, Guy de Montcalm saw his role inspired by history as much as by the Quai d'Orsay, the French foreign office. The Syrian nationalists must come to understand that cooperation with the French would yield great benefits, eventual liberty, possible fraternity, something like equality, and a thriving economy, although he would have to soft-pedal the latter given the worldwide collapse of the markets. He did not underestimate the challenge and he often doubted he was up to the task.

The fastidiously uniformed man across the table was Montcalm's necessary devil. For the short, squat colonel, the tall, spare aristo towering above him was the insufferable Siamese twin from whom he could not shake himself free. Their superiors in Beirut had bound them fast.

"We cannot compromise with rebels and terrorists," Bremond insisted. "They will take what you offer and then find a way of shaping it into a knife that will end up in your back." No coarse, blustering soldier, Colonel Bremond was an "Apollonian," as he was fond of saying, thereby insinuating his knowledge of Nietzsche as well as hinting at a classical education he did not possess. The colonel had risen through the ranks and had layered on tact, polish, and guile with each promotion. Montcalm was slightly in

awe of him—the colonel had been in Syria a long time and had even served as a staff officer with the famed General Gouraud, the soldier who had driven King Faisal out of Damascus. The delegate knew that his own self-esteem was based on ghosts, a distinguished family line that went back to the Hundred Years' War against England. So the delegate felt uneasy in the presence of the self-made officer, as if he were wearing two left shoes, although shoes of the finest leather.

"Come now," Bremond said good-humoredly. "We know where the insurgents are. Here are the havens—here, and here." He pointed at little red counters on the map. "From these locations they resupply and rearm. We need to strike them before they can carry off something spectacular. That's what they want, you know, something to grab the headlines." He swept a plump, manicured hand across the areas he had in mind for his push. "Once the lid has blown—"

"What does this get for us?" Montcalm asked rhetorically. "I'll tell you. What it has always gotten for us. More enemies. More money for the resistance."

"Such actions have bought us time," said the colonel confidently. "Besides, our tactics and training have improved greatly over the years. A few pinpricks, that is all. Root out the insurgents with the minimum of damage."

Montcalm knew what he meant of course—a bloody massacre. He pointed the stem of his meerschaum at the red flags. "You can't invade villages without inflicting casualties. On both sides."

"What is your alternative then? Wait? Talk? While we wait and talk, more will die." His tone was accusatory. "My regulars are tired of taking it in the back only to find themselves chasing phantoms. We need to stop the bleeding."

"By bleeding more!" The delegate raised a hand in exasperated protest and then let it drop. He had been in pain all morning with a migraine. He picked up one of the counters from the map. "It seems I am in the minority," he said ruefully. "My advisers chime your tune, Colonel. They think I am too timid. Even Umar Tamiri, whose opinion I value, as you know, urges a more aggressive policy in dealing with the resistance."

"We can't simply wait for the ax to fall," said the officer sympathetically. "Think of what happened in Iraq, sir. The British ran off with their tails between their legs."

"But control things behind the scenes."

"They have set a hideous precedent, sir. They have encouraged Arab nationalism by appearing to be weak. We are reaping the result."

"I shall think on it more," the delegate said wearily, and noticed his secretary poised silently at the open door.

"It's Inspector Faroun, sir."

"Inspector!" said the delegate warmly as if he hadn't seen the policeman in a dozen years. Faroun was wary of the welcome. The smile was guarded and the atmosphere in Montcalm's office in the Palace of Justice, usually bright and sunny owing to the wall of windows running the length of the wide room, was made a touch sinister by the presence of the scowling colonel. Nevertheless, the delegate listened with sympathy as Faroun expressed his dismay that Special Agent Durac had interfered with a Prefecture homicide case.

"You are bewildered by this turn of events, Inspector," the delegate said in a soothing tone. "However, I'm sure you realize that we all have the interests of justice in mind."

"Captain Martel is a potential suspect in the Vera Tamiri murder case," said Faroun, trying hard to control his emotion. "I was questioning the captain when Durac and his agents drove up to Tel el Saladin and hauled him away and half-conscious at that."

"My good inspector," said Colonel Bremond smoothly. "Neither the delegate nor myself have direct control of Durac's agency. Before my coming here to confer with the delegate, I received word from Durac's office that Captain Martel has confessed to the murder. After Durac is finished with him, Martel will be turned over for military justice."

"The Tamiri case is now a matter of state security," said Montcalm, lighting his meerschaum. He picked up a sheet of paper from the desk. "I was just writing a memorandum to you on the matter."

Faroun stared at the two men with incomprehension. "How could Martel confess in the space of a few hours?"

"Guilty conscience?" the colonel offered.

"Besides, Agent Durac is known for his diligence and his zeal," said the delegate. "That should come as no surprise to you, Inspector."

"No surprise!" Faroun protested. "Everything is a surprise about this case, sir. We turned over the body to Umar Tamiri four days ago and not so much as a funeral notice."

"At Monsieur Tamiri's request," said Montcalm. "He didn't want her funeral to turn into a mob scene and a demonstration. We must respect the wishes of a grieving brother—and her only remaining family member. The matter is out of my hands now and out of yours. The case will be transferred to the Sûreté."

"The Prefecture is to have nothing further to do with the Tamiri matter?"

"My memo will say that in effect," said Montcalm.

"This is an extraordinary precedent," Faroun said numbly.

"Triggered by a French officer's extraordinary confession. Not that your efforts haven't been appreciated, Inspector. Which reminds me," the Delegate said. "I want you to prepare to hand over the Tamiri case file to Agent Durac as soon as possible. My memo will provide you with specific instructions."

The two most powerful men in Damascus stood before him, one a condottiere in gleaming boots who believed the best way to untangle the Gordian knot was with the edge of a sword, the other a nobleman in impeccable tweed bedeviled by indecision. There was nothing for it. Faroun knew he had been sidelined. Perhaps they could not help the patronizing expressions on their faces, as if to say, "Now you know how things stand, go run along and find something useful to do."

12

A stiff spring breeze laden with droplets of moisture was blowing down from the mountains as Faroun stood at the iron railing overlooking the city. Bypassing his office in the Ministry Building, he had turned south in the direction of Mount Hermon and up the winding road that led to the crest of the stony hillock that marked Abel's Tomb. He scarcely felt the drizzle or the chill, and the prospect of the walled city below him seemed shabby and dreary, as if it had collapsed on itself.

He struggled to look past his humiliation to discover the motive for the delegate's capitulation. How else could he explain Montcalm's decision? Either Montcalm had bought into a scheme cooked up by Bremond and Durac to save face for the military by burying Captain Martel in the military justice system or—the delegate had decided to knock Faroun down a peg. If the former, then Faroun was at a loss to explain why Montcalm should team up with Bremond. If the delegate's aim was to weaken the Prefecture, then it diminished his administration's police powers—but why would he do that? Unless the plan was deliberately aimed at frustrating Faroun, at burying the Vera Tamiri case in limbo, at even erasing the memory of her life and death. In which case the delegate had bent to outside pressure, most likely that of Umar Tamiri. But what was Umar's motive? The delegate's turnabout was based on the flimsiest of excuses, the supposed confession of Captain Martel, a confession that Faroun deeply doubted. None of it made sense, the sudden appearance of Durac at the Tel el Saladin, the confession, the delegate's shelving of the case.

Faroun was not inclined to give up what he had started. He couldn't allow the case to fall away. Let Durac poach on his territory and there would be no end to it. He began to turn his anger to productive ends, as long years in confinement had led him to do. Harness the unruly energy and turn it into useful power. He began to review the facts of the case from the moment he had set eyes on the corpse of Vera Tamiri. As he thought again of Vera's ransacked apartment, going from room to room, he spied a blue Bugatti coupe racing up the winding road. For a moment, he thought the car would veer off the slippery incline, but the wheels turned just in time.

Before long the Bugatti pulled up and the side window rolled down. The rain and the wind had picked up considerably, and Faroun caught a toss of a blond head, red lips, and a hand gesturing for him to go around to the other side.

"You need better company than the weather, Inspector," said Eugenie Poquelin as he closed the door. She reached below her knees and drew up a small woven basket. She handed Faroun the linen napkin on top. As he wiped his hands and face, she produced two sandwiches and a bottle of Bordeaux.

Faroun accepted the sandwich and a glass of wine. "How did you find me?"

"Your secretary was not very helpful—she doesn't like me very much—but I ran into your Sergeant Kabir, at the Ministry Building. You like to take your midday meal up here, he tells me."

They touched glasses. She was looking pretty in a raincoat and bright red silk scarf around her neck in a shade that matched her lipstick. He complimented her. They touched glasses again. Faroun bit into the chicken sandwich, hungrier than he would admit. "Why go to this trouble to find me?"

"You did ask me to contact you if I had any further information about Vera Tamiri, didn't you? So, as you can see, I am here."

"Then you have discovered something useful for me?" Faroun wondered for a moment if he should tell her about the new disposition of the case—after all, if she gave him any new evidence, she might run into trouble herself—but his curiosity drew him on. Her information might be useless. But he could not be sure.

"I know I haven't been entirely honest with you, Inspector," she was saying, "so I thought I might try and make it up to you."

"And in what way have you not been honest, Madame Poquelin?"

She turned a bright smile on him. "If you insist on calling me Madame Poquelin, I shall drive off now and leave you standing stupidly in the rain. I am Eugenie." She reached into the basket and pulled out a tiny, clothbound notebook. "This belonged to Vera. I do not know if it will have any bearing on the search for her murderer, but if it helps . . ."

Faroun opened the worn book and skimmed through the pages. A running list of mathematical calculations in a minuscule hand, some with the dates written beside them, additions and subtractions, some of the figures crossed out, but without any reference as to their purpose. On the last page of the book, he found a small diagram, a hand pointing downward, letters inscribed on each fingertip. Faroun held out the open page to his companion.

Eugenie shook her head. "A charm perhaps. I do not know what these things mean." She put her sandwich down to pour some more wine. "But the figures—it's a ledger of some sort, don't you think?"

"How did this book come into your possession?"

"After Vera was burned out of her clinic, she gave me the notebook for safekeeping. From time to time, she would visit and ask for it. She would ask for privacy and then make entries in the book. When she was finished, she would return it to me."

"You never asked her about this?"

"What business was it of mine?" Eugenie explained. "Besides, she did not volunteer any information. She could be secretive about things. And not only about her lovers."

Faroun skimmed through the pages again, then slipped the book into his pocket. "I thank you for this—Eugenie. I would also appreciate your keeping quiet about it too."

"Of course." She turned in her seat to look at him with a bold and searching glance. Scurries of rain dashed against the windshield. "I think you know you can trust my discretion."

Faroun looked at her a moment, then averted his eyes. "You're almost there."

"Have I not been truthful with you?"

"You told me something about the lovers. But not about the gambling. Surely you must have known."

Eugenie folded her napkin into a neat square. "What would her gambling have to do with anything?"

"It might explain why she was murdered, Eugenie. Where did she get the money to play the tables? Did she have money of her own?"

"That miserable Umar held on to her money. She would complain bitterly about that. All he did for her was pay for her apartment and give her a pittance to live on. To control her, you see. To keep her in line." Eugenie smiled grimly. "It didn't work. It just made her more crazy."

"Do you know for a fact that she had money of her own?"

"Her father had left her a special account. It was supposed to go to her when he died. But somehow Umar got hold of it."

"Then she must have had some other source of income. Think of any of the men you met or knew about, Vera's men—outside of Captain Martel, who lives on an officer's pay—who would have financed her habits."

Eugenie shook her head again. "No one. Unless it was that new friend of hers. Teddy."

"You never met Teddy, you said. But did you ever meet a man named Salim al Quassi? He was seen with Vera at one of the casinos."

She placed her hands on the steering wheel. On her right hand, she wore a small cameo ring, the design a classical nymph drawing a bow. "The name is familiar to me—but I can't put a face to it. Vera often traveled in a crowd, especially after the firebombing of her clinic. She felt safer that way."

"Were you ever a part of her crowd?"

"Oh, my, yes—when I could. As I told you, my husband disapproved of Vera."

"A dangerous woman, you said."

"Pardon?"

"Your husband thought of her that way, you said."

"Henri is antediluvian in his thinking," she replied as if she had rehearsed the judgment. Then she looked up with an awakening smile. "Surely you don't think that Henri had anything to do with Vera's death?"

"I took your advice and spoke to Madame Hallaf—Vera's nurse at the clinic. She had some interesting things to say. One was about a row that you had with your husband one afternoon outside the clinic."

"I told you Henri did not approve of my work there."

"She told me some other things about Vera too. That Vera was very dedicated to her philanthropies but didn't seem to have the knack for them. She was distracted; she poured money into her projects, such as the literacy program, but never seemed able to complete them. She was out of touch with the very people she was trying to help. Some days they would have to shut the clinic for lack of medical supplies. Madame Hallaf herself often went unpaid, and no regular physician would work there."

"Pressure brought to bear, Inspector. Umar was out to see that she didn't succeed. And the others—those influential men in the city who wanted her closed down. Shut up and out of business. Do you think my husband was one of them?"

"He is not high on my list of suspects, I can assure you."

"Henri may be older than I, Inspector, but he is really much of a little boy, or maybe an adolescent. He is mischievous but he wouldn't hurt anyone." She sighed. "At least no one but me."

"How do you mean?"

She became pensive. "My father had some pretense to a title, but he had no money. Henri has lots of money. Draw your own conclusions."

"So why should he hurt you?"

"When he feels trapped, he lashes out, that's all." She put her glass back in the basket and wiped her lips with a napkin. "But that's mostly in the past. He has found other outlets for his temper. I don't see much of him anymore. Business, he says." She laughed hollowly. "Anyway, you were speaking of your list of suspects."

Faroun flipped through the pages of the ledger. "Someone broke into Vera's apartment, perhaps just before or after she died. I wonder if this is what they were searching for."

"That miserable hole," Eugenie said. "She scarcely went there. Sometimes, especially when Henri was away, she would come and stay with me and the kids. But lately she had been staying somewhere else. Based on things she said, I think she had a little love nest with Teddy."

The rain had tapered off to a thin drizzle. Faroun looked at the comfortable appointments of the Bugatti with appreciation. The dashboard was polished teak, the dials and gauges set flush into the wood, the smell of a new car and old leather softened with sandalwood oil. The automobile seemed to have been made for the elegant young woman sitting next to him. They were sitting close enough that he could detect a trace of her scent, reminding him of an exotic garden of peonies and camellias. Below the steering wheel, he saw the shimmer of a silk stocking. She had removed one shoe to rest her foot on the brake. Her foot was small with a delicate curve to the instep.

"This will be very helpful, Eugenie." Faroun slipped the ledger into his raincoat pocket. "One more question before I go. If one were to have a lover's hideaway in this town—where would one go?"

"Do you consider me a woman of the world, Inspector?" Eugenie asked with a coy smile.

"If one were Vera, I meant to say."

"I'll have to think about that. At least I don't strike you as a matronly mother of two. I'm even a bit flattered."

"I didn't mean to imply . . ." Nikolai looked for some way to back out of the question.

"I'll make you an offer," she said, turning to him, enthusiasm deepening her blue eyes. "I can do a little undercover work for you, quietly, discreetly, of course. I have friends and I know most of Vera's. Perhaps I can come up with something for you. Anything to bring her murderer to justice. Besides, there must be some attempt to keep her memory alive, despite Umar."

"How do you mean?"

"Surely it couldn't have escaped your notice, Inspector, that there has been no public reference to Vera's death. Nothing in the newspapers. There has been no funeral announcement. Umar has given out the lie that Vera is in Istanbul getting a cure."

"I can tell you that the delegate authorized a news blackout. To give us working room with the investigation."

"It's not right." Those blue eyes of Eugenie Poquelin's had now darkened with anger. "Vera deserves a funeral. She deserves more than just being shoved into a dark hole in the earth."

"Umar is a powerful man."

"Too powerful and too filled with fear."

"What do you mean?"

"Vera told me that he is walking paranoiac. He believes there's a dozen conspiracies out there, all aimed at removing him from this earth. He never travels without bodyguards, as I'm sure you're aware. And he has a legion of spies, Vera once told me."

"Did he think Vera might be conspiring against him?"

Eugenie sighed. "Did Umar kill Vera? Is that what you're asking? The answer is, I don't think so. He hated what she had become, her defiance, her bohemian style, her 'disgrace' as he saw it, but he loved her. In the strange way that Umar loves."

"He loved her and he hated her. Spark and fuse."

"Umar was angry that she had brought scandal to the family name, but I don't think Umar Tamiri killed her any more than I think Henri Poquelin killed her."

"Now you have really caught me in a tangle, madame!"

"I want my Henri off the hook. That's the expression you police use, is it not?"

"Henri was never really on the hook, madame."

She gave him a cross look. "So you think that my Henri is too old to plot and carry out a crime, is that it? He may be older than I, but he is no dodderer, monsieur."

"I wasn't trying to imply anything about his age."

"He doesn't need a cane, if that is what you're thinking." And then she added thoughtfully, "At least not yet."

13

Anxious to study the ledger he had received from Eugenie Poquelin, Faroun practically bowled over Mansour on the way
up the stairs to his office.

"Why, my dear Faroun, you'll catch your death," said the coroner, brushing off beads of rain from the shoulder of Faroun's coat.
"Not that I'm opposed to the Grim Reaper, seeing as he keeps me
employed. Your loss, though, would be hard to bear."

"Touched," growled the policeman. "But I'm not in the mood
for banter."

"Then I'm not in the mood for disclosing evidence," said Mansour in a wounded voice. "Besides, you are off the Tamiri case
anyway." Faroun stopped in his ascent and stared down at him.
"News travels quickly around here, don't you know? Bad news
travels at the speed of light." The surgeon held up a little cello-

phane packet as he looked at the policeman over his horn-rimmed glasses. "I suppose I should turn this over to Agent Durac."

Faroun slowly retraced his steps. "The case is still mine, officially, until I receive Montcalm's written order."

"Ah, precisely my thinking," said Mansour slyly. "That's why I thought you might be interested in the fruit of my little study."

"The piece of ceramic found in Vera's hair," said Faroun appreciatively. "What's the verdict?"

"Turkish. That particular shade of pink, almost salmon in hue. Late 1880s, early '90s. Decorative. From a mosaic, I'd say."

"A private home?"

"Possibly, but it might be from one of the charming hotels built at that time for the convenience of Ottoman dignitaries and bureaucrats traveling about the provinces. The question is, how many hotels built in that period still survive? Damascus has suffered the devastation of war since then. You would need to look into that."

"Thank you, Mansour. I can trust you to keep quiet about this? At least for now?"

"Silent as the tomb," came the reply. "Which reminds me, I've got to get back to work." As he continued his descent, he said, "One last thing about the tile. It seems to be part of a molded fish scale. I would say it's from an aquatic design of some kind. Oriental, perhaps. Like those colorful fish with the whiskers." He wriggled his fingers under his chin.

Faroun was trying to remember the name of the oriental fish when he opened the opaque door with PREFECTURE: ADMINISTRATIVE stenciled in faded sans serif lettering, nodded to Rebecca in passing, and closed the door to the inner office. He swept open the dark blue velvet curtains that he kept meaning to have changed. Obscure light poured in from the courtyard of the ministry. Below, a squad of uniformed traffic policemen were practicing in the drizzle, their white gloves pointing and waving in practiced choreography.

Since Rebecca was rarely allowed to make any sense of his papers, stacks of files and beribboned portfolios occupied the tops of cabinets and spilled across the two antique tables he had inherited from his predecessors. On one of the tables was an ugly replica of a bust of Socrates, and hanging above the other table was a large painting of a battle scene, or the aftermath-of-a-battle scene with riderless horses grazing among fallen knights and fat carrion birds settling on the bodies of the slain. He had been meaning to get rid of that painting for some time. At one end of the room was a fireplace that he rarely used because a faulty flue sent smoke back into the room. The molded mantelpiece was made of a cracked slab of stained marble. A wooden statue of Saint Sebastian presided dolefully over the room. It had been a parting gift from his mother before she had disappeared into the vast storm and turmoil of revolutionary Russia. It was made of polished Siberian cedar, the palms of the saint facing outward to proclaim the stigmata. At the other end of the mantelpiece was the woeful toy bear Faroun had recovered from Vera Tamiri's apartment, although he had stuffed back most of the horsehair that had spilled out of the slit stomach.

The bear reminded him of the potential treasure he carried in his coat pocket, so he threw his raincoat over a chair and settled into the wooden desk chair, which always protested with an agonized screech. Unlike the rest of the room, the desk was dusted and organized, his pencil and pens in a porcelain British toby mug he had bought in England during the war and sent to his father, his papers neatly arranged in the letter basket and the white envelope bearing the delegate's seal propped up against the banker's lamp on his desk. He turned on the light and opened the envelope, dreading the instructions that waited. He looked at the folded slip of paper inside and, without viewing the message, slipped the envelope into a desk drawer. He pulled out an oval magnifier and

turned his attention to the ledger, studying each page until he came to the last leaf with its enigmatic diagram.

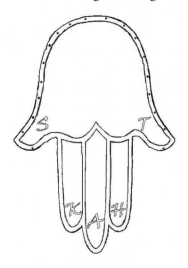

The hand of Fatima. It was the age-old amulet to ward off the evil eye. Superstitious mothers placed it around the necks of their children. Truck drivers hung it over their dashboards. Only there was something different about this amulet. Each fingertip was inscribed with a letter. There was a sixth letter though, the letter Q, and this was drawn within an oval but outside the hand.

Faroun leafed through the calculations again but could see no pattern that linked the accounts with the letters on the hand. All of the transactions were dated and began with entries from the previous year. The accounts, he surmised, were a record of Vera Tamiri's financial dealings. Wherever there was an addition of a sum, Vera had written a star symbol beside it. They were all large sums, nothing under five hundred—assuming the numbers meant French francs. Sometimes the sums were very large, ten, fifteen, even twenty thousand, but they would be followed by other amounts with the star symbol X'd out. These would be subtracted from the previous sums, often leaving her with a hefty negative

balance. The last two entries caught his attention. The next-to-last entry was dated April 13 in the amount of five thousand and had a triangle written beside it. Two days later, Vera had deducted three thousand from this amount, leaving her with a final balance of two thousand. This last transaction had been made on April 15, just one week ago. Perhaps it had been on the day she died. The triangle symbol intrigued. Faroun backtracked and found that several additions or accounts receivable, if he could call them that, had the same triangle symbol beside them, and that all of these had been within the last three months. They were all for five thousand. It seems she had been receiving irregular payments from someone during that period. Faroun wondered if the triangle entries represented gifts from one of her gambling partners or perhaps from her new lover, the one Vera called Teddy. The final entry would be consistent with the fact that she had drawn money from the last payment from "Triangle" to pay down her debt to Monsieur Sezgin. She had paid him three thousand francs.

The policeman was so absorbed in his study that he did not notice the man standing before him until the shadow of his fez fell across the page.

"You wanted to see me, sir," said Ihab Kabir.

Faroun leaned back in his chair, his hands behind his head, and looked up at the high ceiling. He had never noticed the water stains up there before. Or the giant cobweb stretching from the light fixture to the north end of the room. He wondered what kind of spider might be skulking in the shadows. Ihab followed his gaze.

"You were born in Damascus, weren't you, Sergeant?"

"On a farm outside of Damascus, sir, in the town of Jazrail. My father grew vegetables for the market."

"And your family still has the farm?"

"Not anymore. We lost the farm during the time of Faisal. We lost the property to the Shihabs. One of the big Damascus families. They bought up a lot of property after the war. They chased my father off the land and turned it over to one of their relatives."

"What happened to your father?"

"He died of a broken heart, I think." Ihab shifted on his feet uncomfortably. "It's a long story. Besides, I was in Egypt at the time. Why do you ask, sir?"

"I was just wondering how much of the local lore you know. About who controls the strings."

"The French control the strings, Inspector."

"Point taken, Sergeant," Faroun replied, overlooking the impertinence. "The powerful families, the moneyed families, the landowners. You mentioned the Shihabs."

"Among the Sunni Arabs, the Shihabs," said Ihab. "There are the Twelve Families. We all learned about them growing up. If you want to get ahead in Damascus, if you want to keep out of trouble, you know about the families."

"What about the al Quassi?"

"They are also Sunni. The family owns the big transport firm. You see their trucks everywhere on the roads. That is their symbol." He pointed at Vera's ledger, which showed the solitary oval with the letter *Q*. "It's painted on the doors of their trucks. Like this one."

Faroun turned the notebook around. "If that is the al Quassi sign, Sergeant, what do you make of the inscribed hand? Does that mean anything to you?"

"Other than as an amulet, sir?" Ihab was puzzled. "The letters on the fingers—I've never seen those before."

"Who could tell me more about the local history—about these twelve families of Damascus?"

"I worked under Inspector Baramki for a while. He would know. He married into one of them, I think."

"All right then, I would like you to do some special work for me, Sergeant. Find out more about the al Quassi clan for me, the family background, whom they do business with, what kind of influence they wield. I am particularly curious about Salim al Quassi. Find out what you can about him. I don't want you to use known police sources for information. Go underground, out of uniform, and develop your own sources."

Kabir looked at his boss pensively. "Does this have to do with the Tamiri investigation, sir?"

"Any connection to the Tamiri family would be of interest."

Ihab Kabir had a prominent gold tooth. Faroun had to look twice at the smile that revealed it. "I've been waiting for something like this, sir. When do you want me to report back to you?"

"Find out as much as you can as soon as you can. Let us meet in two days at The Hawk. Just before noon when the place is busy. I'll be in Arab dress."

Ihab looked at him sidewise. "To take the pulse of the street, sir?"

"Before I make house calls," Faroun said blandly.

"At The Hawk then," said Ihab Kabir, saluting before he turned on his heel.

Once the door had closed, Faroun placed his hands before him on the desk and sighed. He opened the desk drawer and held up the envelope from the delegate's office. He could not deny he had received it. Rebecca had already dutifully logged it in.

He opened the folded letter, his eyes searching the nearly empty page. There was no memorandum from Montcalm advising him that the Vera Tamiri case had been transferred to Durac's agency. There was no mention of the confession by Captain Gerard Martel. Instead, there was a blue card, a priority pass into the Citadel prison, where political prisoners were held, and Montcalm's written authorization to visit the officer tomorrow morning. Besides the pass, only one word was written on the stationery in the delegate's nervous hand: FRIDAY.

Faroun spun around in his chair and examined the wall calendar. Today was Saturday. Montcalm had bought him some time. He was delaying the formal transfer of the case. This left Faroun with a little less than seven full days to find Vera Tamiri's murderer. He went over to the window that overlooked the courtyard. Except for the guards at the entrance, the courtyard was empty, its brick paving puddled here and there with rainwater. The delegate was playing a curious game. Two hours ago, he had stood in solidarity with his archrival Colonel Bremond. While Faroun could not second-guess Montcalm's motives, he knew a gift when he saw it. Slipping the pass into his suit coat, his eyes fell on the open ledger. He put this into his pocket too. He thought Maxim might be some help in decoding this enigma, and besides, the Ukrainian bistro owner poured a generous glass of arak. But first he thought he would shake the tree by paying a courtesy call on Umar Tamiri.

14

That the rich and powerful prefer stately prisons in which to live Nikolai Faroun knew, for he had grown up in a few of them. He felt a familiar twinge of loneliness and isolation the moment he rolled up to the main gate of Umar's compound in Aldahdah, north of the old city. "Old Family Territory," as his sergeant called it, fortified estates with high walls built on gently rising hills. These families ruled over fiefdoms, and Tamiri had hired *qabaday,* street thugs, to guard his territory. Two of them met Faroun as he stepped out of the patrol car and presented his badge at the gate, one a surly brute with a shaved head and a crescent scar down his right cheek. The guards were not in the least intimidated by the fact that he was Prefecture chief and frisked him before they sent word of the unannounced visitor. After a few moments, Scarface led him into the vestibule of Umar's house.

A cream-colored residence of three levels, mosaic flooring, whitewashed columns, and Romanesque pilasters, the house evoked Syria's pagan past, except for the antique alabaster cross hung in a votive niche just inside the main door. The floor was made of dark travertine marble shot through with veins of scarlet. Here and there the terra-cotta bust of an implacable Babylonian god, impaled on a pedestal, spread malevolence from the potted palms. A broad-shouldered house attendant, wearing a white linen tunic, baggy trousers, and sandals, brought him to the door of Umar's study.

The room was decorated in dynastic style with painted lotus-shaped moldings and a statue of an Assyrian griffin, tall as a man, lurking in a corner. Chill and still as a tomb, the only sound that of Umar flipping through the pages of a document. He presented a dapper image in his gray pinstripe and brass-button spats, but he could not hide his irritation. An inlaid chessboard was on his desk, the pieces already engaged in the hunt for the king. Faroun picked up an ivory knight, appreciating its heft and workmanship.

"Do you play?" Umar plucked the piece from Faroun's hand and returned it to its square on the board.

"I've won a game or two," Faroun said simply.

"I play by mail with an Egyptologist in Cairo," said Umar. "This particular game has been in progress for about six months. He is losing—badly—as you can see. However, I do not think it is chess that has brought you to my door this afternoon."

"I apologize for the intrusion, Monsieur Tamiri. There has been a development in your sister's case."

"You have some news concerning my sister's murder?" He set the papers down on his desk. "Ah, but the delegate telephoned me earlier today. Congratulations! You have found her killer! Agent Durac has extracted a confession from him. An army captain. He is being held in the Citadel as we speak." Tamiri leaned across the desk with a prepossessing smile. "Does it surprise you, Inspector, that I have that kind of information?"

"What if I were to tell you I didn't believe it?"

The businessman looked doubtful. "Then you have other suspects?"

"One, or two." Faroun took the measure of the man across from him. With strips of brilliantine hair running down the sides of his head, the curious pointed ears, the smooth-shaven cheeks with the spasmodic tic, he resembled a creature out of an old bestiary, part badger, part fox. "I need to reconcile a few details, before I turn the case over formally to Agent Durac."

"Naturally, if I can be helpful." Umar plucked a cigarette out of a silver canister.

"What can you tell me about Salim al Quassi? It seems your sister had some contact with him. They were gambling companions."

"That doesn't surprise me. The al Quassi brothers are an unsavory clan. I know of Abdullah, a ruffian of the worst sort. Salim is the younger, but I know little about him. As I've explained to you after I viewed Vera's body, my sister and I didn't speak of her—male companions. That just made things between us worse than they were already."

"Could they have been worse, Monsieur? After her husband died, Vera left in a storm and never came back. She traded all this"—Faroun's eyes drifted to the gilded molding above—"for a squalid apartment in Kasaa."

"As she chose to live, much to my dismay. Vera was willful and . . ."

"Disobedient?"

"Independent."

"Perhaps so independent she deserved a dressing down."

Umar blew a short, round puff of smoke in Faroun's direction. "What are you angling for, Inspector?"

"Someone torched Vera's clinic to teach her a lesson."

"There is a scratch in your recording. I had nothing to do with that business. I've told you that."

"And you've told me that you were supportive of your sister's philanthropies, and yet the more I learn about your relationship with her, the more I suspect the opposite. Some of the clinic's money came from wealthy donors, but apparently, you weren't one of them. In fact, you so were practiced at tightening the screws on your sister she had barely enough to live on. She had to resort to gambling to earn money."

The businessman glared but did not rise to the bait. "Nothing could be further from the truth. I gave her money regularly and, if I say so, generously. She gambled because she was addicted. And she lost all the cash I gave her. That is why I begged her to return home. And I didn't need to burn down her clinic to persuade her. In fact, we were talking about her returning home just before I lost her." Umar straightened the facing of the queen on the chessboard. "I don't know where you obtain your information, Inspector, and I do not understand what it is you are trying to prove. Are you telling me that Salim al Quassi had something to do with Vera's murder? Or that he was fleecing her? I'd believe the latter soon enough. But from all I've heard about the young man, he seems quite incapable of anything so meticulous as murder."

It was a subtle chase, Faroun realized, and it had turned back on him. "I am simply trying to understand why you would derail the Prefecture's investigation."

"Why should I do that? The delegate called me about the transfer of the case; I didn't call him."

"Then can you tell me why you are behaving as if your sister were still alive? It is a matter of time before her friends discover that Vera is not in a hospital near Istanbul."

Umar Tamiri stood up, straightening his coat. "Now you are sticking your nose into family business, Inspector Faroun. And that is none of your concern. Is there any other reason for your visit? If not . . ." Umar picked up the sheaf of papers, shaking them as if to conclude the interview.

"Just one more question, Monsieur Tamiri. You are a building contractor, are you not?"

"I am a broker for building contracts."

"In short you are the one who facilitates large building projects. Government projects, for instance. Obviously, you do not perform such services for small-scale construction."

"Obviously." Umar's feathers were ruffled. "Are you suggesting there is something irregular in my business, Faroun?"

"Not in the least!" Faroun objected, as if he had been misunderstood. "The delegate has utmost confidence in you. I'm just curious how you make ends meet these days. There's a depression on and it has brought government spending—and construction—to a standstill. Damascus is not in the midst of a building boom."

"More's the pity," said Umar. "But the Tamiri firm has weathered such economic slumps before." He pulled out his pocket watch and clicked open the golden facing. "One looks to the future and places one's trust in God."

Faroun picked up the ivory knight from the chessboard once more. "A noble Christian sentiment, sir. However, I would not look to the future of this game. I am afraid your Egyptologist in Cairo has stolen a march on you." Faroun moved the knight three spaces and removed Umar's bishop from the board. He held out the fallen prelate to the businessman. "Mate, Monsieur Tamiri, in three moves."

"I can tell you what it reminds me of," said Maxim, jabbing a thick finger at the diagram in Vera's ledger. "These secret societies and nationalist groups that make Damascus their base of operations— they all have their signs and symbols and codes. It could be I've seen this somewhere before, but I can't place it."

The Ukrainian put a polished glass on a shelf behind him and picked up another, wrapping his bar towel around it. It was early afternoon and except for a pair of lovers billing and cooing at the end of the bar, the club was empty. Maxim's little fleet of Egyptian sailing ships was anchored in the circular harbor at the other end of the bar where he and Faroun were conversing. "Who does this belong to anyway?"

"It belonged to Vera Tamiri."

"You just used the past tense," said Maxim.

"She's dead," Faroun confirmed. "Murdered. At least we have a confession. If it is a confession. But you didn't hear what I just said and you didn't hear it from me."

"No mention of her death," said Maxim, flipping through a newspaper. He set it aside to pick up the ledger again. "So you think this might provide a clue? Who else knows about the book?"

"Only those who dare not speak."

Maxim appreciated the irony. "So what is it I'm not supposed to know?"

The policeman pushed away his empty glass. "I thought I might tap into that long memory of yours."

"In this business it is best to have a selective memory," said Maxim. "However, I have made a few friends over the years." The bar owner rolled the tip of a pencil on his thick tongue and set about copying the diagram onto a slip of paper. "I may have someone in mind."

"The oval with the letter Q. I have reason to suspect that stands for the al Quassi family."

Maxim stopped writing and studied the image. "The trucking firm?"

"I'm not sure."

"Abdullah al Quassi," Maxim said reflectively. "He runs the business. A mean customer, that one. He started out about eight years ago, 1925 or 1926. There were a lot of firms competing for hauling contracts, for private French firms and for the government. Al Quassi began eliminating the competition, and by that I mean shooting the competition. He was a mobster. Perhaps he still is one." Maxim shrugged his shoulders. "There were a lot of gangsters back then. Now we have gangsters and terrorists and you can't tell the difference. They wrap themselves in the Syrian flag or the flag of Islam. Or both. Not much difference. They all want the same thing."

"And what is that, my Ukrainian friend?"

"Power, *mon ami*. Power."

15

Near the village of Quetife on the road to Aleppo, Salim al Quassi took a pistol out of his coat pocket, pointed it at the driver, and told him to stop. When the sedan pulled over to the side of the road, Salim put his arm over the seat and looked back at his wife. She had half of an Armenian sweet roll stuffed in her mouth. Crumbs clung to her heavily rouged lips. Her kerchief was knotted loosely under her jowls, and with the chador she wore over her dress, she appeared huge, crowding out the little girl who sat on her right and the other who sat on her left. The little girl on the right was four and was holding an orange in her lap. She had poked holes in the fruit with her fingers, and juice had stained her new dress. Her mother had not noticed that yet. The little girl on the left, two years older than her sister, held a wooden doll on her lap. The doll was half-bald. Salim grimaced.

Hanan was always pulling the hair out of the heads of her dolls. He did not like to think what she would be like once she grew up and had a husband. He looked at his wife again, her cheeks bulging with pastry and told her to remain calm.

"Where are you going?" she asked, swallowing after she spoke. She did not seem alarmed. She knew her husband was crazy and this was just his latest stunt.

"I am taking leave of you," Salim said. He stepped onto the road, a valise tucked under his arm.

"Don't be ridiculous," said his wife. "Put that gun away."

Salim pointed the weapon at her forehead. "I would like you to be very calm now, so that I do not get nervous. I am leaving you here. You and the children are to go on with the driver to Aleppo."

The woman wiped her mouth with a handkerchief soaked in cologne. Salim hated that scent. He drew back from the window and, holding his breath, waved the driver on. "Don't stop until you get to Aleppo," Salim told him.

The driver nodded and was happy to move along.

His wife leaned out of the car as it sped off and looked back at him as if he were a simpleton standing in the middle of the road.

The highway was empty and the sun was getting to be hot, so he took some shade beneath a plane tree. He leaned against the trunk of the tree and began laughing. It was the first time he had laughed since Vera had died, and he laughed and he hooted with the exhilaration of being free. When he stopped enjoying the joke, he pulled a workman's homespun robe out of the valise and pulled it over his elegant silk suit. He fitted a checkered kaffiyeh over his head and straightened the agal. Holding a pocket mirror before his handsome features, he smiled with satisfaction. He waited under the tree for almost an hour before a battered bus came along. It was covered with dust and filled with villagers bringing produce and livestock to the market. As the bus heaved to a stop with a gaseous backfire, a bearded goat leaned its head out a window and brayed at him. Fleetingly, he thought it would have been much better to have taken the Mercedes sedan and make his wife and the children walk to Aleppo. But he knew he must adhere to his plan. He dare not attract attention. For this reason, he had decided to wear a simple robe and kaffiyeh. Then he noticed his shoes. Italian, soft leather. He should replace these with sandals to complete his disguise. He sighed. Even an impostor must have his comforts. He was not going to part with his shoes.

The driver held up three fingers for the fare, and Salim al Quassi dug into his purse for the coins as the bus cranked back into action and rattled down the road to Damascus.

16

At the Villa Artemis, Faroun was finally making some progress unpacking. He had nearly emptied the first crate of books. There were shelves in the study, so he had begun arranging the volumes there, including a rare edition of Diderot's *Encyclopédie* left to him by his father. A half-shelf of fiction, some Balzac, some Zola, and a well-worn copy of Lawrence's *Revolt in the Desert*.

He took up a private edition of the *Sayings of Gurdjieff* and carried it to the kitchen, where he had just made a pitcher of fresh-squeezed orange juice, and poured a glass. He tipped in a jigger of arak. A radio station program featuring new jazz platters was playing Nina Rette's version of "The Sheik of Araby," but the music died as soon as he lifted his glass. Perhaps it was a cosmic warning, but the frequency, beamed from Beirut, usually cut out about midnight due to atmospheric storms in the mountains of the Anti-Lebanon.

Jules—Faroun could not remember that he ever had a last name—had introduced him to the ideas of Gurdjieff, a Russian spiritualist who had, in his early days, wandered throughout Central Europe and the Near East in search of men of truth. Jules referred to him simply as the Teacher, and his enthusiasm for the Russian's ideas was infectious.

Faroun had met Jules toward the end of 1924, after he had been transferred from the military prison in Lyon to do hard labor in a coal mine in the Saar. With his long stretch of isolation over, Faroun found being around others a difficult adjustment, but he was hungry for new things to learn. The military prisoners lived in a camp just outside the slag heap, wretched wooden and tarpaper barracks that did little to keep out the raw winter wind that blew over the coalfield, but they were at least fortunate to be able to burn coal chips in makeshift stoves and keep reasonably warm if not always dry. The prisoners had pooled their few books into a lending library, and Jules was the unofficial librarian. A love of reading and chess brought Faroun and Jules together, and their discussions would often take them down the meandering paths of thought until the lights were turned out. Gurdjieff had been the mischief behind Jules's landing in the stockade. As a young soldier, he had met Gurdjieff in Paris and fallen under his powerful sway. Once you met Gurdjieff, Jules would say, you either sat at his feet because you had met a saint or ran off screaming because you had met the devil. Jules had decided to stay on at the school at Prieuré outside Paris because he felt at home in the "madhouse." When he first arrived, a stocky, ferocious man with a full flaring mustache ordered him to take off his uniform, handed him a shovel, and told him to bury the clothes in a deep pit. The complication was that it was the dead of winter, the ground was frozen, and he was naked except for his underwear and boots until he had dug a hole about six feet deep. Later, the stocky man came to oversee his progress.

"You are burying your old self," the man had told him as he began to shovel dirt over the uniform. "Remember that." When he had finished his own burial, Jules went back in the house, where the other students had a good laugh at his expense. Then the overseer, none other than Gurdjieff himself, gave him cast-off clothing that was too big for him, clapped him on the back, and invited him to dine at his table, a signal honor. The following day he was outside again digging—this time a latrine. Jules was angry because this was the same work he had been doing in the army. At some point, Gurdjieff came over to persuade him that the work he was doing was different from army work, as if he had been reading Jules's mind. He would just have to find out how it was different. This challenge reinvigorated him and he redoubled his efforts. He became skilled and proud at digging just about anything. He had other adventures with the "Mage of Prieuré" as the locals called him, but the army tracked Jules down. He was court-martialed for desertion and sentenced to seven years of hard labor.

Jules didn't seem to mind digging in the mines either; at least he never complained. He would stomp around the little hut and swing his arms and stretch his neck like a turtle, and he claimed these exercises helped to keep him self-aware but not self-conscious. Faroun told him he couldn't see the difference.

Jules picked up a lump of coal from the muddy floor. "You see this thing, Faroun? It is just a piece of black rock. It is inert. It is useless. Until one puts it in the fire, that is. Then its true worth is recognized. That's us," he said, tossing the lump into the stove. "We are sleepwalkers on this earth. We are inert. We are useless. Until somebody tosses us in the fire."

Jules had been digging in the mines long before Faroun arrived, but he never spoke of a getting out. One evening, he gave Faroun this same tattered copy of the *Sayings of Gurdjieff* and gravely shook his hand. "Be watchful," he said. "You are about to meet the master." The next morning there was a cave-in and Jules was buried alive. To Faroun's mind, Jules had gotten the thread of destiny confused. Two days after Jules's death, Faroun was called up from the mine shaft and told he had a visitor. He was a stocky man with a bald head and intense black eyes and an extravagant mustache, just as Jules had described Gurdjieff. He had another name though and it soon became clear he worked for French intelligence. The winter of 1925 was drawing to a close. Spring was at hand. The man asked Faroun if he would like to go Syria. He had to decide immediately. There would not be a second offer. "And get out of here?" Faroun asked. "No more stockades," said the other. "But there will be chains."

He looked down at his unbound wrists with some surprise as he stood in the study where his father used to spend so many solitary hours. A beautiful orange tree was just outside the study window. The spring was persuading it to blossom. Tayeb Faroun had died in this study in 1922, but his son, Nikolai, did not know about this until many years later. His housekeeper had found him sitting at his desk with his head lying on his stamp album. The page was open to the czarist issues of Russia, he had learned. He was dreaming of her at the end, that tall, pale, beautiful aerialist with the red hair and the gray eyes who once traveled Transcaucasia with the circus. She had left him with a son and a memory so profound that every time Tayeb Faroun cursed her name, he fought back tears.

Faroun put Gurdjieff on the shelf and returned to the kitchen. He sat at the table unmoving for a long time, lost in thought. At last, he roused himself with the knowledge that he would meet with Captain Martel again. The blue-colored pass into the Citadel was on the table and he picked it up. Perhaps Montcalm was not happy with Martel's sudden confession either. In a strange way, he felt that the delegate's five-day reprieve was a call for help. Something was not right. "Be a friend to him," Madame Montcalm had said. But how could he help if he did not know the cause?

The wind was kicking up again and it whistled through a crack in the kitchen window. The trees in the garden were cast in a dance. He remembered that shack on the slag heap in the Saar where no tree grew. Once more he saw the gaunt, coal-streaked face of his friend Jules. He had just moved a bishop to king's pawn three, thereby tempting Faroun with his exposed knight. "Until a man uncovers himself, he cannot see," Jules said with a wry smile. "That was one of his sayings, you know."

Another saying came to Faroun's mind later that morning as he stood at a fruit stand, enjoying a glass of orange juice, near the Khan Suleiman Pasha, a large warehouse where the crafts of Damascus were made and offered for sale. The saying had to do with the Street Called Straight, a boulevard of such antiquity that it had earned mention in the Bible, albeit grudgingly because the author of the passage had lamented, as many have since, that Straight was an impostor. Rather, the street meandered, much like a clever thief, through the heart of the Old City from the vast souk at Al Kumeileh until, a mile farther on, it became something else again as it reached its terminus at the Bab Charki or Eastern Gate, the Gate of the Sun. It had always been a commercial avenue and had in Turkish times been covered by a great awning. The awning had since fallen into disrepair until it was shot through with great rents and holes that let the sunlight through in a maze of patterns in which played motes, and insects, and swirls of smoke from the many food stands that lined the avenue. Beneath the tatters, shoppers gawked and laborers scurried, the latter bearing hides and stacks of bright cloth or wheeling carts of scrap metal and earthenware.

"By the Street Called Straight we come to the House Called Beautiful." That was the saying Nikolai had brought to mind as he savored his drink and waited for his friend Maxim to show. The juice was cold, for the vendor kept his oranges on ice, and it was filled with succulent pips just the way Faroun liked it. The saying had always been a matter of curiosity to Faroun. As a boy wandering the city, he had overheard an American clergyman mention it and the phrase had fired his imagination. He had immediately set off in search of this mysterious House of Beauty but ended up in a blind cul-de-sac as one always did when looking for something in Old Damascus. To this day, a part of him was convinced the House Called Beautiful did exist and that all he would have to do is turn a corner off Straight Street and there it would be, its façade sheathed in gold and embellished with precious stones. Inside, he would find cool fountains surrounded by exotic flowers and the air buzzing with honeybees and off the courtyard would come the laughter of beautiful women and the delicious sound of wine being poured into crystal goblets.

Such was his fancy, but Faroun knew that the famous street led to other places, dark and sinister and far from beautiful. In these backstreets and warrens, men preyed upon each other like jackals, women sold their bodies, conspirators hatched bloody plots, and outcasts wandered about in darkness gibbering like ghosts. And these were the honest folk, for they could only be what they were. The street had earned its ironic name because it was a moving mirror in which all of humanity was reflected and, for a brief moment, exposed. Nikolai's father had told him long ago that every house in this most ancient of cities contained the truth behind its doors. One had only to follow home the honored father and husband to see the handiwork of the brute, hear the mullah who secretly cursed his God, and witness the loyal wife who sent secret messages to her lover. The day human beings became straight, then perhaps the House Called Beautiful would be revealed.

On his own secretive errand, Faroun caught sight of Maxim inside the khan. Wearing a white tunic and peasant's trousers, he was admiring an antique falchion, the upper edge of its blade engraved with a passage from the Koran, its hilt encircled with gleaming gold rope. The stall of the armorer glittered with burnished swords and dirks fashioned from Damascus steel. Medieval warriors paid dearly for such blades and lost their lives to others who wielded them.

"Audi bin Tyi, Faisal's lieutenant, once told me that the secret of Arab sword-making came from Japan, for a Nipponese master had been abducted by some Muslim pirates and persuaded to teach his craft to the armorers of Damascus. I know not if this is true," said the Ukrainian, deftly swinging the blade, "but the steel is."

"You will not find another blade like this in all of Damascus," said the merchant encouragingly in a long stream of hookah smoke. A dwarf with a pointed beard swathed in white muslin, he gained in lordly stature by perching on a hassock covered with rich carpets.

"Alas, I have no need of a blade," said Maxim.

"Then may God protect you from harm in Damascus," the merchant cried after them.

"I have located a man to help you in deciphering that symbol you showed to me the other day," said Maxim as the two men strolled past the carpet merchants, and stalls piled with silks and embroideries. "He is a recluse who values his privacy above all things. A good man, though, for I rode with him during the Arab Revolt. When the Englishman, Lawrence, joined Faisal as his British adviser, Azad al Abila chose Lawrence's bodyguard. But he gave up the soldier's life long ago. He became a Sufi."

"Then he has made quite a passage," said Faroun.

"From warrior to mystic," Maxim chuckled. "He's a ripe old heretic is Azad, a scholar with a long memory. If he can't help you, I don't know who can."

Suddenly the air was heavy with fragrance. Maxim stopped to sniff from a flask an eager merchant held out to him. His stall was lined with arrays of colored perfume bottles, for no people love scent like the Arabs. Maxim's broad nostrils flared as he inhaled. "Wear this," said the merchant in a confidential tone, "and she will deny you nothing."

Maxim waved him off. "I wear that stuff and Shammara will think I'm sleeping around and shoot me."

"I thought she didn't care for you," said Faroun.

"She doesn't," Maxim admitted with a sigh. "But she would shoot me anyway. Just to prove what she would do if she did love me."

"Where do I find our Sufi scholar?"

Maxim nodded a greeting to a young man braiding an agal as they stepped out of the khan and into cream-colored sunlight. A fountain dedicated to a long-dead emir shot water into the air from five different sculpted founts resembling lotus flowers. Mothers in purple scarves and blue veils watched as their children chased each other around the iron railing.

"You know the village of Maraba north of here? I have sent word to Azad to expect you."

"I appreciate this, old friend."

"It is nothing," said the burly man as he clapped Faroun on the shoulder. "Now where are you off to?"

"To interview a prisoner in the Citadel."

Maxim made an involuntary shudder. "Pity the poor bastards in there. The place is accursed. I remember when we rode into Damascus with Faisal in 1918. There were rumors flying about that the Turks had murdered all the Arab prisoners they held in those filthy holes. So I was sent with a detachment to the Citadel. Murder, right enough, but none of the Turks' doing."

"What do you mean?"

"We dragged body after body into the courtyard. A bloody mess, I can tell you. Many were wearing, you know, what the French call 'the last smile.' " Maxim slid his finger across his throat. "Seems the Turks had set the prisoners free. But then the prisoners had old scores to settle with each other. There's nobody like an Arab to hold a grudge."

17

The monolithic, red stone edifice of the Damascus Citadel covered the northwest quadrant of the Old City, the walls towering over fifty feet in the air and lined with artillery pieces. Once it had been a veritable city within a city with tiled palaces and mosques and seraglios and splashing fountains—the essential ambience for any Eastern potentate. The first potentate to inhabit the Citadel was also the fifth caliph of the Umayyad line, Abdul Malik, who built the original structure in the seventh century. Subsequently it had been destroyed and rebuilt, and from this famous redoubt and headquarters the succeeding caliphs had fought off their rivals, driven back the fearsome Mongol khan, and defeated the princes of the crusading Franks. Now the successors of those infidel Crusaders, the French army, claimed the fortress as their own, though the massive building, still formidable, was useless against modern artillery. Several hundred soldiers, mostly un-happy Senegalese and Moroccans, were quartered there along with an infantry regiment and cavalry brigade of the Foreign Le-gion. The Citadel also housed ammunition and supply bunkers and the administrative offices for the French regional command, a vast area that stretched to the state of Aleppo in the north to the Bekaa Valley in the west, south to the border of British Palestine and into the Great Syrian Desert. The French military police, the gendarmerie, were headquartered here as well as the Durac's in-terrogation apparatus. The prisons were extensive, deep, and ter-rible by reputation. The worst of the terrorists and insurgents were kept here as well as French military prisoners. Captain Ger-ard Martel was incarcerated in Cell 3B77, awaiting his fate by mil-itary court-martial.

Faroun could never enter the forbidding confines of the Citadel without a tightening in the chest. There was pain and misery here; fear had seeped into the cracks in the walls. His mouth became dry and his palms began to sweat as he followed the sluggish guard through the iron gate and down to the first sublevel. Two levels below, the guard cranked a heavy iron key into another gate, and with a wrenching screech of metal Faroun entered a long, bare corridor of cells concealed by riveted doors. Behind one of them, Faroun could hear someone weeping.

The weeper was not Martel. The officer crouched on his cot, his arms crossed over his knees, reminding Faroun of a pensive but dangerous leopard. The bare bulb overhead cast a bleak light on the bare walls. Martel had drawn back against a corner of the wall, his head hidden in a pool of shadow.

"You want me to stay?" asked the guard, sliding a forefinger un-der his bulbous nose.

"Leave me alone with him," said Faroun.

"Then you've got fifteen minutes," said the guard. He paused before he locked the door. "Just remember, I'm not responsible."

"You're not responsible," said Faroun. A metal plate suspended from the walls by chains like a portcullis served as a table. Faroun took the rickety cane chair in front of it. He studied the man studying him.

"I can understand your cutting her throat, Martel. Maybe she had it coming. But why did you do that other thing to her?"

The officer tensed but did not move out of his shadow. "You found that, did you?"

"Just tell me why you did it."

"I like to bite people, Inspector. Women, I mean."

Faroun was pleased with the answer. "You didn't kill Vera Tamiri."

"Bravo," said the other stiffly, clapping his hands with a measured and ironic beat. "Only you're too late. I've already confessed. Or didn't you hear? I hated the bitch. She said I wasn't a real man. I was drunk. So I killed her. Simple as that."

"I don't believe it."

The officer unlimbered from his crouch and stretched his long legs over the side of the bed until he found the floor. His feet were bare. And bloody. Propping himself up, he leaned forward out of the shadow. "Believe it," he said.

The sight of the man's torn and battered face, the eyes nearly swollen shut, the lower lip torn and hanging loose, did not catch Faroun entirely by surprise. He knew Durac's methods. Still, this had been a more than thorough job.

"It took six of them," Martel grunted. "Put that in the book."

"I'll do better than that, Captain. I'll do my best to get you out of here. But you've got to tell me the truth."

"What can you do?" he asked scornfully. "Why should I tell you anything?"

"Because we're the scum of the earth," Faroun said quietly.

Martel sat very still as he measured the policeman against the phrase by which former Legionnaires identified themselves. "You don't get out of the Legion unless they carry you out. Or you finish your contract," he said.

"Who finishes his contract?" Faroun asked.

"Or you desert."

"That doesn't exhaust the possibilities."

"All right," said Martel. "I could use a cigarette."

Faroun reached into his pocket and pulled out two packs of Gitanes and two boxes of matches. The soldier fit a cigarette between his split lips and let Faroun light it for him. "You were following Vera Tamiri off and on for a few weeks, you said."

"Just to scare her."

"Then it's likely you saw her with another man during that time. One man in particular—an Arab, well-dressed, her escort to the casinos."

"The man I saw wasn't that well-dressed and he wasn't Arab. He was French, European at any rate, although he kept himself well covered. I never got close enough to identify him. Besides I didn't think it wise."

"How is that?"

The soldier grimaced as he exhaled. "Because whoever it was, he had bodyguards and they weren't local. That's how I figured he must be French. I saw him and Vera together, twice. The black sedans were nearby."

"The Sûreté? Maybe the two of them were under surveillance."

"Somehow I didn't get that impression. That's when I decided to call off my surveillance."

"Where did you see the two of them together?"

"At the souks, Al Kumeileh, and then at the old Turkish bazaar on the Street Called Straight. They were walking along as if they didn't know each other, but Vera was nervous and gave herself away. Once I saw him slip her a package."

Faroun left the cigarettes on the cot and stood at the cell door. "One other question, Captain. When you and Vera met, where did you go?"

"The first time I got leave for Beirut and we met there, but things were never cozy with us. All the time I felt as if she were acting out this fantasy of hers; she was trying hard to be somebody else. So she liked to experiment. But then she started to cling. She was drinking too much and gambling too much and we fought a lot. I don't embarrass easily, Faroun. But she embarrassed me. I was sorry for her, I mean. The thing is, she was a lady and she couldn't change that. I don't know what her problem was, but I decided it was too damn complicated for me. So I broke things off. Then she turned desperate."

Faroun rapped on the cell door and told Martel he would do what he could for him. The soldier shrugged. "Here's my question for you, Faroun. What happened with you and the Legion?"

"We parted ways after the summer push in 1918."

Martel looked at him searchingly. "So you deserted, after all."

"I didn't desert. I just put a gun to the head of a bastard and blew his brains out."

"Well, that's what you were paid to do, wasn't it?"

"There was a problem, Martel. The bastard was wearing French epaulets."

The officer tried out a grin, but it was painful to see.

It was nearly noon by the time Faroun left the Citadel, and he made his way to a little kebab stand he frequented across from the Umayyad Mosque. Its grand dome, slate blue, was flanked by two graceful minarets that seemed to float in the heavens. Flocks of white pigeons flew above the ornamented walls. Faroun took a seat at the food stand, ordered coffee and kebab, and listened as the compelling voices of the muezzins called the faithful to prayer. The great mosque had a chameleon history, first being a pagan site consecrated to the ancient Syrian god Haddad, then a Roman temple, a Christian church, until it took its present unearthly form, at the behest of the worldly caliphs known as the Umayyad. At the same party where he had met Vera Tamiri months ago, he had listened for a while as a comely and erudite French widow, Ariane De Lesseps, had explained to him how these pleasure-loving medieval rulers of Syria had celebrated beauty, to the horror of the Islamic fundamentalists of their time, but Faroun, intrigued by the beauty of his tutor, had somewhat neglected his lesson.

The policeman thought he might visit the sumptuous courtyard of the mosque after lunch. In a curious example of the cooperation between religions in a bygone time, the builder of the mosque had allowed the Tomb of John the Baptist to remain in a chancel off the courtyard. Christians still visited the site for miracles, but not while the Muslims prayed.

The sunlight beating down on the crowded boulevard was nearly warm, and Faroun enjoyed his broiled lamb and hummus as he withdrew from the tumult about him to reflect on what he had just learned from Captain Gerard Martel. There was a third lover, so to speak, a circumspect European lover, with whom she may have shared more than a romantic interlude. Perhaps this was the man who had been feeding her gambling habit, or one of her benefactors, and he was obviously well connected in the government or he wouldn't have merited the attention of Sûreté bodyguards. Only officials with clout rated that kind of treatment. He could be any of a number of men in the ministry labyrinth or at the delegate's palace. If there was a third lover, then he was suspect too. And that gave him the paths of two men to follow, for he was quite sure Martel had no part in the murder. But he had confessed and the military had their hands on him. Faroun knew that once they had their hands on you, they didn't let go.

He decided to forgo the pleasure of visiting the mosque and instead continued his walk down the boulevard. As he stopped to adjust his tie by his reflection in a storefront window, he caught sight of a familiar rotund figure hurrying across the street. Umar Tamiri, homburg tilted at a slightly jaunty angle, was taking a brisk springtime stroll, so Faroun decided to follow the businessman at a discreet distance, especially when he noticed the two bodyguards tagging along. He followed Umar past Saladin's tomb, fronted with its gigantic equestrian statue of the great Saracen warrior, past the Arab Academy, where the sons of the Syrian elite were prepared for college, until Tamiri suddenly disappeared from the avenue entirely. Faroun thought it likely he had turned left, down a narrow backstreet where metalsmiths plied their trade, the heat given off by their furnaces turning the day from spring to summer, the sharp, acrid odors of molten iron and solder in the air. The backstreet curved again to the left, and this dank lane led to the back of the German Bank of Palestine, its clock tower adorned with the red, white, and black swastika flag since the beginning of the year, when Chancellor Hitler had assumed the helm of the German state. A man in a blockish, dark suit and low-slung fedora stepped out of a cellar doorway as Umar approached, and the two men shook hands cordially. They fell into step, Umar swinging his gold-tipped cane back and forth with his stride, the other fingering his worry beads, until they arrived at a little circular plaza of cafés frequented by Jewish merchants and tradesmen. Here they took seats under the awning of Café Pegasus. Faroun took a post opposite, trying to get a look at the man, but the brim of his hat was pulled down. They chatted in an animated way, Umar's companion seeming to enjoy a joke, then he looked at his watch, bid Umar adieu with a curt nod, and strode back down the avenue and right past Nikolai Faroun.

Faroun stood in shadow and he turned a little to the side so the man did not see him. He saw enough of the man's profile to place him. When Faroun had taken over the Damascus Prefecture six months before, his first case was to break up a protection racket operating out of the Maidan district. The merchants being "protected" were terrified and wouldn't speak up. They were terrified of the man who had just walked past Faroun, Mustapha Ni'mat, an enforcer for one of the district hoodlums. The Prefecture broke up the racket, but they couldn't make a case against Ni'mat. The word was that he had gone straight and gotten involved in the construction-supply trade.

Faroun knew Mustapha Ni'mat better than that. He also knew that it was more than the need to exchange a few pleasantries that had brought Umar Tamiri into the orbit of a man who was more skilled at merchandising fear than selling lumber by the pallet and nails by the barrel.

18

The road to the town of Maraba skirted along the base of rugged Mount Kassioun before it broke into the hill country north of Damascus. It was a comparatively safe road considering the army made frequent convoys to a mountain base in the Anti-Lebanon. Still Faroun always felt a little uneasy taking the route, especially when he was alone and on motorcycle, but he was keen to make the appointment Maxim had arranged. Besides, he could put the Triumph through its paces on a road like this, and with a broad if frozen smile on his face, he sped by wheat and millet fields, the soil newly turned, and past groves of almond and olive trees. On the green and open hillsides, shepherd boys drove their flocks along to pasture.

The town of Maraba was typical of the villages that populated the fertile Syrian plain, with red-stone, square houses roofed with timber and mud, the shutters painted a pale blue or yellow. The walled compounds of the wealthier townspeople had red Moroccan-tile roofs and gardens steeped in roses, morning glories, and clematis. Faroun's path took him to the end of the main street, chickens and dogs scurrying out of his path until he found the compound of Azad al Abila. The iron door swung open at his approach, and he found himself in a charming paved courtyard surrounded by grape arbors and lilacs and with a stone well at the center.

He was met by a young woman in a bright print dress, who led him into an airy home of many windows and up a polished staircase to a book-lined study. Outside a window, hummingbirds sipped nectar from cream-colored honeysuckle blossoms. Hunched over a small writing desk, a snowy-bearded man, his head wrapped in the round turban of the Sufi, carved a design into a wood block. Over a white cotton shirt with wide sleeves, he wore a rust-colored vest. He turned his milky blue eyes in a sightless gaze of welcome. He seemed to be following Faroun's keen interest in the tidy little library.

"When I had read every book in this room, my eyes clouded over and I could not see," said the Azad al Abila in a mellow voice that rose and fell as if in a kind of singing. "At first I thought it was a hard punishment for one who loves to learn, but then I realized that God had other lessons planned for me. For these, my sight was a hindrance." Azad asked the girl in the print dress to bring coffee, and only when she passed did Faroun notice that she was sightless too. "Everyone in the house of Azad is without sight, for only the blind can lead the blind." Azad smiled. "However, you will not find a Pharisee among us," he added with a chuckle.

Faroun learned that Azad had been born in Cairo and had been an Islamic scholar in his youth. In 1885, he had heeded the Mahdi's call in the Sudan and had fought with the Khalifa's army against Kitchener at Omdurman. Azad became a professional soldier, fighting for hire wherever there was a war in the Middle East, and he was never without work. During the Great War, he had joined the Emir Faisal and the Arab Revolt. He had been one of the trackers for the Englishman Lawrence, the man the Arabs called El Aurens or, as some wags called him, El Aurum, the Man with the Gold, seeing as Lawrence was Faisal's British paymaster.

"The matter on which you have come to see me," said Azad after they had finished coffee, "has to do with those times, but after the war, when Faisal was king of Syria." The old man took up a pen and with a few deft strokes replicated the diagram in Vera Tamiri's ledger. He pushed it over to Faroun. "My friend Maxim the Ukrainian—did he mention we rode together with Faisal during the Arab Revolt?—told me you had found this symbol, but he did not tell me where."

"In a notebook," said Faroun. "It seems to be a ledger of some kind."

"Did you bring this with you?" The old man took the book from Faroun and ran his hands over it, closing his eyes. He skimmed through the pages, until he came to the place. His finger made a circle around the original diagram, and he closed the book and sat in silence for a moment. "You are a policeman, Maxim tells me. So this book has to do with a case you are trying to solve."

"It does."

Azad sighed. "I am sorry she is dead."

"Maxim told you about her."

"Maxim told me nothing except about the diagram. She was murdered, wasn't she? There is about this book much confusion and pain. The things she wrote down come to a sudden stop. She did not finish her plan. The Hand of Maisalun comes at the very end."

Faroun regarded the old Sufi for a moment. "I have heard of Maisalun."

"As well you should, Inspector, for it was the last battle that the Emir Faisal fought against the French. Out of that last fight, a compact was made. One sealed in blood. I know, for I was there."

The story that Azad told Faroun might have come out of the legends of Saladin or some medieval pageantry, but it had been as recent as 1920. Faisal al-Husseini, the tall, stately leader of the

Arab Revolt, had tried to rule his self-proclaimed Kingdom of Syria, with Damascus as its capital, for close to two years. His claim was disputed by the French, for Lebanon and Syria had been handed to them to rule as a mandate by the League of Nations. The French sent an army under General Gouraud to defeat Faisal. At the battle of Maisalun, Faisal's bedu charged armored cars and artillery with swords and carbines and lost the day. The king of Syria was forced to take his government into exile.

On the night of his bitter defeat at the hands of the French, Faisal had called together representatives from the major factions into his battlefield tent and swore them to an oath of loyalty. Each man was carefully picked by Faisal himself, men he thought he could trust. There were five of them, each representing an important family in Damascus. One family was Sunni Muslim, one Shia, one Druze, one Jewish, and one Christian. They were to wait and work together for his return, for, if God willed, Faisal would come back to Damascus with a new army to reclaim his crown. Azad described a sad and moving scene. Each of the five bowed down to Faisal and, kissing his robe, swore allegiance, and undying hatred of the French. Then each of them embraced each other before Faisal, swearing eternal love and brotherhood. And with that, Faisal took the remnants of his shattered army and withdrew into the Great Syrian Desert.

"The hand of Fatima became their symbol, with the inscription of the initial of the last names on the fingertips; that is how it came to be known as the Hand of Maisalun. These men were bound in a very special way. But, alas," Azad said mournfully, "the oath of loyalty did not last. The rest of the story is an Arab tragedy."

"The eternal brothers fell out."

"After Faisal was defeated, there was civil war in Damascus. Revenge killings, shops blown up with dynamite and grenades, compounds assaulted. Sometimes, a score of bodies lay in the street, and a few hours later, there were another score. The French couldn't do anything about it. Or didn't want to."

"And this was all attributed to the Five?"

"Greedy men snarling over spoils. They were replaced by the equally greedy Franks. That is the calamity of Damascus. I was part of a local militia trying to restore order. I was wounded." Azad rubbed a forefinger across his brow where there was a long, white, jagged scar. "When I woke, I had had enough fighting and killing. So I came here, where I had a piece of land given to me by Faisal for my service. And here I returned to my roots, as I have always loved learning. Here my eyes were sealed. Here my eyes were opened."

"I thank you," said Faroun, getting to his feet and picking up the ledger. "This other symbol on the last page of this book. The letter Q in an oval. I believe it to be the sign of the al Quassi."

"And I have written the family name on this paper along with the other family names," said Azad, pushing it over to the policeman. "You have much of the story here. Except why the murdered woman had written these things in her notebook. What is her name?"

"Vera Tamiri."

The old man clicked his tongue in sorrow. "She was the daughter of Farid Tamiri, the sister of Umar. That is the letter T on the diagram. Farid was the Christian in the original Five. How sad the way bloody things get handed down."

"The diagram places the al Quassi outside of the Five."

"Nayef al Quassi—a Sunni from a powerful clan. He had two sons as I recall. Nayef was exposed as a Turkish spy and hanged within a few hours after Faisal's men took Damascus in 1918. They hanged him from a lamppost. A pity. The family became outcasts."

"Who exposed their father?"

"That I cannot say. There were many scores to settle back in those days. As I have told you. I can scarce remember them all. I have tried to forget those times. For many years, I was troubled by bad dreams. But then I learned to dance."

Faroun smiled. "As a Sufi."

"You should learn how to dance, Inspector. I could teach you."
The old man rose from the desk and took Faroun by the arm. "It is
the easiest thing in the world. And the most difficult."

As Azad slipped his arm into Faroun's, he paused before one of
the bookcases and a ran a hand lovingly over the bindings until he
stopped and plucked a volume from the shelf. He handed the
leatherbound book to Faroun, opening the cover.

"The *Arabian Nights* in the Burton translation."

"You are fond of these stories, are you not?" asked Azad.

"Very."

"I thought so. I could tell that about you when you entered the
study," said the Sufi. "Some men carry their books about them. If
one has eyes to see," he chuckled, "pardoning, I hope the figure
of speech." He snapped his fingers. "One of Scheherazade's tales
came to me as we were speaking. It was the one about an evil
prince who cleverly sets about turning two brothers against each
other. He destroys them for sport. Yet I cannot remember the
name of it."

Faroun felt at a loss, as if a volume were missing in the edition he
had so carefully placed in his head over long years. He drew a blank.

"Well, it is of no matter," said Azad, as the two began descending the staircase. "It was not important. Stories are important but
not their titles. The same with men and their titles." His ears
perked up when they went into the courtyard, for white pigeons
were cooing in the grape arbors and blinking at the two men.
Faroun straddled his motorcycle and was about to kick-start the
engine when a slim, white hunting dog of the desert, a saluki,
came trotting up and with its tongue hanging out looked up lovingly at its master. Azad rubbed its muzzle.

"Beautiful hound," said Faroun.

"My other self," said Azad, touching Faroun's arm in farewell.
"At least he thinks he is. Sometime you must tell me about this
other burden you carry. Dancing will make you weightless, believe me." The old man burst into a nearly toothless smile. "You

must come back and see me," he said, wagging a finger at Faroun. "When you remember that story."

Faroun made a joke about the vagaries of memory and, starting the Triumph's engine, rumbled out of the gate and through the village of Maraba. The bearded village men in homespun robes and turbans paused in their smoking and games of trictrac to stare at the motorcycle, resplendent in black and chrome, a modern charger. Once the policeman made the highway, he gunned the machine into a ferocious roar and tore down the road, scattering gravel and stones, and nearly hitting a lamb that sprang across his path.

The road ahead had opened up and Faroun pulled back on the throttle so that the cry of the engine rose from a throbbing piston-driven chop to a high-pitched whine. The sudden surge of speed saved his life, for the first rifle shot merely sang past his ear. Suddenly they were everywhere, men with rifles leaping up from the side of the road and taking aim. He could barely hear the crack of the carbines above the Triumph's cry, but his momentum brought him to the next bend in the road and out of the firing zone. There was a indistinct dust cloud ahead, however, one that resolved itself into a line of heavily laden camels. The bandits he had just escaped had apparently been lying in wait for this prize. The appearance of the caravan caused him to brake quickly, and the Triumph pulled up short, its rear wheel sliding in a fishtail that he was just barely able to control. He came to a sharp stop just before the caravan leader, a tall man with a long-barreled French Lebel that probably dated from the Franco-Prussian War. He stood over six feet in broken sandals, a many-colored cloak falling from his lanky shoulders, a matted beard spread across his chest like a spade. For a head-covering, he wore a ragged kaffiyeh that had been pinned with paper currency: French francs, German marks, Italian lira, Turkish piasters, decorated his headdress. He nodded and smiled with a kind of benediction on the policeman, revealing an uneven line of blackened teeth.

"I would wait for a French patrol, caravan master," said Faroun.

"And why is that, friend?"

"Did you not hear the firing up ahead?"

"Was there firing now?"

Faroun considered that the men might be hard of hearing and raised his voice. "Bandits up ahead!"

"Bandits up ahead!" echoed the other in the same volume. The other camel drivers came forward, and they were smiling too and poking each other. They were carrying an odd assortment of arms, percussion rifles and sabers, and one man held a German machine pistol in his upraised hand.

"They shot at me," said Faroun a little uncertainly.

"Yet you seem not to have come to much harm, friend," said the other, sizing him up.

"They were poor shots."

"Then I will crack their heads and whip their stinking hides!" announced the tall man. "For I certainly thought I had taught them to shoot better than that."

Faroun watched as the tall man lowered his carbine until the tip of the barrel pointed at the center of Faroun's forehead. The man's companions began chuckling and poking each other some more, for it was a great fun to have surprised this foolish traveler in such a humorous way. "Now empty your pockets and give over what you have to Kemal." A broad-shouldered ruffian pushed a disdainful camel out of the way and thrust out a grasping palm. The policeman went through his pockets and placed in Kemal's outsize hand the bills and coins he carried in his pockets.

Trapped in this narrow, rocky defile, there was no way for him to break out and make for the open fields. He was unlucky in this, he thought, as it was likely he would meet his end in this desolate spot. Syrian highwaymen were cutthroats of the worst sort and did not take prisoners for ransom. They were constantly on the move, fighting other bandits as well as French patrols. He was lucky in one thing: he was not carrying any identification with him and he was unarmed. Frenchmen caught by bandits did not come to quick and merciful ends. The same could be said for Arabs who worked for the French. He could pass for an Arab, but the new Triumph was a liability—that he would have to explain.

"You are trying to make me laugh," said the leader of the gang, looking at the ten francs. "I think you are trying to mock me."

"That is all I have, sir; I am not a rich man."

"Looking at that pitiful blue serge you wear, I would say that is true. But how did you come by this beautiful new motorbike? Don't tell me you are thief."

"That is exactly what I am, good sir. I stole this motorbike from my master, may God curse his name! He is an infidel of the worst sort. He beats me."

"Servants were meant to be beaten," said the other, unimpressed.

"He has also used my wife unlawfully and sold my children to be Kuwaiti slaves."

The bandit chief lifted a wiry eyebrow. "This is not so good of him. You were right to steal his motorbike. It will fetch a fine price, I think."

"Many hundreds, sir," said Faroun helpfully. "Perhaps thousands."

The bandit chief rubbed his hands together. "So who was this bad man you stole the bike from?"

"A terrible man, sir, by the name of Tamiri."

"Did you say, Tamiri?" The brigand took a menacing step forward. "There is only one Tamiri I know, a Christian swine by the name of Umar, son of Farid Tamiri." He spat on the ground and ground the heel of his sandal over the spot.

"You have heard of him, sir?"

The bandit drew himself up in indignation. "Know of the man who cheated my family and threw my father off his own land? I am an outlaw to this day because of that man."

"As he did with my family," Faroun said eagerly, pleased that his lie had opened a door. "I am indentured to him and treated no better than a slave."

"You see how he is," said the brigand, scratching his beard.

"Our lands originally belonged to the al Quassi. Nayef al Quassi gave the property outright to my father, as my father had done him a good turn. That was in the days before Faisal became king. When the French came, the Tamiri took the land and said it belonged to them."

"A great injustice!" Faroun agreed.

"Tamiri said that the al Quassi land was his, a gift from Faisal. Since my father could produce no deed of transfer, Tamiri sent his gunmen to drive my father off. It killed him. Farid Tamiri killed my father!" He shook his rifle in the air and discharged a round. His men followed suit, firing their rifles, their anger echoing down the defile. The brigand returned his attention to the shiny Triumph, running his hand over the handlebars the way he might fondle a woman.

"What is your name, traveler?"

"Abu Ihab, sir."

"I will relieve you of that stolen motorcycle, Abu Ihab. That's small compensation for my family's loss. I will also relieve you of your shoes and that gold watch you keep trying to cover up by pulling down your sleeve. You can keep the suit."

"Then I am free to go, sir?"

"You are only as free as Mahmoud al Harani lets you be." He tapped his chest grandiloquently. "We have both suffered injustice at the hands of the Tamiri, so I will make you this gift. You will be free to make a run for the open fields," said the chief as he nodded to the big man to remove Faroun's watch. "I will count to one hundred. After that, I will send a half dozen of my men after you. If you elude them, you will be a free man. If they catch you, then— let's just say they will have sport. Your chances are small, but perhaps you will bless the name of Mahmoud al Harani nonetheless."

Faroun scratched his head with a show of perplexity. "I wonder if I might have a word with you in private."

Faroun tried to strike a deal. Since he doubted that the bandit knew how to drive a motorcycle, or any other of his rough-and-ready cutthroats for that matter, he offered to provide him with a lesson, if Mahmoud al Harani would set him free. The tall bandit chief studied Faroun carefully, trying to spy the trap. Satisfied, he made a broad, toothy smile and clapped Faroun on the back. Then he pulled out an old British service revolver and put the gun to Faroun's temple, telling him he would ride behind him with the pistol cocked just in case his tutor had any wild hope of breaking for freedom.

Faroun turned the Triumph around, the bandit chief clambered behind him, and he set slowly back down the road toward Maraba, looking for the one slim opportunity to make a breakout. The embankment a hundred yards farther down was about two feet lower, and a sudden acceleration could send him over it, when a better proposition suddenly presented itself. Another plume of dust directly ahead announced the arrival of a French armored car, making a routine patrol. A soldier standing in the turret of the great camouflaged beast must have recognized the bandits, for he opened up with machine-gun fire. As Mahmoud's comrades scattered, Faroun took a deep breath of courage and rammed the throttle as he shifted into a high gear. The sudden tug of speed unbalanced his passenger, and Faroun jabbed his elbow hard against the man's stomach. As the pistol fired close to his ear, Faroun hurtled toward the armored car at full speed. He had just enough time to see the French soldier in the turret point at him as he turned the wheel into the embankment. For the briefest moment, he felt the thrill of being suspended in air and then acceleration as Mahmoud fell away. The Triumph would sprout no wings, however, and the giddy plunge to earth sent Faroun flying over the handlebars.

Faroun must have been out some minutes. When he came to, he was lying spread-eagled in a farmer's muddy field. There was still some machine-gun chatter but it seemed to come from far away. Remembering his passenger, he sat bolt upright, with a sudden twinge in his chest. The only vestige of Mahmoud the bandit was the British army pistol, which lay in the mud next to the tangled wreck of the policeman's Triumph. A bit gingerly, and favoring his left leg, he struggled across the field back to the main road, pistol in hand. He clambered over the embankment there to greet a French soldier drawing a bead on him with his carbine and telling him in Arabic to drop the gun and lie down in the dirt of the road.

19

A bdullah al Quassi stared at the telephone receiver as if he would strangle it.

"What do you mean he got away?" he asked as he returned the instrument to his ear. "How could he possibly get away?"

The voice on the other end was a painful squeal. "Put Anwar back on the line," said Abdullah.

The voice that replaced that of Salim's wife was less hysterical but lisped and stuttered at the edge of panic. Abdullah insisted on a detailed retelling of what had actually taken place on the road to Aleppo.

"Did he say where he was going and what he was going to do?" asked Abdullah.

"All he did was wave a pistol in my face and tell me to get going," cried Anwar. "And then I went to Aleppo as you ordered."

"I ordered you to drive my brother and his family there. You arrived in town without my brother. That is not going to Aleppo!" Abdullah shouted into the receiver.

As Anwar continued to make excuses, Abdullah al Quassi took the telephone over to the wide office window that overlooked the noisy confusion of the warehouse. To the cries of foremen and the rumble of truck engines, sweating stevedores hauled and off-loaded cargo from waiting trucks. Mechanics checked undercarriages and changed tires. His office reeked of diesel fumes and Abdullah al Quassi breathed it all in. He was the pharaoh of a transport empire. Alas, that his father had not lived to see this triumph.

Abdullah felt hemmed in by the memory of betrayal at one end of the family history and the reality of a scapegrace at the other. What hadn't he done for Salim? He had raised him after their mother's death; he had fed and clothed and educated him; he had seen him grow up to be a handsome young man and an unalterable fool. Now he had become a dangerous fool. He would return to Damascus and he would stir up the waters, the dark and dirty waters where that Tamiri slattern was supposed to lie. Salim must muck about and make a mess of things. Even if it killed him. In any event, Abdullah would have to find him and stop him. Anwar continued to drone excuses. Abdullah clicked the receiver back on its stand.

While his older brother stood looking down on the bustle of the Al-Quassi warehouse, Salim was making his way down El Hammam Street, hungry, and not the least bit sure how to go about finding the one responsible for his lover's death. Of one thing he was certain: he could not bring a murderer to justice without something in his stomach. The smell of freshly baked bread made his mouth water. The intoxicating aroma was coming from a coffeehouse just ahead. Tea and bread, that was the thing. Then renewed and reinvigorated, he would . . . do something. He would figure out a plan.

The coffeehouse on El Hammam known as The Hawk was just

a few blocks south of the Gate of the Moon and close to the Christian quarter. Raised five feet above the level of the street, and shaded by a green-and-white-striped awning, its broad veranda offered a commanding view of the activity along the avenue, and for this reason the promontory was guarded by the Noble Order of the Cups. Beginning every morning about ten, this band of old, cosmopolitan Arabs manned the veranda as if it were a battlement. They stayed for lunch and continued their watch throughout the long afternoon, playing backgammon or draughts from time to time, but mostly sipping cups of thick, sweet coffee and drawing on their hookahs. They wore red tarbooshes out of affection for the glory days of the Ottomans. Behind dark glasses, their eyes roved ceaselessly like itinerant lawyers in search of misfortune.

Their talk was personal, that is to say, political. The names of fathers and uncles and grandfathers were invoked with a solemn fervor, and the posts of responsibility they had held under the sultans were recited in a loving litany. In the old days, any man with an official seal—a postal clerk, a salt-tax collector—could support his extended family of twenty, for there was a tax or duty on just about everything, and everyone paid the tax at least twice.

"The infidel French still charge twice but keep it all for themselves," said the one known as Hisham. He called for another ball of the heady Anatolian tobacco delicately laced with Persian hashish.

"There were trays of sweetmeats at my grandfather's every night of Ramadan," said his companion with a rheumy tear. "Every night, we children ate until our stomachs ached."

"The stomachs of our children ache still," added another, an ironic sage whose eyebrows rose and fell like the wings of a hawk. "With hunger, in these dog-ridden days."

"When will we ever see the last of these cursed Franks?" Ahmad wondered aloud.

"God will punish them," said Abu Jerrius fervently. "With fire, plague, and the sword of Saladin." He spat into the street below.

"God be praised, but King Faisal's army will come out of Iraq and sweep the infidel into the sea," said the first, his leg rocking rhythmically, while his fingers worked a string of amber worry beads.

There was no immediate reply to this delectable wish. Something else delectable had caught their attention.

"Isn't that Noor's sesame buns I smell?" wondered one of them aloud. He lifted his nose in the air and licked his lips. "I think they just came out of the oven."

"Eleven o'clock," said Hisham, clicking open his pocket watch. "You can set your watch by Noor's buns," he cackled, gurgling on his pipe.

Ihab Kabir, wearing a tradesman's leather apron and a stained cloth cap, sat a table in The Hawk overlooking the street and stirred a fifth spoonful of sugar into his tiny cup of Turkish coffee. He scarcely acknowledged the other Arab in a gray-and-white-striped robe who took a seat beside him and signaled the waiter.

"You make a convincing peasant, sir," said Ihab quietly.

"Keep that in mind," said Faroun, his features concealed by the folds of his kaffiyeh. He wondered if Ihab might not be making a jest but shrugged it off as impossible. "And drop the *sir,*" he cautioned. "What have you learned about Salim al Quassi?"

"He is in Aleppo."

"That's interesting."

"You have to know something about the two brothers. Abdullah is the oldest. He owns the trucking company. Salim is the playboy and lives in his brother's shadow. His older brother has been bankrolling him but he tired of the losses, that's what I got from one of the servants. So Abdullah sent him to Aleppo to open a new branch of the business."

"Conveniently puts Salim out of the way."

"That was my thinking too."

"Did you learn anything about Salim's relationship with Vera?"

Ihab twirled the spoon slowly in his cup, then lifted his cup using both hands. "Hints, perhaps. He despises his wife. Two girls but no son, and so Salim haunts the nightclubs and casinos. Madame Salim cries a lot, but not when her husband is around." Ihab looked past Faroun at the crowd passing in the street. "The al Quassi cook told me that Salim had a mistress he was crazy about. Someone special. But the cook thinks Salim was thrown over. His mood has been dark and melancholy and he has been taking it out on the staff. She showed me a big bruise on her arm. The cook also told me Salim's wife knows about the affair."

"But we don't know if this someone special was Vera."

Ihab tilted back his head and finished his coffee. "We don't know."

Faroun dipped his sesame roll in some olive and garlic and washed the morsel down with coffee. His eyes drifted to Ihab's plate. He was munching a Damascus specialty, tiny pickled frogs mixed with pearl onions and radish. Why did everything about Ihab Kabir have to be so damned melancholy? Faroun pushed away his plate. "What do you know about Aleppo, Ihab?"

"I went there once. About two years ago. My wife has relatives in that place. I went there to tell them she had died."

"Well, you're about to make another trip. I want you to introduce yourself to Madame Salim al Quassi. It may be she's not feeling very forgiving about her husband and might volunteer a little information. And we don't have much time. I want to hear from you by tomorrow afternoon. Call me with your report."

Faroun left The Hawk a few minutes after Ihab and mingled with the crowd. A French patrol lorry was making its way down Hammam Street and a gaggle of Damascus street urchins converged in its wake. Half-naked, spindly, their heads shaven, they ran after the soldiers and held out their hands for baksheesh. Hooting and jeering, they called for coppers or candies or anything the soldiers would spare. When the hot, bedraggled troopers just stared back at them with tired eyes, the boys picked up stones and hurled them at the truck. Cursing them roundly for being cheap damned infidels, they performed a little victory dance in the street and flitted away.

Salim al Quassi sat in The Hawk picking at the last of his cheese pastry with sticky fingers. Who would know what had happened to his beloved Vera? How would he track down her murderer? Perhaps Abdullah was right. He was nothing but a useless fool. He had ruined any chance now of making something of himself with the new company branch in Aleppo. He would be back to checking manifests again. But he wasn't going back to that hand-me-down kind of life. He was going to find Vera's murderer and then he was going to do something to make her proud of him. Just as they had planned. As if she were alive.

But she was dead. And there was nothing he could do to bring her back. He held a teaspoonful of sugar over his cup and let the sparkling grains slowly slide into the black coffee. Then he remembered that night, that terrible night when he'd found Vera's body and he'd had to get Abdullah to get rid of it and clean up the mess. They'd waited in the Rolls Phantom on the poplar-lined street outside the hotel. He remembered the two men, shadows, really, for he had never seen them. But they had carried Vera out and taken her to the river. Abdullah would not say who they were. He said he had done business with them before. Business of this nature. Just people he knew.

20

Faroun was pleased to see that Rebecca was in a good mood the following morning. A vase of fresh-cut flowers was on her desk, and the policeman wondered if that young man from the Intelligence Division had stopped by. He was sweet on her, and for her part she seemed sympathetic, considering him mal-nourished. Offering her boss a baklava wrapped in pink tissue pa-per, she began to tell Faroun the plot to an American movie she had seen about this Texas cowfellow on a horse who wooed his sweetheart with a six-gun and a guitar. Faroun cut her off before she could unravel the preposterous tale but accepted a piece of baklava, which he threw in the trash once he was in his office. He couldn't stand the taste of baklava. The files he had requested were on his desk, bound and yellow with age. This confirmed that the young man from Intelligence had indeed come by.

He plunged into the background of the five families whose symbol was the Hand of Maisalun. In addition to the Christian Tamiri, the Shihab clan represented the Sunni, the Kuabbahs the Shia, the Al-Atrash for the Druze, with the Jews represented by the Hamra. Wealthy landholders, the families had been among the political leadership and professional elite of Syria for generations. The dossiers provided by Intelligence did not reveal any profound connections among the families, except for their prominence. They did not intermarry and their only political connection was through the Club of Damascus, originally formed to agitate against Turkish rule, and their support for King Faisal, which was noted in the summaries, although there was no mention of Maisalun. The Intelligence Division of the Prefecture, apparently did not know of this connection. With the exception of Umar Tamiri, whose willingness to do business with French authorities was well-known, the other families had held aloof, unwilling to be perceived as pro-French, or unwilling to rock the boat. Still, Faroun knew that the nationalist groups backing the resistance were getting their money from well-connected Syrians.

Disgruntled by the Intelligence Division's lack of rigor, he was about to leave off the files when he spied a report in the al Quassi dossier that caught his attention. It confirmed the story he had learned from Azad al Abila about the family's forlorn history. The al Quassi had once been among the twelve ruling families of Damascus. Nayef al Quassi had agitated against Ottoman rule and been an early supporter of the Arab Revolt. The members of the Five, however, were late converts to Faisal's standard and fought in his cause only after the emir had claimed sovereignty in Damascus in 1918. It would seem Nayef had been closer to the prince than the heads of the other Damascus families. Yet he had been executed by Faisal's troops within hours after they liberated the city. The report said he had been exposed as Turkish spy and had been accused of taking part in an assassination attempt on Faisal's life. There were no further details. Obviously, the other Syrian families had distanced themselves from the al Quassi clan. The family had been ostracized and disgraced. So Nayef was a traitor. The question remained, who had betrayed him and why?

Who had the most to gain?

Perhaps part of the answer lay in the Office of Land Claims and Assignments. Documents might survive to tell Faroun what had happened to the al Quassi property during the brief period of Faisal's rule. It seemed reasonable to suppose the al Quassi had forfeited their property following Nayef's execution. The brigand Mahmoud al Harani had provided a curious bit of lore. His father had been an al Quassi tenant farmer but had been thrown off his land by Farid Tamiri. It might be a tale made up to excuse a life of crime, but the story deserved checking.

Nikolai turned to Vera's ledger. Her financial transactions had something to do with the Hand of Maisalun diagram. Otherwise, why would they appear in the same notebook? It was reasonable to suppose that somehow she had learned of Faisal's secret pact with the heads of the five families. She had written down the al Quassi insignia beside the diagram. Did she know of Nayef al Quassi's treason? And what would she do with such information? Money. She was getting money from someone to cover her gambling debts. Salim was the likely candidate. If she was getting the money from Salim, then it could be that Vera was blackmailing her lover. Payment for keeping quiet about the dark al Quassi history. More than a little—for there had been three payments of five thousand francs. Perhaps the extortion had become too much for Salim and he had killed her. Far-fetched, perhaps, but the presence of the diagram invited speculation. Too much speculation.

Then there was Umar. Not only was Vera a family scandal, she was mixed up with an outcast like Salim al Quassi, son of a man who had betrayed Prince Faisal—a double motive for retribution. It also suggested a purpose for Umar to have coffee with a bottom-feeder like Mustapha Ni'mat.

Time to seek out Mustapha. But not before he had a chat with

Inspector Baramki, whose office was just down the hall. Before he left, Faroun asked Rebecca to do a little research at the Land Claims Office.

Younis Baramki glowered over a stack of files when Faroun poked in his head, a wolf disturbed in his lair. He had a vulpine look about him too, short, dark hair flecked with gray and the steady gaze of a hunter. He was renowned for his tenacity, and Faroun thought it best to get down to business immediately. The tension would be there whether he made pleasantries or not. Faroun knew that Baramki still smarted over losing the prefectureship to an outsider. An outsider and an unknown. Nevertheless, he rose and politely offered Faroun a chair.

"They have ruled this city for a thousand years," said Baramki, warming to the topic once he knew Faroun's business. "Some call them the Twelve. Or simply the Families." Baramki went on to explain that they had become a special interest of his when he'd begun investigating the links between crime syndicates in the city and the resistance. Besides, in social standing, he was on the fringes of the Families, his father having married a distant relation of the Shihabs. This meant his parents had been invited to several of the annual fêtes thrown by the Twelve when he was a boy, although relegated to one of the lower tables. "My father was proud of the association with the great clans even as he was stung by their indifference. And yet he could hope for some preferment down the line, if he could prove himself useful. He was, from time to time, but never enough. He died wondering what else he could have done. They offer. They withhold. That is how they manipulate, a fine art with the Twelve."

"Then more so with the elect," Faroun said, adding, "the Hand of Maisalun."

"If you've gotten as far as Maisalun, then you know more than most," said Baramki with grudging appreciation. "Faisal wanted to weaken the power of the Twelve. He wanted a cadre for his future return to Syria, a return that is not likely to happen. Instead he sowed the seeds of discord and there was much bloodletting after the French drove him out. Cleaning house, as I think of it. But they settled their differences. They always settle their differences."

"Except with the al Quassi clan," said Faroun. "They were ostracized."

"Were they?" Baramki looked across the desk at Faroun with an expression of conviction, while lowering his voice. "If there is one thing you need to know about the Families, it is this. They are invisible and indivisible."

"And into everything?"

"Anything that's worth their while."

"And not above doing business with the criminal class?"

"Invisible, sir."

"I'm just trying to figure out what business a man like Umar Tamiri would have with a crook like Mustapha Ni'mat. You were in with me on the breakup of that protection racket. You remember Mustapha."

"That's interesting," said Baramki. "He's gone straight, I hear."

"Building supplies."

"Maybe it is business. Umar is a contract broker, isn't he?"

"Construction contracts."

Faroun got up to leave.

"I heard about the Tamiri case," said Baramki. "You don't think Martel did it, do you?"

"Durac forced his confession," Faroun admitted.

"Don't trust him."

"I don't."

"Don't cooperate with him."

"I won't."

"If you want me for anything . . . you can count on my help."

"To be honest, I was wondering if I could."

"It's not because you're Prefect chief and I'm not." Baramki had put it out in the open at last. "I don't hold that against you."

Faroun was sure that he did. "If it's any consolation, Baramki, I didn't want the job in the first place."

"God disposes." Faroun knew Baramki was referring to the high commissioner's office in Beirut. Faroun offered him his hand. The two men shook on a truce.

"I can pull in Mustapha for a little chat," Baramki offered.

"Thank you, Inspector, but I think I'll pay him a visit myself."

"You can check out my permits and my license," said Mustapha Ni'mat, pulling the documents from the top drawer of his desk as if he had been expecting Faroun. "I've been a respectable businessman ever since my last run-in with the law." Nature had marked him for meanness, an ascetic gaze set in a sallow, pockmarked face. Narrow as a knife blade in a pinstripe suit with one shoulder cocked higher than the other. Faroun knew his dossier. He had spent his childhood picking pockets but graduated into running his own gang. After that he had specialized in making victims cough up money even they didn't know they had. Now he claimed he had gone straight, but instinctively Faroun reached inside his coat to be sure his wallet was still there.

"Businessman, perhaps," said the policeman, looking about the office. "Respectable is a stretch." They were close enough to the Gare Maidan that he could hear the afternoon train huffing into the station.

"Look all you want," said Ni'mat defiantly. "Go through my inventory. You guys do what you want anyway."

"We may get around to that," said Faroun, "but I'd like to know what business you have with Umar Tamiri."

"The name's familiar," said Mustapha, rolling his eyes.

"Familiar enough to have coffee with at the Café Pegasus."

"*That* Tamiri," said Mustapha, tapping his forehead.

"Your papers might be in order, Mustapha, but your acquaintances might not. So why don't you tell me what you and Umar had to talk about the other day?"

A worker opened a door that led to a warehouse, and Mustapha nodded for Faroun to follow him. The air was pungent with sawdust and tar. Barrels of nails and screws and spikes lined the walls, and whole sections of the shed were filled with neat piles of lumber and bags of cement. A panel truck was backing into the shed piled with more building supplies. A foreman in a leather cap ran up to Ni'mat and held up a clipboard. Mustapha flipped through the pages and signed the manifest.

"Things look busy."

"Don't you look around the city, Faroun? Or are you too busy harassing honest businessmen to notice? There's a boom going on."

"That's funny. I walk around town and don't see any construction going on."

"You see all this?" cried Mustapha over the shouts of workmen and the rumble of engines. "I can't keep up with demand. If there isn't any boom going on, there is going to be a boom going on."

"Is that what Umar had tell to you?"

"I don't know what you're talking about."

"Then it would be inconvenient if we closed you down for a few days so the tax boys could conduct an audit and inventory?"

"What do you want, Faroun?" The man with the narrow eyes turned and glared at him. Faroun was glad to see the level of exasperation.

"Perhaps I didn't see you and Umar Tamiri together after all. Maybe I was dreaming."

Mustapha's eyes narrowed more. "I told you I had a talk with Umar. He's a construction broker, isn't he? But I don't have anything to do with building contracts."

"What contracts, for instance?"

"Why don't you ask Umar himself?"

"I think I will."

"Look, why are trying to break my back?" cried Mustapha. "Can't you see I'm trying to make something of myself?"

"I'm humbled when a crook turns to the path of righteousness. It restores my faith in mankind. But what kind of contracts are we talking about?"

"Go ask Umar," Mustapha muttered, and hurried off, clapping his hands in the air and screaming at the workers that he wanted one man per bag of cement, not two.

Faroun allowed himself a smug little smile of satisfaction as he crossed the Rue Kadem and ambled toward the little pedestrian bridge that lay across one of the water channels that fed into the Banyass, the second river of Damascus, although it was little more than a stream. He dug his hands into his pockets and looked into the murky water below, considering how Mustapha Ni'mat, clever thug that he was, had a gift for tripping himself up. He had done this the first time Faroun had made his acquaintance, and it had led to the breakup of the protection ring. Now this business about Umar's contracts was most interesting, and Faroun did not doubt that there were deeper layers to the onion.

He was about to move along and leave this particularly drab and depressing district of the city when the call for afternoon prayers went up from the minaret of a nearby mosque. The cry was echoed from spire to spire throughout Old Damascus, a peremptory and lyrical call to surrender that reminded the Muslim faithful that the world was but a place of passage and that only the obedient would be pleasing in the sight of God. To Faroun it seemed as if the city held its breath, and then, the elemental communion reaffirmed, exhaled its busy citizens back into the tawdriness of the day. The muezzin's call reminded him that he was at the center of a force both powerful and mercurial, for Syria and the lands of the Arabs burnt with a restless flame, one that could erupt at any moment and consume the unbelievers in its path.

Restless himself, Faroun was about to move on when he spied

a sleek Rolls-Royce Phantom, the tawny color of a lion, pulling up in front of Mustapha Ni'mat's place of business, followed by a black Renault sedan filled with toughs who looked as if they had just been sprung from prison and given cheap black suits. The uniformed chauffeur hopped out to open the door of the touring car as a tall, husky man uncurled from the backseat. Straightening his cashmere coat, he looked around cautiously before he stepped into the office of Ni'mat Building Supplies. Faroun had seen this Rolls about town before, for there were perhaps three or four in all of Syria. He had been with Ihab Kabir at the time. "That's Abdullah al Quassi's Phantom," he had told Faroun admiringly. "A man might even kill for one of those."

Faroun didn't doubt that the owner of the Phantom had. Abdullah and Mustapha, an interesting convergence, if he could make anything of it. He would give anything to be a fly on the wall of Mustapha's office.

Perhaps Umar would be part of the discussion. Faroun felt sure his visit to Ni'mat would prompt a telephone call from Monsieur Tamiri himself. That would be just fine. He had a few items to discuss with Vera's brother.

"The transfer documents are in some disarray," Rebecca said apologetically when he returned to the office, "but I've done the best I could." She opened an accordion file. "Many of the records from King Faisal's reign in Syria were destroyed when General Gouraud's troops shelled the Ministry Building in 1920. Other records were carried off by Faisal's staff. But this is interesting." She pulled a yellowed and slightly singed paper written in Arabic and bearing the king's seal. "The al Quassi lands were confiscated following Nayef al Quassi's execution in 1918. This document verifies the confiscation and the assignment of the property into an entity called The Royal Land Trust." She pulled out a booklet from underneath the other papers. "This is a copy of the rules and regulations governing that trust. According to the mission statement, the trust was set up by the new king to manage confiscated lands. It became defunct in 1920 when King Faisal went into exile."

Faroun looked up at her as she stood over his desk. "Then what happened to the disposition of the lands?"

"This is where it becomes a paper chase. The trust was transferred by the king himself to a new corporation just before the French army arrived in Damascus."

"Why should this be of interest to us? The al Quassi lands went to a trust and then to a company. That seems to be the end of it."

Rebecca gave him a shrewd look. "I think you had better speak to Monsieur Lavette about that."

"So old Lavette was less than cooperative?"

"You know how our head of the Land Office is with his precious documents. Like a miser guarding a hoard of gold."

"I'll drop in and have a chat with him. It helps if one speaks his language." Faroun opened one of his desk drawers and rummaged about until he produced a cellophane pouch filled with a colorful assortment of seeds. "Birdseed," he confirmed as he slipped the pouch into his pocket.

Rebecca gave him a wondering look. "Before you speak to Monsieur Lavette, call Sergeant Kabir. He left this number in Aleppo." She handed him a memo slip.

The electricity had gone out at the ministry for the second time that day so the lift was out. As Faroun climbed the stairs to the top floor, he pondered the information Ihab had just relayed to him by telephone. Faroun's subordinate had revealed two important facts, one of them troubling. Ihab had been able to persuade Madame al Quassi to talk, for it seemed she was fuming about her husband and willing to expose his "decadence." She knew all about Salim's latest affair, for she had intercepted a letter from his lover. The letter, which Ihab had seen, was addressed to "Teddy." It was filled with gushing endearments and sweet talk and hinted at intimacies that made Ihab uncomfortable even as it made Madame al Quassi cry with self-pity and vindication, for here was demonstrable proof of her husband's outrageous infidelity. She would make him suffer for that, she assured the sergeant. He had deserted her and the children on the road to Aleppo, and this was the second part of the message, the part that made Faroun uncomfortable. Salim had vanished. Salim's wife suspected it had something to do with his mistress and that he had returned to Damascus. The woman had driven him mad. As for the identity of Salim's lover, Madame al Quassi had no idea, but if she did, she would scratch out her eyes, this evil vixen, this Madame or Mademoiselle "V," for that was how the letter was signed. Most likely a infidel European, she hissed, for all foreign women were whores.

Faroun made his way through the cluster of desks inside the Office of Land Claims and, waving off Monsieur Lavette's secretary's cries that he was not to be disturbed, took a flight of stairs that led to the roof of the Ministry Building. Behind a decorative battlement sheltered from the wind, the director of the Land Office was cooing soothingly to a half dozen pigeons in a wire loft. He turned a baleful countenance on Faroun, until the policeman produced the pouch of seeds.

"From that same excellent mix?" Lavette inquired. Faroun nodded. "Very thoughtful of you, Inspector." Elias Lavette's smile was not less intimidating than his glare, for his appearance made most people uncomfortable. He had been blinded by chlorine gas and wounded by shrapnel at Verdun and left for dead on the battlefield. One of his company found him and carried him back across no-man's-land. It took the rest of the war for the medicos to stitch him back into something that resembled a man, but the surgery left him scarred with suture marks like barbwire gouges from his forehead and across his scalp and down his left cheek. He had lost sight in one eye and wore macroscopic spectacles, one lens made of black glass. He had also lost all but the thumb and forefinger of his left hand. These ravages he had borne manfully, and his staff referred to him, in some awe, as the Librarian for his encyclopedic memory. He did not inspire affection, though, and so he often came up to his pigeon loft to find it.

"That is a scandaroon, is it not, Monsieur Lavette, a new one?" Faroun pointed at a bird with a rosy beak who found the policeman an equal curiosity.

"That is a very close distinction, Inspector Faroun," said Lavette. "You see those little white chevrons on the wing? That is what distinguishes the Tunisian flier from the scandaroon."

Lavette opened the packet the policeman had brought and slipped it into a suit pocket. "I saw my first Tunisian while I was convalescing in Arras," Lavette recalled. "Oh, they were the bravest of the brave, these little fellows, I can tell you. No private in a frontline outpost was so naked and alone. But they flew, zip, zip, zip"—he demonstrated with an expressive choreography of his hands—"through a rain of bullets, through artillery barrages. Those contemptible Boche aviators would even try to shoot them down. But they came through with messages from the front, time and again. When the telephone lines were cut by explosions, who do you think conducted the business of the war? Why, the generals were blind without them." He made a wry expression. "The generals were blind in any event, eh, Faroun? Which reminds me, what time do you have?"

"Nearly eleven thirty."

Lavette pulled out a brass-tipped spyglass form his coat pocket and went over to the parapet, a slight stoop to his gait. "But you did not come here for pigeon talk," said the director of the Land Office. "Your secretary was in my office this morning, stirring things up. Something about King Faisal's Land Trust. I finally had to shoo her off with a few pieces of paper."

"Rebecca can rub people the wrong way, but she means well. Tell me about King Faisal's Land Trust."

"A royal scam," said the other as he scanned the sky. "Faisal set it up in 1918 as a way of rewarding his followers. Much of the land belonged to the Turkish government in Istanbul. Faisal claimed these lands under his authority as the newly self-proclaimed king of Syria. He included within its purview lands confiscated from his political enemies."

"Including that of traitors."

"Oh, yes. Or those Faisal believed to be traitors."

"And who were the recipients?"

Lavette lowered the spyglass and turned to Faroun. The sun glinted on the dark lens of his glasses. "Who do you have in mind?"

"I'm thinking of the al Quassi family."

Lavette grunted. "You might say Nayef al Quassi was the biggest loser of them all, for he had a great deal of property. They hanged him, you know. As a Turkish spy."

"What happened to the al Quassi lands, Monsieur Lavette?"

Lavette turned back to his search of the sky. "I don't know if I should be telling you this. That matter is a little too close to the seat of our political pants, if you catch my drift."

"Yet it would be a matter of record, Monsieur Lavette."

"A matter of deep record, Inspector. It is almost impossible to discover these documents."

"Unless someone knew where to find them."

"I am grateful for that wonderful mix you bring for my girls, Faroun. Perhaps I might inquire into the name of your supplier."

"A policeman must be guarded with his sources, Monsieur."

"Yes, yes. Of course. But you do have more?"

"I feel sure I can guarantee an uninterrupted supply."

"Then you are the only official in the French Syrian government who can make such a claim," said Lavette with amusement. "I suppose I can tell you that the Nayef al Quassi's great loss was Farid Tamiri's gain."

"The father of Umar Tamiri, you mean."

"I believe Farid had a son by that name."

"So Nayef al Quassi is hanged for a traitor and Farid Tamiri gains his lands by royal decree. Cause and effect, do you think Monsieur Lavette?"

The director shrugged. "Who is to say? Ah, but there she is. Right on time." Lavette pointed to a speck in the northern sky.

"I merely speculate that Farid Tamiri must have been high in King Faisal's estimation."

"Kings still do what they will, Inspector. And dictators. Especially in this age of failed republicanism." The speck in the sky had become a pigeon on the wing. It alighted silently on the parapet to the appreciative cooing of her mates in the wire loft.

"King Faisal is king no longer."

"Not of Syria at any rate." Lavette gently gathered the bird into his arm. He turned his inquisitive eye, magnified by a thick lens, on Faroun. "I think I know where you are going with this, Inspector. The former king did make certain provisions for the perpetuation of the trust before the French removed him from power."

"And these provisions are still current?"

"As far as I know. I can provide you with the documents in question, but you'll have to take up other matters with the Legal Department."

"I am in your debt, Monsieur."

"And I await your next batch of ambrosia," said Lavette. He removed a cylinder from the homing pigeon's leg and placed her in the hutch. As he popped open the cylinder, he turned his back to Faroun. Reading the note, he made a long *ooohhh,* just like a pigeon. Faroun wondered if the rumor was true, that old Lavette had a beautiful Syrian mistress stashed away in a northern suburb, and that they exchanged love notes by cupid's winged messengers.

When he returned to his office, Faroun was bearing a slender file and scarcely able to contain his excitement. Rebecca was typing furiously, a half-eaten piece of baklava beside her typewriter. He scrawled a note on a memo pad and handed it to her. "Take these documents and this note and run it by the Legal Department for me, will you?"

When he was sure Rebecca had left the office, he took out an envelope from his coat pocket. The note was written in a petite, elegant hand on woven paper. A faint trace of her scent clung to it, just enough to entice, and to warn.

21

The Hotel Nurredine was, like many buildings in Damascus, a prisoner of history. The Ottoman architects who built it had demolished an Orthodox convent just as the Christian builders before them had cleared away the ruins of a temple dedicated to the lascivious goddess Cybele to make way for the nunnery. The current structure, dating from the 1880s, was a Moorish-inspired gem, its guests mostly bureaucrats and military officers traveling to Syria and Palestine. Made of red Syrian granite and fitted with a layer of ivory stucco, the hotel was hidden behind a line of cypresses and a tall wrought-iron fence, and this kept it at a discrete distance from the constant traffic moving down Bab Charki Street a block away. Faroun arrived at the black-painted portal in an unmarked police car and rolled up the circular gravel drive, whose centerpiece was a reflecting pool and fountain. He opened the scented note one more time. This was the address.

While a marble putto sprayed an irreverent arc of water over the back of a bronze tortoise, Faroun parked the unmarked car next to a vintage limousine. It was a Graef and Stift touring car from the early twenties, beautifully maintained, most likely by the lean older man with a shock of unruly white hair who was lovingly polishing the hood.

"That's the only one I've seen in Damascus," Faroun said by way of a compliment.

"The only one you'll find too," said the spindly man without missing a swirl of his chamois.

"Are you the owner?"

The man who stepped off the running board was in his early sixties with a prickly white stubble on his drawn face and rheumy eyes. Pulling up his faded gray trousers, he looked around as if he were being watched. "I owned it once. Before she got her hands on it."

"And that would be?"

"That would be a demoness from hell named Moulmenian, though she's had other names before she stole mine." At the mention of her name, the light seemed to fade in his eyes. "You'll find her inside. At the desk." He went back to waxing. "Scheming," he cautioned, as Faroun walked away.

The policeman stepped into the foyer and, for a moment, took in the cool confines of the hotel. Graceful rounded archways led to shadowy alcoves and recesses adorned with potted plants and porcelain lamps. Colorful mosaics had been embedded in the wall above by the staircase that led to the upper floors. Faroun stood on another mosaic, an inlaid scene of bedouin warriors racing their camels across the desert, heading toward an old ruin in the distance. To the right of the front desk, flanked with vases of marigolds, was a sunny reading room lined with bookshelves and accented with antique urns stuffed with papyrus plants. A chubby, redheaded boy sat on a stuffed ottoman drawing on a sketch pad. He paused in his artwork to stare at Faroun with large blue eyes.

"Tradesman's entrance is in the rear," said the concierge, coming from behind the front desk like a terrier. She gave Faroun's wrinkled white linen suit an unfriendly appraisal. She was a voluptuous Armenian woman, round in the hips and shoulders, striking by virtue of her imperious features and high cheekbones. Doubtlessly, she had turned heads in her youth. However, her temperament, made sanguine by having to deal with peddlers and others who got in her way, had compromised her beauty. Her attire didn't improve matters, for she wore a long burgundy and blue dress that might have been fashioned from a worn Persian rug, trimmed with excessive furls of lace at the wrists and neckline. Around her waist, she wore a thick leather belt, laden with a key ring and old iron keys, bringing to Faroun's mind the image of a keeper of a medieval madhouse. She looked him up and down as if he might have stolen something. "You . . ." Her long eyes narrowed. "I know you, don't I?"

"I don't think so," said the policeman, removing his beret. "I gave up moving linens and soaps a long time ago."

"Then why are you here?" she demanded.

"I believe I come as a guest. Suite 308."

Madame Moulmenian involuntarily placed a hand over her bust as if she had a sudden palpitation of the heart and returned to the front desk. Picking up the phone, she made hurried conversation and bustled back with an officious smile.

"Suite 308, monsieur, awaits you," she said apologetically. "I made an unforgivable error."

"No harm done," said Faroun.

"If you need anything, even the tiniest attention, do not hesitate." Now she was all coquettish and purring. "The Hotel Nurredine I am sure you will find is famous for its ambience—and discretion." He could have sworn that she offered him a congenial wink until her eye fell balefully on the grizzled man who had been polishing the touring car. He had just picked up a broom like one assuming the afflictions of Job. "Cesar," she barked. "What are you ogling?"

Cesar cringed at the summons. "Take this gentleman"—she nodded grandiloquently at Faroun—"to his suite." Casting a spiteful glance at Madame, Cesar crooked a finger at Nikolai Faroun as he mounted the stairs.

The door to Suite 308 opened on a sedate, well-furnished living room, with comfortable rattan chairs and a coffee table decorated with fresh-cut roses. A hallway lined with watercolors of crowded souks and city scenes from the time of the Ottomans led to a bright and airy dining area. Tall windows overlooked the pleasant garden at the back of the hotel. A decorous flower arrangement of cut roses and geraniums sat in the center of a small, round table covered with white lace. A bottle of champagne cooled in a bucket, and covered dishes waited on the table as Eugenie Poquelin, smiling, brought him a glass and offered a toast.

"Welcome to the Hotel Nurredine."

"What is the occasion?" Faroun asked in a puzzled tone.

"No occasion, Inspector, but I thought you might like to visit the hideaway where Vera Tamiri met her lovers."

Eugenie had prepared dainty egg salad sandwiches and, as a side dish, asparagus smothered in labneh and olives. Faroun kept to the sandwiches as he questioned her about the hotel. She knew very little about the Hotel Nurredine, she claimed. When Faroun asked her how she had learned of Vera's hideaway she affected a mysterious smile and, touching a linen napkin to her lips, pushed her plate away. She asked if it would annoy him if she smoked, and although it would, he nodded his assent. She lit up a gold-tipped Sobranie, gold bangles jingling down her wrist. "I've told you all I can, Inspector. I don't know how many men she met here. She met Teddy here, I can tell you that."

"Yet you know nothing about Teddy."

"We shared many things but not everything. As you know, Vera did not confide about her current lovers."

"Past amours then. So it is reasonable to assume that you knew about this hotel."

Eugenie waved a finger at him playfully. "You are trying to catch me up, aren't you, Inspector? Surely you would understand if I told you that I must respect my sources."

"I can respect that, of course."

"And I hope you can have some respect for Vera. She had her flaws—and all of that is too painfully coming out. She cared about her work at the clinic; she cared about the women who came there. After the firebombing, it was her plan to reopen the service, even expand it. If she had lived . . ."

"How long did Vera stay in this suite? It's obvious she spent little time at her apartment."

"What are you trying to get at, Inspector?"

"It seems to me she must have lived here."

"For the past few months. It is possible. Ever since she got rid of Captain Martel. She was rarely at her apartment but she told no one about this place. I do not know how to explain it."

"Then we might suppose there was someone special she shared time with here. I mean, it would have made for inconvenient scheduling if she was seeing several men."

Eugenie gave him a sharp look. "I asked you to respect her memory and what do you imply? Vera Tamiri was not what you think. She did not hop into bed with every man. She was in love with Teddy. I can tell by the hints she dropped."

"And that is an important fact to know."

"Who knows what good things she might have completed had she lived? I cannot explain to you those rages in her soul that put her in conflict with herself. But I do ask you to respect her memory. That's the only reason I am helping you. For her. And to bring down the monster that took her away from us." She bit her lip to stop the tears, and, awkwardly, Faroun took her hand. She squeezed it and walked to the window. When she had regained her composure, she gave him an anxious look. "Anything we said here would be the strictest confidence, wouldn't it? I mean, if anyone knew we were meeting like this . . ."

"I did not know it was you I would be meeting." A half-truth admittedly, and one that allowed for interpretation.

Her nervousness had given way to a playful smile. "But you are not disappointed?" Far from disappointed, thought Faroun. She was pretty in a festive dress with flounced sleeves trimmed with red embroidery. She had done something different with her hair, curls at her ears in the Andalusian style. She reminded him of a Gypsy, but it might have been the dangling earrings.

She tilted the bottle of champagne. Faroun placed his palm over his glass. She lifted his hand aside, poured some more wine. "Now—who is trying to catch someone up?"

She broke into an intimate laugh, then became solemn. "I hate this place. I hate Syria." Then she brightened. "Before we came here, though, we were in Morocco. I loved Morocco." She lifted the glass to her lips and a little of the wine spilled over the rim. "That is to say I loved Moroccan men. I even made love to a Tuareg warrior once. A young Legionnaire had a crush on me and so I persuaded him to arrange a meeting with one of their bandit chiefs in the desert. We rode out to his camp. While my Legionnaire waited outside by the campfire, the sheikh and I had— coffee. He was a ferocious coffee drinker, fabulously thirsty, and he never took off his veil the whole time. The Legionnaire brought me back to town but he was so downcast that I told him to spread a blanket in an oasis. We made love before we returned to town. He was as keen as the Tuareg, but being a young man, he fumbled so."

"Quite an exotic little adventure," said Faroun. "Naturally, husband Henri was left in the dark."

"Actually, I did tell Henri about it; I don't know why. I suppose I was feeling some Catholic schoolgirl guilt. Do you want to know his reaction?"

"Let me see," said Faroun, looking into the air.

"He laughed at me," she said indignantly. "He thought I had made the whole thing up! It is typical of Henri to laugh at his own cuckoldry. Well, it's not as if he doesn't have his share of adventures. And mistresses!"

"An active fellow, Henri."

She blew out a puff of smoke with irritation. "He hasn't touched me since our youngest, Celine, was born. I am grateful for that. Really."

"That is a terrible waste," said Faroun, and suddenly he realized it was the champagne slipping into his speech. He pushed the glass away. "I will confide something to you, Eugenie."

"About your lovers?" she said, putting her pert chin on her hand and looking over at him as if she might be reading his mind. "Tell me about your lovers."

"A boring tale for the most part, believe me. The last one was a German."

"An *allemande*? How dour. Were you so lonely?"

Faroun could see where this was going and caught himself. "Let's talk about Teddy. What if I were to tell you I know who Teddy is?"

She lifted an eyebrow. "That would be interesting."

"I've had Teddy's identity confirmed by his wife. One of my officers spoke to her in Aleppo yesterday. She had seen some correspondence between them. Teddy is Salim al Quassi."

She wrinkled her brow. "You mentioned him before. A man she gambled with. I can never keep Arab names straight." She looked over at him carelessly. "With your pardon."

Faroun pulled a billfold from his coat pocket. "I have a photo of him here. It's a newspaper photo from a groundbreaking ceremony at his brother's trucking firm about a year ago. A little grainy—perhaps you can recognize him." Faroun slid it before her and excused himself to go to the washroom.

The bath was just off the corridor. Closing the door, he turned on the faucet and splashed water over his face. He stood there, cooling off, the beads of water coursing down his forehead and cheeks. He was an idiot for meeting Eugenie at a lovers' hotel. They weren't having an affair. He smiled wanly. Or were they?

He caught sight of something reflected in the mirror. Wiping his face with a hand towel, he went over to the bathtub. It was a cast-iron antique with a porcelain veneer and gilded lion's feet. But it was the tile wall behind the tub that had Faroun's attention. The design was aquatic, large pink and orange fish swirling among flowering water lilies. A lively, charming scene. Oriental koi caught in a graceful dance. Faroun had seen that tint before; he had seen that shade of pink in a tile chip that Philippe Mansour had found in the hair of a dead woman whose body had been fished out of the Barada River. Faroun stepped into the tub and ran his hand over the design. In the center of the inset, the tiles were cracked. He traced the crack and found a hole where a piece of tile had been chipped away. It was the same size and shape of the tile Mansour had found. He stood against the wall. Vera was about a head shorter. The crack in the design came at just about the place her head might have been had she been standing in the bathtub. At the place where she might have been forced against the wall with such force that her head cracked the tile.

Vera's final scene came to him as if he had been there. It was late, perhaps after midnight. She had spent an evening losing at the tables and had come to the love nest to take a hot bath. She was expecting someone. He came into the apartment and made his way to the bath, where he surprised her. And frightened her. She defended herself. He overpowered her and drove her head against the wall. The blow might have been enough to kill her, certainly to knock her out. Then he pulled out his knife to finish the job. But how had the body been transported out of the hotel without attracting any attention?

Drying his hands, he went back to the sunny room where he had dined with Eugenie. Her glass was still full and the photograph was on the table, but she was not there. He called for her but there was no answer. He went from room to room but he did not find her. He discovered an open back door off the pantry that led down three landings and on to the garden at the back of the hotel. The back gate to the garden stood open. Instead of Eugenie, the chubby little boy with the sketch pad sat on the lip of a fountain as the grumpy Cesar tugged at some weeds in a flowerbed.

"She is not here," Cesar said. "There was a taxi waiting and she took it." He shook his head. "Women!" he grumbled. "Can you not figure them out? When you do, it's too late, believe me, far too late."

Faroun walked over to the boy, who jumped off his perch and, wordlessly, saluted the policeman.

Cesar stood up, his hand to his back as he straightened. He rubbed the boy's tousled red curls. "He thinks you are Napoléon."

Faroun smiled and returned the salute.

"His name's Toni. Show him the drawing, boy." Tony pulled out a sketch that showed Faroun standing in the foyer of the hotel wearing the signature bicorne hat of the first emperor of the French. His hand was tucked neatly into his waistcoat in the signature pose. Toni's talent was impressive. A few deft strokes of charcoal and colored chalk. "It's his hobby, drawing the guests and clients of the Hotel Nurredine. He sketches everyone."

"Why isn't he in school?"

"He is dumb, poor fellow. Some childhood malady. I cannot say for sure. Toni is not my son. The harridan was married before.

Toni was born and the papa ran off. Not hard to figure out why, at least not for me, and it has nothing to do with this boy. I love him like my own. He's the reason I'm still here. That and the fact that the demoness has got a lock on everything I own." He grimaced. "Or used to own."

Faroun's attention drifted to the third-floor window overlooking the garden. "Let me ask you something about Suite 308, Cesar. Perhaps a week and a half to two weeks ago—do you remember who lived in the apartment?"

"Why do you want to know?" Cesar asked suspiciously. "You are a policeman, is that it?"

"The Prefecture."

A look of uncertainty played across the old man's features. "I don't pay too much attention to who comes and goes around here. It's not in my best interest, if you can understand. Besides, I'm in my cot off the scullery by nine."

"And what about Madame?"

"She retires early too. Not in the scullery, I'm glad to say. At least I have that to myself. Besides, you won't get anything out of Lady Medusa. She sees even less than I do."

Toni pulled out another sketch and held it up for Faroun's inspection. Eugenie Poquelin, leaving the garden by the back gate. Her slippered feet were off the ground, a fairy princess with wings.

"He draws people as he sees them," said Cesar.

"And he draws everyone he sees?" the policeman asked.

Cesar chuckled. "He has stacks of drawings in his room."

"I'd like to see some more of those drawings," said Faroun. "Any renderings Toni has done in the past two weeks."

"Cesar!" Their conversation was interrupted by the screech of Cesar's nemesis. She had rounded the corner of the building and was making for them with ungainly speed. "What are you doing here, lollygagging? What do you think I'm paying you for?"

"Paying me with my own money," he cursed under his breath. "Tomorrow afternoon," he whispered. "There's a sweet shop around the corner. I take him there once a week for a treat."

Faroun paused to see Madame Moulmenian send Cesar scurrying to clean up the lawn. As she walked off, firing a scowl in Faroun's direction, she pointed Toni to the front of the hotel. He followed her, his shoulders slumped, dragging by a string a cigar box in which he kept the tools of his art. Perhaps in sympathy, Cesar dragged his rake through the grass as he trudged back to the flowerbeds. He gave Faroun a look of bleak despair. Poor bastards, thought Faroun, the brace of them.

The policeman left by the garden gate, as Eugenie had done. He looked down the poplar-lined street as if she might be there waiting for him. The street was empty. As he closed the black iron gate, the thought came to him that this portal would provide a convenient exit for someone carrying a body in the dead of night.

22

Salim al Quassi paused before the pawnbroker's shop on the Rue Aladam and peered into the dusty window. It was hard to see much of anything. Only a dim bulb glowed from within, and the store window was crowded with furniture and crockery, a draftsman's table and tools. Costume jewelry glittered in faded felt-lined boxes mixed with an assortment of pocket watches and wristwatches.

He had followed a maze to get to this place, the maze of the Damascus underworld, or what his brother jokingly referred to as "the lower depths," ignoring that he was a diver in those waters too. Mustapha Ni'mat had provided the key that had brought him to the pawnshop. Not that Mustapha had been inclined to be cooperative. It had taken a bit of persuasion. Perhaps a touch more than necessary. However, Salim needed information and he needed it quickly, for there was no telling but that Vera's murderer might flee the city or take up a disguise or otherwise elude him. He might even strike again and ruin some other man's life, for, as Salim had so painfully discovered, there was no hell on earth greater than losing one's heart, losing one's soul. In the end, Mustapha, the only business associate of Abdullah's he could recall, had recognized his urgency and come around with the names. These names were painted in bold black letters on the sign overhead, MARDAM & NASIB BEK.

"Perhaps Monsieur would like to see a gentleman's diamond. We have several new ones on consignment," said Mardam, coming round from behind the counter, bowing and rubbing his chubby hands. "Perfect for the pinkie," he said, waving a monogram ring on his left hand. His round, pockmarked face was lit up with an unctuous, predatory smile. Tufted eyebrows arched to his forehead making him appear to Salim like a messenger from the infernal regions. "Ah, no!" Mardam exclaimed, as one who had a sudden inspiration. "I can see it is about a lady. Something for a lady. Yes, yes, come with me." He led Salim over to a jewelry case loaded with bracelets and bangles and piles of cheap jewelry. Stepping behind the counter, he unlocked the case and drew forth a blue felt box. He blew the dust off it and popped open the top. "Have you ever seen one like it?" he asked, holding up a necklace of cheap stones, red and yellow, and blue. "The latest thing from Paris. Ladies of refinement—"

"I could use a wristwatch," said Salim, showing his bare arm. His own watch had been missing since the bus ride into Damascus. No doubt he had been the victim of some low thief.

"I knew it would be a watch, didn't I?" The merchant hummed tunelessly as he swung a long pole into the shop window, snagged one of the watches in the window, and dropped it on the case before Salim. "What a treasure this is, monsieur. Just come in on consignment. Made by the Egyptian jeweler Nasser—you see the little red fez on it. Just like the one I'm wearing." He shook the black tassel of his fez at Salim. "Appreciate the solid-gold clasp. Once belonged to Egyptian royalty—look at the initial on the back. You see that: *F* with a crown—that's *F* for Prince Farouk."

"I'll take it," said Salim, slipping it on his wrist. "Is that the right time?"

"Yes, correct," said the other, holding up his watch. "Two in the afternoon. I never skip a second."

"Judging by the dust on all this stuff," said Salim, looking around the gloomy shop, "it doesn't seem you have all that much business, Monsieur Bek."

"Times are hard. The Franks—may God damn their eyes— have ruined us!" said the pawnbroker, shaking his head. "Never fear! Since you are such a special customer, I have in mind for you a special price."

"Times are hard," repeated Salim. "So I am sure you are available for other kinds of work."

The other looked up from a pad of paper where he was working through a complicated set of calculations. "I'm sure I have no idea what you mean, monsieur."

"I mean work of a special kind, but not like your prices for this junk you peddle. I mean disposal work. Of a kind."

Mardam Bek put down his pencil and, placing his hands on the glass case, gave Salim a searching look. "Monsieur?"

"I mean like the work you performed some nights ago at the Hotel Nurredine," said Salim, pulling out his pistol. "A poor, dear woman had been murdered there and you and your brother cleaned up the mess and took care of the body. Do you remember that disposal job?"

"Who are you?" asked the shaken man.

"Where is your brother?"

"In the back. In the appraisal room."

"Is there anyone else around?" Salim asked, going over to the door and flipping over the sign, while keeping the gun trained on Mardam. He flipped off the light. "I thought not. Then let's have a

little chat, Monsieur Bek, in the back room. We are going to rene-
gotiate for this overpriced bangle you are trying to sell me. I'm a
disgruntled customer and I do not like being treated like a country
yokel. There are other matters on the agenda too."

A block down from the Hotel Nurredine on the Street Called
Straight was an Armenian-owned patisserie. The patisserie lifted
its patrons right off the street with mouthwatering aromas, its
cinnamon-and-nut-stuffed pastries and colorful selection of iced
sherbets. Toni Moulmenian was enjoying some of each while Cesar sat next to him sipping his coffee and Faroun looked through a
collection of the boy's sketches. Like the ones he had made of the
fairy princess Eugenie and the policeman as Napoléon, the boy's
drawings were steeped in his own symbolism. There were several
renderings of Cesar. He appeared as a white-bearded man with a
nimbus and a look of infinite suffering, like a kindly mage who had
been trapped and forced to perform drudgery under an evil spell.
The spell-maker herself appeared in the background, glowering
and grimacing with long teeth, and curling lip, her hands on her
hips, and eyes like orange saucers. In one drawing, the "demoness," as Cesar called her, was shown in a less formidable pose,
cringing before a man with massive shoulders, a fearsome devil in
long camel-colored coat. The giant's eyebrows and lips were lowering and brutal, and his hands had sharp talons that clawed the
air. A tiny, terrified child with red hair stood next to her, holding
on to her dress, a piece of paper in one hand, a broken piece of
chalk in the other.

"Toni calls him the Afreet," said Cesar. "I don't know who the
monster is, but he was at the hotel nearly two weeks ago, and as
you can see, he scared the boy. I remember the night because the
Medusa woke me up about three in the morning and told me to get
up, grab my mop and pail, and clean out Suite 308, the very one
you visited the other day. She said if I found anything there, articles

of clothing, or anything, I was to give it to her. And I was to keep my mouth shut. Anyway, Toni showed me this drawing the following day." He tousled the boy's hair. "I had to calm him down—Toni and I speak in signs, you see, because it's not smart to write things down with her always looking over your shoulder. He told me the Afreet had come around the night before and had threatened his mother. He said something would happen to the boy if she didn't play dumb. Then he gave her some money, Toni told me."

Toni looked up from his sherbet and made a couple of quick hand movements. "A big packet of money," Cesar translated.

"What did you find when you got to Suite 308 that morning?"

"That was what was so strange about it. It looked like somebody had just been there cleaning ahead of me! I mean the bathroom had just been scoured; everything washed down and by someone in a hurry. So I just went to work and cleaned again. But you know something . . ."

"What is that, Cesar?"

"There was a strange feeling to the place. I can't describe it, as if something evil had seeped in and no amount of scrubbing could get it out. Something very bad had taken place there."

"Did you find anything out of the way? Signs of a struggle?"

"You mean like bloodstains, don't you? Nothing. I examined the rest of the suite. The furniture was in order. I checked the closets. Nothing. As if no one had ever been there."

"Can you remember what night this was?"

Cesar counted back on his fingers. "A Sunday morning. A week ago, I think."

"But someone had obviously been there that night."

Cesar shrugged. "You know what the Nurredine is like. People come and go."

"Lovers come and go."

"Lovers. Friends. It's not for married people." Cesar took a bite of his croissant. "Not for married people married to each other, that is."

Toni went through the little stack of drawings he had brought with him and, pulling one out, handed it to Faroun and nodded gravely at Cesar. The drawing was of a Arab man with a thin mustache and aquiline nose, a handsome fellow dressed in evening clothes. Flowers were growing out of his shirtsleeves. Bunches of flowers instead of hands. Between his hands he held a stuffed toy bear.

"That was one of them."

"Teddy."

Toni nodded and grinned.

"Yes, that's what Toni calls him. Although sometimes he calls him the Flower Man. He was always bringing flowers to the woman in that room."

"Was Teddy there that night, Toni, the night the Afreet came to see you and your mother?"

The boy nodded as he scooped a spoon into his orange sherbet.

Faroun set the drawing down on the seat next to them. "You said one of them."

Toni pulled out another sketch and handed it to Faroun.

"This man arrived before Teddy on the same night."

Faroun stared at the figure in the sketch. He was as thin as a knife blade and was wearing an outsize hat that cast a sinister shadow over his features. He carried a suit coat in one hand while he knocked on the door with the number 308. His shoes were much too big for him. He wore a black shirt and a white tie. "What do you call this man, Toni?"

Toni looked up as if he was trying to think of a name. He signed to Cesar. "Black Shirt. He just calls him Black Shirt."

"Last question, Toni. Did you ever make a drawing of the woman who was staying in Suite 308?"

"The boy never saw her," Cesar said nervously. "Mostly she arrived late at night by the garden gate, and whenever I saw her, just once or twice, she was always covered with a scarf or a veil. We just called her the Mystery Woman. She never returned after that morning I cleaned. That's all I know."

"The gate is left open?"

"Locked," said Cesar. "But the Mystery Woman had a key. I don't know if she had others made."

"Our Mystery Woman would enter the hotel compound through the gate and then let herself in via the back door to the suite."

"Yes, of course."

Faroun reached into the pocket of his raincoat and pulled out a box of tin soldiers, brightly dressed in Napoleonic uniforms. "Here's the Little Corporal himself," said Faroun as he pointed out the rotund figure with the hand in his vest. "And that's Marshal Ney. The horsemen with shining breastplates are called cuirassiers. And the last one—one of the Old Guard. I'd like to make a trade, Toni. All these soldiers are yours for one of your drawings. This one here."

Toni stood up to salute Faroun as he left the shop. Faroun fired off a sharp salute in return. Cesar came out into the street with him. "He won't forget your kindness," said the old man. "Here," he said, pressing into Faroun's hand an object folded into a piece of fabric. "I want you to take this. But don't open it now. And don't ever ask me about it, because I can't tell you any more than I'm telling you now." Cesar nodded gravely in the direction of Toni, who had already lined up his army on the table, ready for Austerlitz. "When I was cleaning that suite, there was something trapped in the drain, the bathtub drain."

23

Faroun had Toni's drawing in hand when he entered the lobby of the Hotel Nurredine. It was full afternoon, and since Cesar and Toni were still at the patisserie, Faroun decided to have a look around. The front desk was deserted, but from somewhere on the first floor came the crackling strains of an old recording, a drowsy piano and a clarinet that sounded much like an Arabian oud.

He followed the sounds down the corridor that flanked the front desk, taking a left at the empty kitchen, Cesar's "scullery," clean and polished and lined with shiny pots and pans, until he came to an apartment with the door open. He knocked at the door, but the music was so loud he doubted if anyone heard him. He stepped into the parlor, a room that seemed to have been frozen in time, for the furnishings recalled a previous decade, Tiffany lamps with beaded shades, a mahogany traveling bar and intricately carved coffee table, and rich Moroccan carpets in maroon and dark blue. The carved, upholstered chairs and couch were embroidered with leaping gazelles like those in medieval tapestries. A portrait of Madame Moulmenian and Toni hung on one wall. Faroun traced the scent of sandalwood incense to an alcove in one corner of the room. The space housed an elaborate candlelit shrine, its centerpiece a gold-framed photograph, surrounded by smoking joss sticks, of an exotic veiled dancer, her head thrown back and limbs poised like Shiva. Crowding this central deity were publicity photographs of the same woman in seductive costumes and expressive poses, flower petals beneath her dancing feet.

The music faded away.

"Have you seen quite enough?" demanded a familiar and peremptory voice.

Faroun scarcely recognized the woman standing at the other end of the room. She wore a gold-embroidered caftan and a matching turban adorned with a peacock feather. The jewelry was gold and Egyptian-inspired in a style fashionable in the twenties. Cleopatra making a comeback. She joined Faroun at the shrine and lit a stick of incense with one of the candles.

"She was the toast of Beirut," said Madame Moulmenian, her eyelids heavy with blue shadow and her speech slurry. She touched one of the photographs with her fingertips. "Upon a time. Cynara. Her admirers came from all over the Middle East, from Cairo, Istanbul. An Italian once shot himself for love of her. But it was an English lord who gave me that name. Cynara. He said it was from a famous English love poem." She looked at Faroun as if she had just recognized him. "You were here, when was it, last week—the other day? Your lover is gone. The French blonde. Very pretty, that one. You are fortunate to have a love, monsieur."

Faroun followed her to the coffee table, where she took a cheroot from a brass humidor. He lifted a crystal lighter from the table and applied the flame, still wondering, as he gazed at Madame Moulmenian's fiercely rouged and powdered face, how to reconcile Cesar's "demoness" with the dancer who had once been the toast of Beirut and this sad-eyed revenant who kept a shrine to her lost youth and fame.

"What brings you here?" Her eyes narrowed with suspicion. "At this time, you are something else than a lover, I think."

"I have a few questions."

She was glowering now. "You are a policeman, aren't you?"

"Nikolai Faroun, Prefecture chief." Faroun produced his badge and made a slight bow.

"I have done nothing wrong!" she cried, stamping her foot. "You damned French get plenty out of me." Her eyes fell to a decanter half-filled with a green liqueur. She poured the liquid into two slim glasses and, grudgingly, handed one to Faroun. She threw her head back as she drank, dramatically, and savored the absinthe. She put the glass down on the table with a gesture of annoyance. "I pay my taxes. Twice. Thanks to the assessors, whose avarice knows no bounds."

"This is not about taxes, madame," said Nikolai, putting his glass on the coffee table, untouched. "I want you to look at this drawing."

Faroun unrolled Toni's terrifying scene with the fearsome Afreet. Moulmenian snatched the picture and held it up. "This is Toni's work. Where did you get it?" she asked anxiously. A look of panic came into her eyes. "What have you done with my Toni?"

"Nothing, madame," said Faroun calmly. "He is safe with Cesar, at the sweet shop."

"With Cesar?" She put a finger to her temple as if to banish her confusion. She tipped the absinthe glass so that the last drop passed between her lips. Then she laughed. "He was handsome once. Cesar. But he let himself slide."

"This man—this caricature that Toni drew. He came to visit you some nights ago, a week ago perhaps. I want to know who he is."

"This picture is nothing," she said dismissively. "My son imagines—things."

"I have seen other drawings. Toni has imagination, yes, but he records what he sees. His eyes are the eyes of the Nurredine. He draws those who come and enter. This man may be a monster," Faroun said, pointing to the creature in the camel-colored coat, "but that does not make him any the less real. He came here some nights ago and threatened you and your son. Something happened that night and he wanted your silence. And he gave you a sum of money."

"Who said anything about money?" Her eyes widened with betrayal. "It was that bag of bones, Cesar, wasn't it? I will starve him!" she bellowed. "I will beat him black-and-blue, that lying old man." She balled up her fists as if she might strike him. "The two of you are in this together, is that it? Trying to frame me!" She grabbed her arms to stop her trembling. "I have done nothing wrong."

"I know a terrible crime was committed in Suite 308 of this hotel. I had the opportunity to search that suite the other afternoon. I will not tell you what I found. The man in the camel-colored coat, the same man we see in Toni's drawing, was here that night. I know that man was involved in the murder of the young woman who was staying in the suite."

"Murder?" she mumbled, fidgeting, seeking a way out. "We have no murders at the Nurredine." She looked at him defiantly but could barely control her trembling. "This is a respectable hotel."

"Madame, you do not realize the grave trouble you are in. I could arrest you on suspicion of conspiracy to murder. I can have this hotel shut down on any number of pretexts."

"You wouldn't dare."

"I will, madame, if you do not tell me what you know."

Moulmenian began pacing back and forth, wringing her hands. "You don't know him," she was saying as if to herself. "You don't know what he can do. He will kill my boy."

"That's why I am here. To see that doesn't happen."

She stood still and turned, her cheeks stained with mascara. "He will find a way, believe me."

"Tell me the truth and I will arrange a guard for the hotel. Just give me his name."

"Something happened up there that night," she said, lifting her clouded eyes. "I don't know what it was. We have lovers' quarrels. Of course we do. From time to time. They are messy, sometimes." She shook her head. "I know nothing about any murder. I did not see anything. That night, the man, this thing Toni drew, he came here. Yes, he threatened me. He had a gun. I was to keep my mouth shut about the woman who stayed in that room."

"What was her name?"

"I don't know. Some French name. Deslibes, I think. Our guests are discreet in the matter of names. She was Syrian though. And beautiful."

"And what else?"

"I was to keep my mouth shut about the man who was visiting her, about everything. Then he said I had a nice boy and patted Toni's cheek, but my son was so scared. He clung to me and buried his face in my skirts. Then this man handed me an envelope of money, for cleaning services, he said. He said I was to send someone up to the suite after he left and scour everything thoroughly. He went away. He has not come back. He must not ever come back."

"Did you go up to the room yourself that night?"

"I did not. I would not. I sent Cesar. And we didn't talk about it. Not since that night."

"Good, madame. You have done very well. Now I need the name of that man. You know him, don't you?"

"He will kill us."

"He will not harm you. I promise that."

"He has killed many men, they say. They say he can reach into every home in Damascus, this Abdullah al Quassi."

"Toni's devil."

"Oh, yes, that man serves in hell," she mumbled. "You will protect me? You will protect me and my son?"

"We will."

"I will hold you to that promise, Inspector Faroun."

Faroun left the hotel grounds by the garden gate, the same gate the murderers had used to carry out Vera Tamiri's body, he was now sure. As he examined the lock, he heard the screech of tires. Agent Philomel Durac stepped out of the rear door of a black sedan, leaving one of his henchmen standing on the running board with a toothpick in his teeth and hand over his bulging breast pocket.

Wiping his hatband with a handkerchief, Durac offered a tight smile that might almost have passed for congenial. Faroun regarded his adversary through new eyes. Toni's drawing confirmed that the agent had been at the hotel the night Vera died. Faroun had trouble imagining Durac with a woman, much less a beauty like Vera Tamiri, and what he could imagine wasn't pleasant. "I hope you had nice chat with Captain Martel the other day," the agent said.

"He didn't have much to say actually. He kept spitting out teeth."

Durac grinned. "The tough guys are always the first to crack. Well, he won't be speaking to anyone for a while. The captain has been transferred to solitary. Visitors upset his equilibrium."

"Is that why you've been following me—to keep me informed of Captain Martel's health?"

Fedora back in place, Durac dug a hand into a coat pocket and pulled out a crumpled pack of Gauloise. "Actually, it's your health that concerns me."

"I appreciate a colleague's concern, but I manage pretty well on my own. Lots of exercise in my line of work, and I try to drink healthy too. I'm down to one bottle of arak a day and I mix it with orange juice."

"Here's my health tip, Faroun. I don't want you coming

around to visit my wards in the Citadel, and I don't want you bothering people at the Hotel Nurredine. I don't want you bothering anybody connected with the Tamiri case. The delegate is trying to buy you some time, but what good will it do? Martel is a confessed murderer. He lost his head with a dame and then dumped her body in the river. End to a tragic love story. Nothing you'll learn from anyone in the hotel will change that."

Faroun knew he was being provoked and would not allow himself to be drawn out, entirely. "As you point out, Agent, the case is still open and I run it. Martel is a fall guy—so let's drop the pretense. I don't know what you're trying to cover up, but I mean to bring in Vera's murderer. If any of your goons"—he nodded at the sedan—"get in my way, I'll haul them in for obstructing a civil criminal investigation."

"Be a blind man," Durac muttered as the policeman walked off.

24

Nikolai Faroun searched around the kitchen of the Villa Artemis for a corkscrew. After some ten minutes of increasingly agitated searching, he found it in the flour canister. How had it gotten there? he wondered. What night was that? And how much arak had he drunk? Unable to solve this mystery, he turned his attention to the greater one that he had been carrying around all day.

He took his seat at the kitchen table and examined the object that Cesar had carefully wrapped in a square of cloth. The policeman placed the lustrous black pearl in the palm of his hand. The earring matched the one Mansour had found tangled in Vera Tamiri's long, dark hair. Combined with the cracked tile inset he had found in the bathroom of Suite 308, the earring confirmed the place of death, and it gave him a timeline. Since Cesar had been awakened by Moulmenian at three in the morning to scrub down the suite, the murder had occurred that same night, perhaps between midnight and two, allowing time for the cleanup crew, the murderer, or his hirelings.

A timeline to work with, and thanks to Toni's imaginative sketches he had suspects—three of them. Three men had visited Vera's suite the night she died. Teddy, or Toni's Flower Man, was undoubtedly Salim al Quassi, a nickname confirmed in several instances, including the letter intercepted by Salim's wife and the mangled toy bear that sat forlornly on Faroun's office mantelpiece. Madame Moulmenian's admission had confirmed the fact, since it was Abdullah al Quassi who had bullied and bribed her into silence. This fact led Faroun down the line of speculation that it was a lovers' quarrel, after all, that had brought about Vera's death. The feckless Salim had become jealous, killed his lover, and then called in Abdullah to cover up the crime.

A lovers' quarrel. Or two. Toni's drawing of the sinister Black Shirt led him down another path. Could there be any doubt that Philomel Durac had visited Vera on the night of her death, that he had perhaps visited her before that? It required an act of imagination to believe that the beautiful Vera Tamiri would kiss a toad like Durac, but he had to entertain the possibility. If Tamiri had become his mistress, then Durac was the man Captain Martel had seen with Vera in the souk. If Durac was keeping his mistress in gambling funds, and she suddenly turned up dead, then the agent had a compelling motive for a cover-up with Martel as the convenient scapegoat. Her betrayal might even have been the catalyst for murder. It was not far-fetched to imagine a jealous Durac showing up at the hotel just before his rival arrived, doing the deed, carving the cross-shaped wound in her abdomen to suggest a religious complication, and leaving Salim and Abdullah to clean up the mess and ensure Moulmenian's silence.

Two plausible scenarios then, two possible murderers, but that didn't exhaust the possibilities, for Faroun had this nagging feeling that Umar was somehow caught up in the crime. Vera's ledger with its records of mysterious transactions and symbols, most importantly the diagram of the Maisalun hand, took the policeman into waters as murky as the Barada where the victim had been found.

Vera might have stumbled across something compromising about her brother and the family history, information Umar might want suppressed. That would explain the five thousand franc payments Vera had received over the past few months. Valuable land had changed hands, as the brigand Mahmoud al Harani had confirmed. Thanks to his interview with Lavette, Faroun knew how much the Tamiri clan had benefited at al Quassi expense. Driven by some old score to settle or driven by greed, perhaps Vera's father had fingered Salim's father as a traitor to King Faisal. Is this what Vera had learned? The best way to know would be to sound out Monsieur Umar on the issue.

That test would come as soon as tomorrow morning, for Faroun had been right in suspecting that his visit to Mustapha Ni'-mat might stir the pot. Umar had telephoned Faroun's office in the afternoon to set up a meeting at his compound in the Aldahdah district.

But tonight . . . tonight, exhaustion had set in . . . and a sense of unease, of creeping despair, of things beyond his reach. Even as he closed in on the facts surrounding Vera Tamiri's murder, there were complications he could not have anticipated. Salim al Quassi was on the loose somewhere in Damascus, and if he had gone underground, there was little hope of tracking him down before Montcalm's deadline expired. The newly planted suspicion that Durac was the murderer placed a spiked barbican in his path—he had no direct evidence that Durac had committed a crime, and one of Faroun's witnesses was in prison himself for Vera's murder! As for Umar . . . even if he was involved somehow in his sister's murder, and Faroun could prove it, Vera's brother was a close friend of the delegate's. Montcalm might waver; he might even try to shield Umar. With that protection, Umar would be untouchable.

Faroun rested his head on his hands. He had scarcely slept since the visit to the old Sufi in Maraba and the bandit ambush. But he would not sleep yet. He still had two days before the case became Durac's property.

Wrapping his robe over his pajamas, he stepped out into the cool spring night. On a night like this in 1925, he had stepped foot once more on his homeland's soil. He had left as a callow young man in 1917, thirsting for adventure. Faroun had blamed his father for driving his mother away, of banishing her to Russia, of removing the font of love and affection in his childhood. He was still haunted by the image of a tall, athletic woman with the bundle of auburn hair and eyes as gray as a wolf's. Most of all he had remembered her smile, a deep, tragic, and curiously ironic regard, as if she doubted she had brought a child into the world and was continually surprised at the novelty. By joining the army, he had punished the man who had made him suffer. He had furthered his own ends too, for now he would be his own man, no longer his father's captive son. He was just not prepared for—how could he be prepared for?—death's monstrous feast, the carnage that was the Western Front during the Great War.

He had left a callow young man and returned . . . What had he returned as? When the prison gate in the Saar had opened and Nikolai Faroun had stepped out of the slag heap and into the world once more in the company of a French intelligence officer, his heart leapt up at the possibility of liberty. He knew there would be conditions, but he also knew he had paid for that one rash moment when he had removed from the earth a man who deserved killing. Seven years of his life had been paid. He little suspected that he had merely traded one form of reckoning for another. He had the trappings of freedom, for he was, in his handler's parlance, an asset. He knew the towns and villages of Lebanon and Palestine for, since his fourteenth year, he had accompanied his father on business trips throughout the region. They had journeyed to Egypt and North Africa, and the possessions of the expiring Ottoman empire in what was now Iraq and Syria. He had been to Istanbul and Tehran and had traveled by steamer to the ports of the Black Sea and the Caucasus. He was an asset too because he was a devourer of languages, Turkish and Russian, French, German, English, and Italian, as well as Arabic in a dozen dialects. His handler, a French intelligence operative whose sobriquet was Jacquard, introduced him to other more exotic tongues, Japanese, Chinese, and Tartar. He was an asset most of all because he was a murderer. A murderer can be trained in the craft in ways an innocent man cannot. A murderer is useful, and yet, as he learned through the long year of training that followed, a murderer is expendable. For who mourns a man with blood on his hands? Who remembers?

That cool spring night nearly a decade ago, he had stepped off a steamer in the port of Tripoli in north Lebanon and met his contact, a hard-driving Maronite Christian who called himself Le Hache, the Ax. His teeth were black from chewing tobacco, and around his neck he wore the dried ears of Muslims he had killed in combat. They had traveled over rough country by horseback to join a group of partisans fighting for French interests in the western Bekaa Valley. The revolt against French rule had begun in the Jebel Druze and spread from town to town and village to village across the mountains of the Anti-Lebanon and into the Bekaa. Faroun and Le Hache had launched their first operation against the Muslim village of Katoun. The partisans crept up on the sleeping village and began torching the houses. The village men were shot as they tried to escape their homes. The women and children were rounded up to watch the conflagration and then marched to the outskirts of another village to spread the word of the terror. After that, Faroun had continued to spread the word, but he did not exercise the Ax's zeal. The cries of Katoun followed him from killing ground to killing ground and echoed in the thickets of his memory. . . .

He had done his work well since then, a man in the shadows for an exclusive club. His branch of French intelligence did not even have a formal name, and few knew the identity of its director. Faroun had never met anyone who had met him face-to-face. Gradually his handler had extended Faroun's leash, and he had been entrusted with other assignments designed to tighten France's grip on its mandate in the Middle East. So he had pleased those who pulled his strings and had even landed a proxy post in the high commissioner's office in Beirut. There he had been groomed in police work, a stepping-stone to his assignment as Prefecture chief of Damascus. The Tamiri case was the first real test of just how effective he could be in his new cover. If he failed, then his usefulness would be at an end, and he knew what the penalty would be. He did not entertain the illusion that he might somehow escape. But this led him to ponder the outcome if he succeeded. They had something special planned for him, and that is why they had placed him in Damascus. His handler dangled before him the charm of freedom. Should he complete this last task, then the slate would be wiped clean. Jacquard had been fair with him thus far, although he could never hold out a crumb of hope without a threat. What task lay before him, he did not know. He only knew that there would, at some point, be a telephone call. And that is why every jangling of that instrument delivered a jolt of alarm.

It was not the telephone that pulled him out of his reverie, however, but the insistent beep of a car horn. Faroun went through the garden and out to the main gate of the compound. He opened the gate and the headlights swung to the side and the blue Bugatti came to a stop in the driveway.

"Do you *live* here, Inspector Faroun?" Eugenie asked as she removed her soft leather driving gloves, surveying the bare, unpainted walls of the Villa Artemis. Her eye settled for a moment on the curtains Gert had left behind and looked away as if she had seen something unspeakable. "God, do you have anything to drink?"

"What brings you out here to the lonely foothills of Mohajirene at this time of night, Madame Poquelin?" Faroun asked as he fumbled about in the cupboard and brought out a fresh bottle of arak. "Rather late for a social call."

"I lost my way three times coming out here. At last a farmer down below pointed the way." She removed a scarf imprinted with rose blossoms and unbuttoned her coat. Folding it over the back of a kitchen chair, she took a seat at the table while Faroun poured. She was wearing a black satin blouse and trousers, around her neck a gold choker.

"You disappeared suddenly yesterday."

They clinked glasses. "I didn't come here to talk about that."

"It's after ten, Madame. What did you come out here to talk with me about?"

Eugenie grimaced as she tasted the arak.

"Perhaps you would like something else," Faroun offered. He realized that he was wearing only his bathrobe. He straightened the lapels.

"This stuff has ruined my taste for anything else." She pushed the glass away. Her blue eyes had misted over, but whether from the drink or her burden he couldn't say. She looked down at her hands, twisting her wedding ring. "I've come here, Inspector, on behalf of a friend." She hesitated, as if she were summoning the courage to go on. "I am not at liberty to say whom."

"And how I can be of help?"

"My friend is not entirely sure you can, so you might say this is something of a gamble."

"Does this have something to do with Vera?"

"It may." Eugenie stood up and, crossing her arms, drew a deep breath. "It is about the delegate. He is in a great deal of trouble. He needs your help. Only he doesn't know he needs your help."

"All right, I'll try and read between the lines."

Eugenie shot him a sharp glance as if to remind him she was on a serious errand. "My friend's worries have to do with Vera's brother, Umar Tamiri."

"Reading between the lines we might say that Umar has some hold over the delegate."

"He has the delegate's ear almost exclusively. Monsieur Montcalm ignores the opinions of the foreign service officers on his staff. He doesn't trust them. He believes them to be out of touch. There is disarray in the delegate's camp. And Monsieur Tamiri is advising a course of action that my friend fears will lead to a catastrophe."

"That is a very strong term."

"It is the term my friend used."

"And this friend of yours, I take it, is well-connected." Seeing the hesitation in her eyes, he went on, "If you came all this way, then you must know I can be trusted."

"I can tell you this, but no more than this. Umar is urging the delegate to take aggressive action against the resistance. That is what my friend is saying. My friend fears that the delegate is being lured into a compromising and dangerous position."

Interesting. Colonel Bremond was urging the same course of action. Faroun thought back to his last meeting with the delegate on the day Martel had been arrested by Durac at Tel el Saladin. Montcalm and Bremond had been arguing as they stood over a table map. The two men had never gotten along; now it seemed the diplomat and the soldier had agreed on a joint plan. More puzzling, if Umar was also urging Montcalm to force the issue with the insurgents. And hard to believe. Umar was a calculating man. What would he have to gain from such a showdown?

Eugenie looked as if she had suddenly realized how ridiculous she must sound. "This is what I was asked to tell you."

"You are not holding something back?"

"No, of course not," she said a little uncertainly.

Faroun went to the cupboard, found a bottle of brandy, and poured a glass for her. "How is it that you are privy to this kind of information?" he asked in a skeptical tone.

Eugenie drew herself up as if she had been stung. "Why?" she asked indignantly. "Is it that I'm only suited for buying clothes and beautifying my husband's arm?"

"I implied nothing of the sort."

"Fine words from a man who lives in a house as bleak as a monastery and greets his guests in a bathrobe," she said contemptuously. "Why don't you pitch your tent in the desert?"

"Fitting place for an Arab," he fired back. "The desert."

"And I didn't imply that either," she said, reddening. "Besides, I have delivered my message." She swung her coat about her shoulders. "I can find my way out."

Suddenly Faroun found himself standing alone in the kitchen. The front door slammed.

He caught up with her before she could get into her car. "You forgot this," he said, slipping the scarf around her neck and drawing her to him. She pushed him away. "What is it you are trying to do?"

"There is more to the message that you brought."

She shook her head ruefully, but a slight smile was on her lips. "You are right. I am not cut out for this kind of thing. I am frightened just thinking about it. But my friend told me that she had no one else to trust."

"She?" Faroun sighed. "Tell her that I appreciate her courage in speaking out. Tell her I will do everything I can." He took her gently by the arm. "I didn't mean to doubt you, Eugenie."

Eugenie turned way. "I've said enough, too much."

"So now you are going to run away again, like you did at the Hotel Nurredine."

"All right, so I ran."

"You recognized the man in the newspaper photo I gave you, is that it?"

"I never saw him before."

"You did not know this man was Vera's lover? You did not recognize Teddy?"

Eugenie looked at him in alarm. "I never saw him before."

"Then why did you run?"

"I ran—I ran because I realized I was in a compromising situation with you, Nikolai Faroun."

"A situation which you had very carefully arranged with all the blandishments, food, and champagne."

"I admit my fault. I thought we might—there was a wild thought in my mind that I might seduce you."

"In the way you seduced that young Legionnaire in Morocco, after your romp with the Tuareg sheikh in the desert?"

A sly smile crept into her face. "I wondered if you might not believe that."

"Do you always make up little stories about your seductions?"

"So there haven't been—many," she said, holding up her head. "Some wives would be proud of that."

"Then it is good you broke things off as hastily as you did."

"It is."

"Especially since the suite in which we had our meeting was the same in which Vera Tamiri was murdered."

"Oh, God. Are you sure of that?"

"Quite sure."

"Then you know who murdered her?"

"Not yet. But if it hadn't been for you, I wouldn't be able to make as much progress as I have."

"Then you are . . ."

"Close."

"Close," she repeated, looking up at him with admiration, and then clicked open the door of the blue Bugatti. "Now, good night, Inspector Faroun." He closed the door of the blue Bugatti before she could get in. She did not move. The chill of the night made both of them shiver. Faroun touched her scarf, but somehow he found his fingers drifting along her cheek and into her hair. He pulled them away and she curled her fingers around his but did not look at him.

"Where is Henri?"

"Where he always is. Out of town on business."

"You don't believe that, do you?"

"I have my children and my empty, frivolous life," she said sarcastically. "What else do I need?"

"You have to go right now." He closed his eyes, wondering at the fact that the two of them were here at all. Should he simply tell her? Should he tell her he yearned for this desirable young woman who smelled of jasmine, whose loneliness and worldly pose had touched and amused him? She stood next to him, shivering, and he put his arms around her. To hold her like this was to open a door that could take them anywhere. Anywhere. She slipped her hand from his and placed her palm against his chest as if to push him away. But she did not.

"I have to go home right now."

"Your children are waiting for you."

"My children are tucked away for the night."

"The nurse is with them?"

"The nurse is with them."

"Then I will bid you good night, Eugenie Poquelin," he said, not moving.

"Then I will bid you good night, Nikolai Faroun," she replied, as rooted as he.

25

The phone rang early the next morning. Faroun tumbled out of bed and made his way, half-asleep, to the foyer. "Are you sure about that?" he said.

"I am here, standing right here," said Ihab Kabir. "You had better come."

"You have contacted no one else?"

"No one."

"Then don't until I get there."

Back in his bare, monastic bedroom, Faroun pulled on his clothes. When he was halfway out the door, he caught himself whistling. A trace of her scent still lingered in the house and clung to him, and so he whistled some more.

He was actually in too good a mood, considering his errand when he pulled up on his motorcycle at the storefront on the edge of the Maidan district. The machine was a vintage Terrot and a replacement for the Triumph being repaired at the Prefecture motor pool.

Ihab led him through the office and into the warehouse where Faroun had talked with Mustapha Ni'mat two days before, and where the man now lay curled up next to a roll of tarpaper. A couple of Ni'mat's day laborers stood about at the entrance to the warehouse, smoking cigarettes and looking out-of-work. The foreman had discovered the body that morning. There was no evidence of a break-in, but the foreman had seen an Arab in a gray and white burnoose the night before when he was closing up. He and Ni'mat were talking familiarly when he'd left.

"A big man?" Faroun asked.

The foreman shook his head. No, this man was short and slight of build, a thin mustache. He was wearing a soiled checkered kaffiyeh.

"Salim al Quassi," said Ihab.

"How can you be sure?" Faroun asked.

"Ni'mat used to work for the big brother, Abdullah. What he actually did, I couldn't discover. But there was a link. I figured to track down Salim, I'd begin with Ni'mat."

"Only Salim, it appears, beat you to it."

"Three bullets in all," said Ihab, pointing at the blood-soaked body. "One in each knee. One to the head."

"Salim wanted information. Question is, what did he want to know?"

Ihab shrugged. "The murder proves one thing though."

"What's that?"

"Teddy is capable of murder."

"And inflicting pain," Faroun added. "Let's find him, Ihab. Let's find him before he kills someone else."

Faroun was sure that there wouldn't be many mourners at Mustapha Ni'mat's funeral, especially no one from the Prefecture, but Mustapha had done a bit of service for Damascus law enforcement by getting himself murdered. The crime provided a little extra leverage for Faroun's encounter with Umar Tamiri. The same two *qabaday* thugs, Scarface & Friend, greeted him at the tall gate, but since he was expected, they waved him through. He pulled up the Terrot motorbike next to an immense ivy-covered urn. Once more, he was ushered into the study, where Umar was glowering in concert with the Assyrian griffin in the corner. Faroun noticed that the chessboard was missing from the desk.

Umar started the interview with a show of pique. "What I want to know is why you are having my activities—I'm looking for the right word here—shadowed. Some of my business acquaintances are distressed. They think I might have done something wrong."

"If you mean Mustapha Ni'mat, I can tell you that he is beyond distress of any kind. He was murdered last night."

It didn't appear that Umar was sleeping well. Purple bruises were beneath his eyes. He suppressed a muffled groan, although Faroun doubted its sincerity. "Who"—Umar dropped into the chair—"did this?"

"I thought a name or two might come to your mind."

"Why should I know about that?" Umar asked distractedly.

"As you said, Mr. Ni'mat was a business associate."

"*Acquaintance*—that was the word I used, Inspector."

With Umar in disarray, Nikolai decided to spring.

"What I am saying, Monsieur Tamiri, is that I suspect Mustapha Ni'mat had some role to play in the murder of your sister."

Umar reached for a cigarette. "That's preposterous. I know about Ni'mat's checkered past. He is—was—no murderer."

"Perhaps not. Pity he's not here to confirm that."

"This is harassment, Faroun! That's why I called you here. There is absolutely no reason to pursue the matter of my sister's death further." Umar expelled a forceful roll of cigarette smoke. His voice took on a more confidential tone. "Of course I realize you are trying to discern the truth."

"I am."

"And for this I thank you. However, I can't have suspicions cast there and everywhere. It just won't do." Umar had drawn his sartorial inspiration from a stereotype of the bon vivant; thus the elegant smoking jacket with royal blue velvet color, paisley cravat with ruby stickpin. The light blue Wedgwood tea service with plate of digestive biscuits completed the picture. He refilled his cup with an aromatic brew and considered a biscuit. "Yet it seems you are bringing your suspicions here."

"You needn't take offense, monsieur. I don't have any evidence that you did any harm to your sister, no more than I have evidence that you burned the Women's Clinic to the ground. I just know you made Vera's brief life a misery. You cannot conceal her death for that long. She must return from Istanbul one of these days, mustn't she? Or do you expect all memory of her to evaporate?" Faroun looked around the room, his attention flitting to a painted mummy's coffin standing upright in one corner. "That's not the foremost matter on my mind, however. I'm trying to understand how you must have felt when you learned that Vera was seeing Salim al Quassi, son of your father's archenemy, or perhaps just his archrival, son of the man he had exposed as a Turkish spy."

"My, but you have been mucking down the dirty alleys of Damascus rumor, Inspector."

"More than rumor, I think. This is not the sort of thing the head of a powerful Damascus line would want known. Compromising secrets have to be carefully obscured. And woe to him— or her—who should shine a light in so dark a place. I wonder if your sister Vera had such a light."

Umar no longer held a look of amused contempt. He rose and set his linen napkin aside with a trembling hand. "Our interview is concluded, Faroun."

"I can even conceive of a situation," Faroun persisted, "in which Vera might have come to her brother with an offer to keep silent about an embarrassing moment in the family history. It wouldn't do for your Damascus peers to learn that a Tamiri had betrayed one of his own."

"So now you insinuate that Vera was blackmailing her own brother?" Umar jabbed a finger at him. "This is nothing but vendetta, Faroun."

Umar's slippered servant entered the room as if he had been listening just outside the room. His host, eyes fixed on Faroun, nodded for the servant to escort the policeman.

"You might wish to know, monsieur," said Faroun, pausing in the doorway, "that name you were trying to think of, the name of Mustapha's killer—I'm very close to bringing him in. Being an intemperate man, lacking in self-discipline, he will, before long, tell us all we need to know."

Faroun followed the servant down the corridor to the landing until the silence was broken by the shattering of crockery from within the study, the sound an expensive teapot makes when it is hurled against a wall.

The sound brought the slightest smile to Faroun's lips. It seems he had stirred up more than the pot.

26

Faroun's sense of foreboding was briefly dispelled by the rich sunlight on the Street Called Straight, as he headed on his motorcycle for the Palace of Justice. Entering the Christian quarter of the Old City, he was caught up in the bustle of the district market. The vegetable and fruit vendors went about their routines, unloading their produce, piling oranges and cucumbers and eggplant in neat pyramids. The morning air was invigorated with the scents of lime and cardamom and cinnamon. The awnings of the dry-goods shops creaked open, and store owners flung up their security doors with a rattle and began setting out their wares. Arab women, their figures hidden under black haiks, emerged from the alleyways, carrying baskets and calling to each other. They moved as if under a quilt of light and shadow, holding up bags of lemons and onions and haggling for the reduction of a centime or an extra leek thrown in for good measure.

A tinker's cart, drawn by a donkey wearing a garland of wildflowers, clattering with basins and bowls, kept pace with Faroun for a brief time as his motorcycle rumbled down the street. A gentle image of old Damascus, Faroun thought, but signs of another city, one gripped by uncertainty and fear, took more disturbing shapes. Fierce slogans had been painted on alley walls. Crimson fists bordered them like exclamation marks, paint dribbling from the clenched fingers like rivulets of blood.

The cracks were beginning to show. Ever the since the tax riot on the day Faroun had found Vera's body, Damascus had seethed and turned fitfully in its sleep. The Old City, rising with the dawn, went about its business, as if its demons were only phantoms of the dark. But one could not really shake off the Damascus night.

As the policeman approached Bab Touma Street, he encountered the first barricades, bristling barbicans of stone and timber and barbed wire. The Christians had decided to wall the nightmare out. The barricades seemed to rise before his eyes like the shadows of no-man's-land that often invaded his sleep. Remembering Talifa and Marit, he visited them briefly. Marit's husband, Gregor, greeted him at the door, shotgun cradled in his arm. Faroun had a late-morning meal with them. Only Talifa, who had seen so much, tried to lift spirits by recounting the mischief of young Nikolai Faroun, and she soon had them laughing at Faroun's expense. Satisfied that they were well protected by the district vigilantes, Faroun continued his journey to the delegate's office, weighing what he could reveal to the delegate about Vera's case, and what he could not.

Montcalm's secretary preceded him into the office. His suit coat flung over the back of his chair, his shirtsleeves rolled up, the delegate for the Syrian state was pouring over a stack of memorandums. His pipe was clenched in his teeth but the bowl had gone cold.

"I've bought you all the time I can," said the delegate without looking up. "The Tamiri case goes over to Durac's side of business tomorrow."

"It's not about the deadline, sir."

Montcalm set his pen aside. "Then you've found our murderer." His demeanor suggested that he doubted that was the case.

"No, sir, but there are a few things I thought you might want to know." Faroun provided a capsule review of the investigation so far, the discovery of the crime scene at the Hotel Nurredine, the evidence that confirmed this, including Vera's earring. He described the contents of Vera's notebook and the diagram of the Hand of Maisalun, and the history behind it. He then told him what he had learned about the visitors to Vera Tamiri's suite in the Hotel Nurredine the night of her murder and the break-in to her apartment in Kasaa. The delegate nodded as Faroun described his suspicions about Salim al Quassi, who may have fought with her over money. When he mentioned his other suspect, Montcalm leaned back in his chair and gave Faroun a keen look.

"This isn't tit for tat, is it, Faroun? Are you positive Agent Durac was in the hotel that night?"

"I have a witness, Delegate."

"What's his game, do you think? Do you think they were lovers?"

"Beauty and the beast," said Faroun, trying to evince a smile from Montcalm. In this he failed, but he had the delegate's attention.

"What would Durac have to do with Vera Tamiri if they weren't playing at romance?"

"I'm not sure, sir. But it does help to explain why Durac beat a confession out of Captain Martell. He has something to hide."

"And I've given you some latitude on that score," Montcalm confirmed. "But what do you bring me? What is this old story about King Faisal and his Five Henchmen? An *Arabian Nights* entertainment, Faroun." The delegate rose from his desk, walked stiffly to the French windows that overlooked the eastern quarter of the Old City. " 'In a city of a hundred silver gates, with silver bracelets my beloved brings the wine of ecstasy and hate.' So sang the nameless Umayyad poet a thousand years ago. Damascus has seen twice a hundred battles since that time. And now she is poised for another one. That's the reality. Things have gone silent, Faroun, and that terrifies me more than ten thousand protesters shrieking below these windows. Of all the enemies a governor must fight, the most formidable is fear. If you have evidence against this Salim al Quassi, then produce it. If you have something on Durac, produce it. If you haven't, then find it before tomorrow noon."

Faroun braced himself for what he was about to say: "There is more, sir. I have just been to see Umar Tamiri."

Montcalm turned on his heel abruptly. "I expressly told you not to involve Monsieur Tamiri in your investigation."

"He asked for the interview, Delegate."

"Yes, yes," said other, waving his pipe in sharp little circles. "You have been meddling, haven't you? And this has made Monsieur Tamiri very upset, no doubt. I will not have my direct orders flouted like this." Checking his petulance, he confided, "I rely on him. He has a wealth of experience to draw on, and unlike most of his countrymen he is a friend of the French."

The delegate walked over to the map of Syria and Lebanon that covered nearly the whole of the western wall of his office. "Here is our Syrian puzzle, Faroun. A patchwork of tribes ruled by powerful families, factions driven by clashing aims, a mix of mutually exclusive faiths, a warren of districts that have little in common but that they once belonged to a Turkish sultan. And here is the touchstone," said the delegate, pointing to Damascus. "Our city has ever been the crossroads of the Near East. Whatever the future holds, it begins here. And I need good men around me whom I can trust. Tamiri is indispensable, don't you see?" The policeman couldn't ignore the familiar note of plaintiveness in the delegate's voice. "Without French guidance, Syria falls into anarchy and ruin. As Syria goes, so goes the rest. Our colonies in Africa and

the Orient are restive. And it will not be long before there is another world war. Hitler is bent on it. Our leaders in Paris don't
want to see it. But I see it. *I* see it." He shook his head at the blind-
ness he perceived in the world. "Given what is at stake, a strong
hand must be employed."

"In what way, sir, if I may ask?"

Montcalm's glance was searching. "As Prefecture chief you have a
right to know." The delegate reached out to touch his shoulder. "I will
take you into my confidence by telling you that I mean to go after the
resistance, crushing them once and for all." Montcalm stuck his pipe
into his mouth and struck a match. "There is no point in having a dialogue with the disaffected nationalists and jihadists. I see that now."

"Diplomacy by other means?"

Montcalm appeared to weigh the sarcasm in Faroun's comment
before lapsing into a study of saintly resignation. Tall and spare
with hollow cheeks and ashen complexion, he looked the part of a
suffering ascetic, but with a new determination, like that of a medieval prelate who had decided to wield a mace in defense of his
faith. "Colonel Bremond and I have agreed on a course of action.
The colonel is moving a very strong force into this area." Montcalm pointed at several villages on the fertile plain to the east.

"These villages have long been pro-French, sir."

"We have intelligence otherwise. The villagers are providing
supplies and storing weapons for the insurgents."

"Is this Umar Tamiri's advice as well? Torch the outlying villages? One would think they had been reading from the same
script."

"That's none of your concern," the delegate snapped.

Faroun knew had overstepped his bounds, but somehow Madame
Montcalm's words came back to him now, her concern for her husband's direction, her distrust of his advisers, his need for someone to
speak plainly. "It is my concern, Delegate, if Umar Tamiri is not who
we think he is," Faroun said, closing his eyes even as he spoke the
words. "I suspect his loyalties, sir. I suspect he may be deceiving you."

The delegate turned angrily on Faroun. "Do you have proof of his duplicity?"

"No, sir."

"Then I will not hear of it." Montcalm was shaking with rage. "You take things up, you make accusations, but you lack the evidence." He waved his hand in irritation. "And spare me an apology." He moved away from the map and back to the windows.

While Faroun stood his ground silently, the delegate went on, "I didn't want you for this post, Faroun. You have been a source of trouble from the first. I'd send you back to Beirut on the next plane. Only the high commissioner won't take you back. I'm stuck with you," he muttered. "You impugn my integrity when you doubt my friends."

"I have never doubted your integrity, sir," Faroun said earnestly. "However, you just pointed out there are rumblings like the ides of March. I can confirm those rumors. With the colonel's troops deployed to the villages, he is bound to weaken the city garrison."

"So now you have become a military expert, Inspector?" the delegate asked sarcastically.

"I have some experience in the field, sir," Faroun replied a bit tartly.

"I've seen your dossier," said the delegate. "An impressive war record. I'm sure it carried a good deal of weight with the high commissioner when he recommended you for the Prefecture." Then he added, "I'm surprised he didn't make you head of our army command."

Faroun ignored the gibe. "I merely point out that while Bremond is out making a punitive expedition, the city lies exposed to an attack. The resistance would find the invitation hard to resist."

Montcalm's reaction was dismissive. "We have the gendarmerie and the district police to keep order."

"The district police have been infiltrated, sir. They cannot be trusted."

"The resistance would need time to plan a major strike, wouldn't they?"

"Yes, sir."

"Do you imply our plan has been leaked?"

"I have no evidence of that, sir."

"What am I to do with these suspicions of yours, Inspector? Your head is swirling with them. You have a case to resolve, don't you? And less than twenty-four hours to do so." Montcalm walked heavily back to his desk and filled up his meerschaum from the crystal humidor, almost empty of his favorite latakia.

"I'm sorry if I have spoken out of turn, Delegate."

Montcalm's annoyance with him was not over. "You have, and it is damned impertinent of you. What principles do you stand for? Outside of the fact that you have the HC's endorsement, I know next to nothing about you at all. You have diligence and yet I feel no fervor in you. Perhaps like other Levantines, you too hold we French imperialists in contempt. If that is so, then what is your side of the game?"

Faroun could not hide the sting he felt at the delegate's remark. "That of a man trying to do his duty, sir."

The delegate sighed. "I meant no disrespect, Faroun." His shoulders slackened. "Perhaps we are just that. Imperialists. But who else is there to govern?" The heavy cloak of resignation fell about him once more. "Be that as it may, as it may . . . I have tossed the dice. If it turns out to be the wrong decision, then I will answer for it."

Faroun followed him to the tall windows. The sunlight had vanished behind a sheet of gray, and the midafternoon sun had become almost completely obscured except for a pale yellow ribbon at the top of the horizon. "All I ask of you, Delegate, is that you allow me, in the time remaining, to follow the investigation wherever it leads."

The delegate looked at him bleakly. "You weary me, Faroun. I can't give you any more time. Not even to save my own shirt. Durac takes the case tomorrow."

"That may be all the time I need. If I have your confidence."

The two men looked out into the uncertain light. "Confidence? Do what you must, Faroun. I don't know who to trust."

When Faroun walked out of Montcalm's office, the delegate's secretary was holding up a telephone receiver. "It is Rebecca," she said. "There's a car waiting for you at the gate."

A somber Ihab Kabir was waiting for him as Faroun arrived at the Bek brothers' storefront on the Rue Aladam south of the old city. Philippe Mansour was not far behind. He seemed almost jaunty as he got out of his Prefecture ambulance, like a man on a holiday, his white lab coat flying in the breeze and black bag in hand. Faroun made a once-over of the pawnshop while Ihab led Mansour through a floor-length curtain and into a back room. The inspector found nothing amiss in the shop proper. It didn't appear as if anything had been stolen, nothing was in disarray, although a costume necklace was spread out on top of one of the glass cases, as if the shopkeeper had been showing the item to a customer before he was called away.

In this case, the owners, Messieurs Bek, Mardam and Nasib, had been called away forever. Confirming the identity of the two brothers would not be easy, for the bloodied mess Mansour was trying to free from its rough cocoon had been carved almost beyond recognition. The body in the burlap bag next to it had been mutilated in the same manner. There seemed little doubt who the men were, however, since each was wearing a black onyx pinkie ring with an initial letter arrayed in diamonds.

"The brothers Bek," said Mansour, standing up and wiping his hands on a cloth. "Former pawnbrokers. One might say, ironically, that justice has been served. These men engaged in usury and extortion at the expense of the desperate and the poor." He shook his head. "Not that the poor don't have it coming."

"It would seem someone objected to their business practices," Faroun observed.

"I think it was more personal than that," said the coroner. "They received very careful attention, as you can see. They were gagged while their tormentor went about his work. When he was finished with them, he sent them off with a single bullet to the head."

"Seem familiar?" Faroun asked Ihab.

"I knew it was his work when I saw the mess on the floor."

"Meaning?" asked Mansour, sliding his gold-rimmed spectacles up the length of his nose.

"Salim al Quassi, Abdullah's brother."

"The transport magnate al Quassi?"

Faroun turned to his sergeant. "When did you spot Salim?"

"Two hours ago," said Ihab. "A tip from a news vendor not far from here. He saw a workman who fit Salim's description turn into Rue Aladam and with two burlap sacks thrown over his shoulder. What caught his eye was that the man was wearing very expensive shoes, certainly no workingman! The street is a cul-de-sac with only three or four businesses. When I saw that the Bek brothers shop was closed early, I became suspicious, so I went around to the back. The back gate to the compound was empty. A woman came up to me and told me that she heard what sounded like two shots. I went in and found the guard dog, its throat slit. Then I came upon them here."

"Tied up in the burlap sacks."

"And Salim gone."

"What do we know about the Beks?"

"When I was working for Vice, the word on the street was that the Beks were the fellows to contact when a cleanup was needed."

"The sacks," said the surgeon, giving a knowing glance to Faroun. "Where else have we seen a body in burlap recently?"

"What do you make of it, Mansour?"

"As Vera died, so did they. Either Salim thinks they are the murderers or they had something to do with her murder. That would explain the mutilation. Unless he's involved in an elaborate deception to throw us off his scent."

"No, I think Salim was after information, just as he was with Mustapha Ni'mat. The question is, did they tell him anything?"

Mansour gave an eloquent Gallic shrug. "The symbolism didn't strike me the first time around. I mean with Vera. After all, a burlap sack is a burlap sack—until it becomes something else."

Mansour had assumed that air of intellectual superiority that so galled Faroun. "This is not a good time for one of your enigmatic riddles, Coroner."

"Then we'll apply Occam's razor," the coroner replied, "but with a bit more skill I trust than the blade wielded by Salim al Quassi. The simplest explanation is always the best."

Seeing the impatience in Faroun's eyes, he hurried along. "There was a practice of the Ottoman sultans that might resonate with these crimes. The last sultan in Istanbul, Mehmed VI, who died in 1926, was also the last to exercise the privilege; at least it is to be supposed that he tried it once or twice. Wearing his gilded slippers, I might have been tempted myself. Had there been dalliance, I mean." Seeing that Faroun's impatience had turned to exasperation, he continued, "I'm speaking of the sultan's henhouse, the seraglio."

"Go on."

"The previous sultans had been more liberal in the application. If one of the royal concubines was suspected of infidelity, say with a eunuch, or discovered passing a billet-doux to a lover on the outside, or even overheard making up a tale of sexual conquest to impress the other girls, she was immediately trussed up, like our two brothers Bek, placed inside a plain sack, one tied with a silken cord, and tossed alive and screaming into the Bosporus."

"A Turkish practice?"

"The Ottoman sultans and caliphs were Turks of course."

Faroun realized Mansour had made something of an inspired leap. There was a provocative link between the cruelty of a Turkish sultan and the sadistic murder of Vera Tamiri, the rough sack into which her body had been stuffed. The disposal of Vera's body had been symbolic, an act of supreme contempt—a settling of old scores. The disposal of the Beks had been symbolic too. Somehow the brothers Bek had figured into the crime. Were *they* the murderers? That wasn't their game. All the signs pointed to a crime of passion—an unspeakable rage. Yet there was trouble with this analysis. If her murder was a crime of passion, and Salim was the murderer, why was he on a killing spree? Was he trying to eliminate those who might have known of his deed? Yet it seemed he wanted information from Mustapha Ni'mat and the Beks before he murdered them. Had he found this information? If so, where would it lead him?

Faroun turned to Ihab. "Salim had already left by the time you arrived on the scene."

The police sergeant hung his head. "I was all too late, sir." Then his face brightened. "Salim has rented a room."

"Where?"

"He was seen going in and out of one of the pilgrim inns between the two great souks. I was on my way there, when I was tipped off by the news vendor."

"South of the Citadel? There are a dozen such inns in that area."

"This one is near the street of the leather workers."

Faroun placed his hand on Ihab's shoulder. "This is what I want you to do. I want you to stake out the Al-Quassi Shipping Depot. I'm told Abdullah spends most of his time there. We don't know if Salim's rampage is over, but it's a reasonable supposition he will, before long, seek the aid and protection of his older brother. Stay there, until I come for you or send for you."

"And you, Inspector?"

"I will see if Salim has gone back to his hotel. There's a good chance he might lie low there for a while. At least it's worth my time to find out."

"You won't get there easily," said Mansour. "The army has restricted traffic in the area of the souks and all the way to the Christian and Jewish quarters because of the heightened state of alert. Durac's flying squads are out in full force too. Your car will only get you part of the way."

"Then I'll chance it on foot." Faroun nodded to the two men and headed for the door that led to the courtyard.

"It's nearly dark," said Mansour, following him. The two of them looked at the pall of the oncoming night. Already visible was Mismar, the Needle, as the Damascenes called the polestar. "You might well become a target yourself if you're out past six. There will be a curfew. A lot of nervous and trigger-happy gendarmes are on the loose." Mansour checked his watch. "You have thirty minutes." He watched Faroun step out the rear gate and into the alley. "What do you want me to do?"

"Tend to the brothers Bek and contact their next of kin. Tell Rebecca to go to her aunt's house in Arnous. I don't think it's safe for her to try and go home to the Bab Yahoud tonight."

Mansour waved good-bye but Faroun was gone. "The brothers Bek," the surgeon sighed. And then he began rubbing his hands. "Will require a lot of stitches."

27

Faroun struck out on foot for the northwest in the direction of the city's largest souk. From the Al Amara district, ever a hotbed of trouble, he heard the tumult of a street demonstration in defiance of the curfew. He went down a backstreet that paralleled the Street Called Straight, the great thoroughfare that cut through the heart of the Old City. He spied two army patrols speeding to Al Amara and slipped out of sight. Before long, he was at the edge of El Kumeileh Square, which led to the souk and the guild workshops. The Citadel loomed beyond that, casting a shadow so immense it seemed like the center of night itself. Along the battlements, searchlights roved and crisscrossed in the darkness.

Faroun waited for a squad of gendarmes to march by and sprinted across Straight to plunge into the warren of back alleys that led to the Souk el Rashid. Here he felt comparatively safe, for the soldiers did not venture into a fetid labyrinth that had been elaborated over the centuries with the ambush of invaders in mind.

As he entered this maze, it seemed that he was finally coming to the end of another. He had been right to put Salim into his sights. The junior al Quassi had spun out of control and had proved that he was capable of anything. Yet Faroun's search had taken an unpredictable turn. Perhaps he was after the right man but for the wrong reason. Perhaps Salim was not the murderer but the *avenger* of Vera Tamiri. If that was the case, then Salim would lead him to the killer.

But if he was wrong about Salim?

So Faroun would have to see if the traps he had laid might snare other game. His investigation was well known to Durac, and the Sûreté agent had taken no pains in warning him from the case. He had even gone to the extraordinary length of trying to frame Martel. Faroun didn't doubt that Durac could turn murderous when crossed. Yet there might be another reason for Durac's interest in Vera, outside of a love affair. Vera's notebook was likely bait. Faroun was keen to test its attractive power.

Beneath this stream of suspicion was Faroun's conviction that another current, colder still, had carried Vera's body to the rough embrace of a fisherman's net. So Faroun had set a net of his own. He had taken a risk in letting Umar know that he suspected Salim. Umar was nothing if not well-informed. Now it was time to see what this undercurrent might bring.

But meanwhile he must keep his sights on Salim.

Faroun had reached the outskirts of the market. The stifling air became thick with the scent of citron and cloves mixing with the stench of garbage and refuse. He passed the bins of mandragora and aloe and Syrian rue where the herbalists plied their trade. Beyond the stalls of the textile merchants, he stepped out of the way of a huge porter grunting under a pile of tanned hides. When Faroun asked him the way to the pilgrim's hotel Ihab had named, the man simply jabbed a finger behind him and trudged on, a muscle-bound Goliath indifferent to curfews or the footpads who haunted these hidden byways of the city. Faroun entered the souk of the leather workers and turned into a narrow side street.

The way ahead was piled on either side with mounds of shoes, cascading out of the dimly lit shops and onto the street as if from a horn of plenty. Fastened in pairs by their laces, the delicate white leather of baby shoes mixed with carpet slippers, the rough cowhide of military boots, and dress shoes of every description. A solitary cobbler pointed distractedly with an awl to Faroun's hurried question. The policeman sidled past a startled apprentice wearing a skullcap and leather apron. A tiny pathway led between two of the stalls, so cramped that Faroun had to squeeze through it. In one of those surprises of space by which Damascus perplexed and intrigued, the path opened up and Faroun found himself standing in the middle of a little square. The blank façades of the houses flanking the space gave no hint as to those who lived within. Private homes, except for one old hostel at the north corner of the square, a feebly lit sign hanging above the entrance by a rusty chain, the Arabic lettering worn by sun and rain into a ghostly script.

Like many hostels of its type, the Ras Algetta had been built to accommodate pilgrims of slender means who were making the hajj. These simple inns could be found in nearly every district of the city, for Damascus had always been the gateway to Medina and Mecca. During the months of the pilgrimage, the city teemed with those yearning to exorcise the devil and purify themselves before the Holy Kaaba. The rest of the year most of the inns stood empty, while their owners kept occupied in other trades. This one showed a light.

The night clerk of this establishment wore a checkered kaffiyeh so rumpled he might have slept in it. He greeted the policeman's badge with a nervous smile. His eyes roved from Faroun to the stairwell, and as he spoke, his voice rose in a nervous whine.

He had seen no one all day, it was not his business to answer the questions of strangers, he was simply trying to run a decent place. Faroun knew the man was giving a signal to someone upstairs.

Faroun pulled out his Walther automatic as the clerk disappeared behind a partition. Mounting the steps two at a time, Faroun crouched low when he reached the landing. Halfway down the murky corridor, a hotel room door was partially open, and as Faroun stood up, he flattened himself against the wall. He crept along the hallway until he was just outside the door. He was about to push the door open wide with his pistol when he heard movement from the staircase. A gunshot went off and he felt a sting in his shoulder. Clapping a hand to the wound, Faroun turned to fire at his assailant, then heard footsteps from the other end of the hallway. The figure lumbered forward, steel-gray pistol in one hand and pointed right at him. He lifted the Walther and was about to fire when Faroun saw the black shirt and white tie, and then the grimace of Philomel Durac, who wasted no time in firing off three rounds. The reports of the pistol were deafening. The sharp odor of gunpowder filled the airless corridor. Reaching Faroun's side, Durac waved for him to remain low.

The agent went ahead, crouching, until he reached the body at the head of the stairs. After peering down the staircase to be sure, Durac turned to the dead man, checking for a pulse. He picked up the dead man's revolver, stood, and as he began walking back, another assassin leapt out of the room with the half-open door and raised a machine gun to his shoulder, Durac in his sights. Faroun fired once to the head. The gunman flew back against the wall, his weapon discharging a spray of bullets into the ceiling. He groaned as he slumped to the floor.

Faroun got to his feet, made sure the second gunman was dead, and joined Durac at the other end of the hall. The man the agent had shot was lying faceup. The familiar scimitar-shaped scar stood out on the cheek of Umar Tamiri's house guard, chalk white against the man's swarthy skin.

The two men went back down the hall. Durac pushed open the door of the hotel room with his Militaire automatic. He stepped inside, pistol at the ready. The inspector followed, pulling out a handkerchief and slipping it under his coat to staunch the bleeding.

They took in the room. An overturned lamp lay on the worn carpet, casting a garish shadow on the small, dingy space. Four folding cots stood against the wall in one corner. A washbasin lay on the floor, its contents soaking into a tattered rug. Wind blew through the open window, flapping the two strips of yellowed cloth that passed for curtains.

"Shit!" said Durac, sticking his head out the window. "I'd complain about saving your miserable hide, Faroun, except that you've gone and saved mine." The Sûreté agent rolled his head against the wall. "I might have got killed out there." His eyes fell on Faroun's shoulder. "Looks like you caught one."

"A nick, that's all."

"Sorry to hear it," Durac said with a laconic grin.

"Glad you could stop by."

"I've had my eye on this place for some time. It's a safe house for radicals. I've got men breaking into places all over town." Durac holstered his pistol. "Our Colonel Bremond has left us all in the lurch. He even pulled troops out of the Citadel to help with this sweep of the villages. His name will be etched in glory if he kills a few sheep and burns a few farmers out of their homes."

"I take it you don't approve."

"The colonel waltzes out of town with two thousand men and leaves the gate wide-open. He might as well invite every fanatic in the city to take a French head."

"On that sole point, you and I agree," Faroun said. "The question is whether or not someone will take up the invitation."

"You've heard the talk on the street. We both know something big is in the wind. Why are you here anyway?"

"After a suspect."

"You are a dog worrying a bone, Faroun. You just won't let this Tamiri thing go, will you? Which suspect is it this time?"

Durac was fishing.

"You, actually."

Durac burst into laughter, the raucous sound of a man who found nothing funny.

"I don't like being followed around by your men, Durac. And I don't like some other police officials trying to swipe one of my cases. It makes me wonder what the Sûreté really has to gain."

"What's this about now?"

"I'm sure you have a reasonable explanation for showing up at Vera's suite the night of her death." The agent wasn't laughing anymore. Faroun wondered if he should reveal all his suspicions but decided to be prudent. Two could go fishing. "Perhaps you wanted her to turn over that notebook of hers. You know the one I mean. The same ledger that your boys were looking for when they tore up Vera Tamiri's apartment after her murder." Durac's look of surprise had turned darkly sullen. "You played your hand when you warned me off the other day at Nurredine. You lack subtlety, Philomel."

Faroun could see he had hit the mark, although Durac did his best to conceal it. "Let's talk about the book, Faroun. What do you want for it?"

"All right, let's talk about the book. What do you want it *for*? Perhaps there are very important pieces to a puzzle that has more to it than a thwarted love affair?"

Durac's brow clouded. "Love affair?"

"Did Vera tell you that she found you a perverse, ugly little man and show you the door at the Hotel Nurredine? If so, I'd say she had come to her senses."

"Vera and me?" Now Durac really did find something funny. "You've been overreaching with this case all long. Vera and me!" He lowered his jaw in a crooked leer. "Not that I didn't have a fantasy or two."

"Out of your league, Durac."

Durac slipped into the familiar sneer. "Let's get back to the notebook."

"A simple exchange, Durac. I release the notebook. You release Captain Martel. We both know he didn't kill Vera. Besides, by tomorrow's deadline, I'll produce the murderer. I know you don't want me to produce the murderer and I think I know why. However, I'll produce the culprit anyway. I'm just a little bit curious why the item is so important. Why would Vera Tamiri's financial information be of any use to you? Unless . . ."

"Out of *your* league, Faroun."

"I'll tell you what I think. I believe you had some hold on Vera. Tell me, was she providing you with information?"

"What business is it of yours?"

"I hold the notebook."

"How do I know this notebook is genuine?" Durac asked stubbornly. "I want to see it first."

"I'll bring it around to your office tomorrow, just before noon, and you can inspect the merchandise before the transfer. Agreed?"

"You said an exchange, not robbery."

"On the other hand, once I produce Vera's murderer, you'll have to release Martel anyway. And I still have the notebook. And you have nothing."

"You have to prove the case against your murderer first. I have Martel's confession."

"I'm willing to take that risk," said Faroun.

"Why should you give a damn about the Legionnaire anyway?"

"Let's just say I owe a debt to an old comrade-in-arms."

Durac was displeased, yet a wry smile crept to his lips. He pulled the dead assailant's gun from his belt and pointed it at Faroun. "There's another solution, Inspector. You were just murdered by some nameless goon in the corridor of a shabby hotel. Who would know otherwise?" The thought that he might call Durac's bluff was fleeting. The walls of the room seemed in motion. A tremor rolled through the building. The two men swayed in place. The agent yelled at him but Faroun could not hear. Part of the ceiling gave way and fell on Durac in a downpour of plaster dust and debris. Faroun was thrown against the wall and, covering his face against the choking dust, he tried to reach out for Durac but, blinded, spun into the corridor. An explosion followed so deafening it was if an artillery shell had burst in the hallway. Faroun braced himself against the wall as he made his way to the back stairwell. He nearly tumbled down to street level. The door had been blown open by the blast, and the bare bulb swaying overhead lit a drunken path to the alley.

Then he caught sight of the Citadel, the mighty fortress become a blazing tower like the cone of an erupting volcano. The fierce red flame at its core roared up into the night, fed by the ammunition stored in the bunkers. Projectiles as brilliant as phosphorus flares hurtled into the sky. They silhouetted a tomcat on top of a compound wall, a mouse wriggling in its jaws. Then the wall shook, swayed, and the creature vanished as an explosion consumed, as it seemed, all creation. Faroun put his hands over his ears against the roar. The ground shook and tilted and the concussion brought him to his knees.

The policeman staggered to his feet and clung to the wall. Lurching forward, he twisted and turned down the labyrinth of backstreets to a little square surrounded by tenements, glass shards littering its length where the initial blast had shattered the windows overhead. A confused babble . . . Heads poked out of the holes in the buildings where the windows had been. A woman thrust a lamp into the darkness as if in supplication. Above them, a great cloud of black debris, deeper than the thick night, was sweeping over the district, and bits and pieces of metal, wood, and chunks of stone began dropping out of the sky. Faroun ran until a sharp pain in his side made him slow down. More than fatigue brought him to a stop.

The sound was scarcely perceptible, but it caused him to turn around with a chill in his heart.

At first, it was just a ghostly streak against the ground, but gradually it took on shape and substance, like a phantom made flesh, transformed into a great white hound. The beast loped toward him silently, and as it came nearer, Faroun could see it was a saluki, one of the hunting dogs of the desert, its sleek head shaped like an ax blade, a wonder of speed. Faroun fumbled for his pistol as the hound approached, but his hand felt as if it were swathed in gauze or cotton and he couldn't grip anything. The saluki came on, right for him, so close Faroun could see the froth on its jaws. As the policeman flung himself against the wall, the hound surged past and vanished just as a stone whistled by Faroun's ear.

"Damn you to hell!" came the cry. A hulking, thick-necked man wearing a white linen kilt and sandals, and brandishing an ancient Turkish cavalry saber, stopped to catch his breath beside Faroun. "Don't tell me that is your damned hound," he rasped.

"No," said Faroun. "Not mine."

"Not anyone's, I think. He's the devil's wretch, he is." The giant drew in a great breath and appraised his companion with some suspicion. The fellow was all broad and rippling muscle below a shaven skull. Fifty years ago, he would have been a likely candidate to guard a sultan's harem or even the sultan himself, had he been willing to forgo his manhood. "What's your business here?"

"Lost my bearings in the explosion." As if in confirmation, the sky behind them brightened with another red spiral, as the fire found more ammunition.

"Insurgents!" the giant spat. "They'll have us in one hell of a mess with the French this time." He introduced himself as Tariq, a truck driver who plied the route between Damascus and Beirut. He explained to Faroun how the saluki had been raiding his chicken coop for the past two weeks. The dog was uncanny, appeared only at night, and outfoxed him every time. Five of his prized layers had been carried off. "Leaps right over the compound wall," said Tariq, "but I will catch him yet." He shook his fist in the direction the dog had gone. "You look like you could use a breather," he said, looking Faroun up and down. "My house is in the compound over there. My daughter will make coffee."

"A kind offer, but I have no time to stop."

"What is this place you are seeking?" asked the giant.

"The Al-Quassi Shipping Depot. I'm looking for a man who might have been running that way."

Tariq gave him a shrewd look and chuckled roughly. "Looking for a man? It's one hell of a night for police business, if that's what you're about." He laughed again, but this time at himself. "Then again, look at me, chasing a phantom. He swung at the thick air with his old saber. "I know the place well enough for I used to drive for al Quassi, but he's a right bastard, Abdullah, and I won't work for him anymore. Follow this lane until the end, then cut to the left. Three streets down. You'll see it on the right."

28

Faroun traveled south from the Old City following the truck driver's instructions, but in the smoke, noise, and confusion in the wake of the Citadel blast, he lost his way and found himself in a bleak terrain of blasted trees and shells of buildings. The billows of smoke that drifted through the streets conjured another battleground, a war zone he had traversed as a young soldier in northern France . . .

Instinctively he sought cover as rifle bullets whined overhead and machine guns chattered from nearby streets. Old women in shawls and widow's weeds scurried for cover among the ruins as the ragged line of surviving infantry advanced deeper into territory the enemy had held for four long years. A horse screamed in agony amidst its traces and the wreckage of an ammo cart. The body of an enemy soldier hung over a broken window frame like a piece of dirty wash. Corporal Faroun trudged forward, bayonet at the ready, following the ragged line of his comrades until he heard hysterical weeping from a building to his right. He went inside and there amidst the wreckage of a French cottage, Captain Legere was standing over Briand. Briand had finally snapped, as Faroun knew he must, for Legere had picked him out for the treatment weeks ago. No one knew what motivated Legere, the atrocities of war, a father who had humiliated him, a girl who had scorned him, who can say what drives a man into sadism that was like a thirst? No one knew how Legere chose the men he wished to break. Perhaps it was an imagined slight, or some misinterpreted word, or simply the captain did not like the look of the man. But once he had settled on a victim, he went about his program relentlessly, methodically. Poor Briand had snapped just as the final push was on; for the Germans were in full retreat, and here he was in a bombed-out building whining and mumbling and shielding his head with his hands while his tormentor stood straddled over him, pricking him and jabbing him with his sword and screaming for the miserable coward to get up and fall in line or he would kill him then and there. Faroun had seen it before and had shrugged it off; it was none of his business and Legere had not singled him out. Besides, to interfere was only to draw on himself the captain's fascination. Yet this was different somehow, this treatment of Briand, who was as amiable a country boy as you would ever want to meet, a former shepherd from the French Alps, a tall, muscular giant who towered over Legere by a foot. It was nearly the end of the war, the German line had at last been broken, the Yanks were driving them back in the Argonne while Faroun's Foreign Legion battalion had fought through the Forest of Retz to drive in the enemy's northern flank. The long nightmare was almost over, and here was Legere straddling Briand and trying to cave in what was left of the poor boy's mind and manhood. Later, Faroun would have ample time to wonder why he took the action he did. Perhaps he was acting out of some vague impulse of leftover humanity; perhaps he had finally snapped too. He walked up to Legere and drove the butt of his rifle between the officer's shoulder blades. The officer had staggered off, and when he turned, a pistol was in his hand. Faroun pulled the trigger of his rifle and exploded Legere's head as if it had been a melon. He coaxed Briand to his feet and together they stumbled into the street. . . .

Faroun stood in the middle of a lane that did not even rate a street sign as the smoke from the exploding Citadel swirled by and the stench of sulfur and cordite smothered the air, lost amidst the wreckage of a city gone mad. Wondering how he was to find the Al-Quassi depot, he spied the ghost again. The hound just stood at the end of the lane, almost indistinguishable from the smoke that drifted by, panting and looking at Faroun with a curious detachment, as if the policeman were the hound and not the other way round. Then it took off. Faroun decided to tail the saluki as it loped down the street and turned the corner; after all, the beast seemed to know where it was going and Faroun did not. He followed the gray ghost through the maze of streets, doubting his judgment along the way, until he came to a familiar knoll on the edge of the Maidan district. By then, his saluki guide had run ahead of him and was gone.

Faroun remembered the place. At its top was a small park originally dedicated to King Faisal and the liberation of Damascus from the Turks. Faisal's statue had long since been replaced by the voluptuous figure of Marianne, the spirit of French liberty. At some point, she had been decapitated by vandals, and so she could not look northward, as Faroun now did, to the terrible conflagration that was consuming the neighborhoods surrounding the Citadel. A fierce column of fire and smoke poured out of the center of the fortress as if it were the very mouth of the underworld. The two great souks of Al Hamidieh and Al Kumeileh were burning vigorously too as other fires, created by exploding munitions, threatened the western half of the Old City. So far the flames had not spread eastward to the Christian, Jewish, and Armenian districts, and the policeman hoped that district fire brigades, pumping water from the Barada, might be able to contain the blaze. South of the Old City, the Maidan Road and the Banyass River provided natural barriers against the fire, but Faroun could see incendiaries at work in the teeming ghetto. The resistance groups had made a daring strike right into the heart of the city. They had infiltrated the Citadel, set off the munitions stores, thrown French forces into disarray, and then spread havoc. Perhaps they had hoped to ignite a general uprising. They could not hold out against disciplined French troops for long, but they won either way. The French would restore order, but the victors would be the lords of ruin.

The Maidan district, home to thousands of restive refugees, would be the tipping point. That explained why Faroun could see torch-wielding men flitting about the warren of streets below. Already there were fires near the Al-Quassi Shipping Depot, on the northern edge of the district, prominent by its huge warehouse and sign. It did not appear in danger, though, for the main gate was guarded by armed workers.

The policeman left the park and set off along the boulevard. Salim al Quassi would be at the depot. If he had been at the hotel, the shoot-out with the assassins would have sent him packing. Now there was only one place left for Salim to run. Besides, it was exactly where Salim wanted to be, Faroun felt sure. Abdullah would be at the depot defending his business against looters. Only Abdullah held the answers to the questions that raged in Salim's tortured mind.

A quarter mile on, breathing heavily from the smoke drifting down from the Old City, Faroun slipped inside an unguarded side gate. He traveled unseen along the chain-link fence until he found a loading dock at the rear of the main building. The door was unlocked and the timber staircase led up to the main office. He pulled out his Walther as he crept up, flattening himself against the wall. Abdullah al Quassi's nerve center was a glass cage, with windows on three sides so that the businessman could survey most of his operation at a glance. The huge space had been divided, with Abdullah's private office to the left and a door to the right that led to a large, and deserted, secretarial and accounting suite. The policeman could see shadowed movement in the office as he crept up the stairs.

The brothers were speaking heatedly, Salim waving a pistol in Abdullah's face. In the shadow thrown off by a banker's lamp on his desk, Abdullah towered over his younger brother like the fearsome Afreet in Toni's drawing. A cold cigar gripped in the corner of his mouth, Abdullah nodded along with Salim's torrent of complaints, humoring him, it seemed, before he descended on him. Faroun moved closer to the half-open door.

"I just want the truth," Salim was saying excitedly. "The Beks said you told them. You know who killed her. They told me you knew all along."

"And why should you believe them?" Abdullah asked. "Why should you believe a couple of thugs against the word of your own brother?"

"Because in the condition they were in, they could only tell the truth."

"What did you do to the Beks, Salim?"

"I did to them what they did to my Vera. I put them in sacks."

Abdullah pulled the cigar from his mouth. "Are you trying to tell me you killed the Bek boys?"

"I did some other things to them first. That way I know they didn't lie to me." Salim became pensive. "I'm not sure they told me everything, but at least I know what they told me wasn't a lie."

"May God be merciful!" Abdullah cried. "Why did you have to kill them?"

"They put Vera in a sack like a bloody animal!"

"The Beks took care of the mess you made!" Abdullah discouraged Salim's protest with a frown. "Calm down, now. Actually . . . actually you may have done us a favor. The Beks were witnesses, after all. Provided no one saw you."

"Look at me," said Salim, throwing off the kaffiyeh. "I was dressed like a day laborer. Just as I was when I saw Mustapha."

"You saw Mustapha?"

Salim nodded energetically. "Mustapha Ni'mat. I remembered you had some dealings with him. He was the one who told me to seek out the brothers Bek at their pawnshop."

"Mustapha told you that?" asked Abdullah, lighting his cigar.

"He said that the Bek brothers did little odd jobs like that for you. Little jobs like disposing of bodies." Salim's face dripped with a feverish sweat, but he wore a disconcerting smile. "Mustapha spoke the truth. I saw to that too."

Abdullah's craggy forehead seemed to raise an inch. "You took care of Mustapha too?"

"He's dead."

"I see you are a little more resourceful than I thought." Abdullah seemed stumped by this new puzzle his brother had introduced. "Perhaps Aleppo isn't for you after all. Perhaps I can bring you deeper into the organization."

"What do you mean 'deeper'?"

"I mean that there is another level to Al-Quassi Shipping. We people of the old families always have need of real talent. I just never suspected that my little brother Salim might prove his worth."

"What do you mean—people of the old families? They have only despised us."

"There are ties that go deeper than any politics," Abdullah confided.

Salim shook his head defiantly, keeping his pistol trained on his brother. "I'm not doing anything you say until you tell me what you know about Vera's murder."

"All right, all right, just don't get excited with that thing," Abdullah replied, pointing to the revolver. "Someone else visited Vera at the Nurredine that night, as we know."

"Yes, we know that," said Salim impatiently, running his hands through his shock of disheveled hair.

"I don't want you pointing that gun at me when I say this to you." Abdullah reached out slowly to take the weapon, but his brother stepped back. "I know this is something you don't want to hear, that's all."

"Your brother is about to tell you that your mistress had another lover," said Faroun, stepping into the room. "That's what he will tell you."

Nervously, Salim spun about and trained his gun on Faroun. "Who the hell are you?" His hand began shaking when he saw Faroun's Walther.

"Meet Inspector Faroun of the Damascus Prefecture," said Abdullah.

Faroun motioned for Salim to drop the pistol. He hesitated and then, bending down, placed it on the floor.

"Kick it over to me," said Faroun. When Salim complied, Faroun said, "Tell him, Abdullah."

"What is he talking about, Abdullah?"

"Do you think that woman was saving her caresses just for you?" Abdullah asked contemptuously. "She was seeing a French officer. And right now that officer is in the Citadel or has perished in the attack launched by our Syrian militias. He confessed to the crime. He went to the Nurredine that night and killed her. Ask the inspector."

Faroun studied Abdullah for a moment. "A French officer is in custody. He confessed to the murder. He confessed, Salim, but that doesn't mean he is guilty."

Salim stared at Faroun widely. "I am in a madhouse with madmen."

"Ask your brother, Salim, how he knew about the other man in Vera's life—unless he was spying on you?"

Salim turned his troubled countenance to his brother. "Is this true? Were you having me followed?"

"What do you think, Brother? I have always looked after you. If there's trouble, you find it."

"You are right, Salim," said Faroun. "Your brother knows who killed Vera. But he didn't say anything to you. Why do you think that is? Let me help you, Salim," Faroun persisted. "When you got to the hotel the night Vera was murdered, how did you get into the suite?"

"Like I always do, through the garden gate and then through the rear entrance, up the stairwell. I have keys."

"That night—think about it—was the garden gate locked or unlocked?"

"I don't remember—everything is confused."

"The policeman is trying to confuse you, Salim," Abdullah scoffed.

Salim ran his hand through his hair again. "Wait—open—the gate was open. I remember now. Because I dropped my key and when I was searching for it on the ground, I braced myself with the gate handle. It opened."

"And the back door of the suite?"

"Open," Salim said wonderingly. "Vera and I. We both had keys. The only keys."

"Except for the set she gave that soldier," Abdullah scoffed.

"I don't believe that," said Salim. "She would not give that key to anyone."

"Listen to me, Salim," Faroun said, keeping his eye on him. "When you got there that night and found Vera's body . . . you found her—where?"

"She was on the—bathroom floor. There was blood every-where. There was blood coming out of her neck, and her stomach. I covered her up with towels. I didn't know what to do."

"So someone had been in the suite just before you arrived, someone who knew Vera was alone. And someone who knew your whereabouts too."

"I stayed on at the casino that night after Vera left. I told her I would be right along. Then I went to the Nurredine."

"How soon after Vera left for the hotel did you follow?"

"An hour—no more than that."

"And we are to believe that Vera's soldier lover—who had keys to the garden gate and the apartment—would have done the deed just before you arrived. Was he a mind reader, do you suppose?"

"She called him when she was alone," said Abdullah.

"Do you believe that, Salim?" asked Faroun. "Do you seriously think Vera would entertain a lover knowing that you were likely to arrive shortly? Vera might have liked to play things close to the edge—but do you think she would do that? Do you think she cared so little for you?"

Salim wrinkled his brow. "I told you. She would never betray me."

"Then who would have taken that chance unless it was someone who knew precisely where you were at the time?"

Salim turned in wonderment to his brother. "Abdullah?"

"Abdullah could have procured a spare set of keys from the hotel owner, Madame Moulmenian. She is terrified of your brother—as many are. I'm willing to wager he has those keys on him right now." Faroun moved his pistol to cover Abdullah. "Empty your pockets on the desk, Abdullah."

"This man is talking nonsense, Salim. He is trying to fool you."

"Do what he says, Abdullah."

Abdullah broke into a snarling laugh. "All right, all right. So I have a set of keys. What does that prove? I told you, Salim, I was looking after you."

"So you were there that night, Abdullah?" Salim demanded.

"I went to see Vera Tamiri that night. I thought this fling of yours would be over in a week or two. And then—when I saw it was going on, I paid her a visit. I brought her a gift."

"A gift."

"Ten thousand francs, my brother Salim. Ten thousand francs for her to cut off this crazy affair with you. Don't you see? This madness of yours was driving you to ruin. She was only in it for the money anyway. That's why she took the ten thousand. And she was grateful for it. Very grateful." Abdullah smiled. "After that, I left and your mistress was still alive. I don't know what happened after that."

"You are a liar, Abdullah," said Salim, his voice rising. "She would never do that. She would never take your money."

"You are an idiot, Salim. That's why she wanted you—for the money and only for the money. That crazy French officer was probably watching and waiting until I left—and he got into the apartment and got in a fight with that woman. He cut her throat and carved that cross on her belly and then took the money and ran. That's what happened. He already confessed. Nothing can change that fact."

This was the moment for which Faroun had been waiting. Abdullah had backed himself into a corner and now he had begun to unravel. The big man was sweating and his eyes moved frantically as if looking for a way out. All Salim had to do was make the connections, but Faroun knew he would have coax him along. "Nothing can change the facts of the murder, either, Salim. You said that you found Vera's body and covered her with towels."

"I did," said Salim.

"What happened then?"

"I went down to my car and told my driver to fetch Abdullah."

"You returned to the suite, is that right?"

"I waited in the apartment. I paced back and forth and then Abdullah arrived with the two men, the Bek brothers, as it turned out. Then the two of us—my brother and I—went down to Abdullah's car to wait for them to finish."

"Did Abdullah see the body?"

"He looked into the bathroom, saw her there. That was all."

"Did he lift the towels? Did he look at the body?"

"No, she was covered up."

"Then how would Abdullah know about her wounds?"

"You told me what those wounds were," said Abdullah.

Salim looked at him carefully. "All I told you was what I saw. Her throat was cut. The rest of her covered with blood. That's all I saw."

"The coroner confirmed the mutilation, Salim—the cross carved on her abdomen."

"This policeman is trying to trick you, Brother," said Abdullah, leaning against the desk, his arms behind him.

"Wasn't your father exposed as a Turkish spy?" the policeman asked. "Was it not Farid Tamiri, Vera's father, who betrayed him? You had waited a long time. So Vera would pay the price. You cut her and carved her as an infidel tramp who deserved no better fate than that of a Turkish sultan's wayward plaything. You had her tied up in a sack and thrown into the Barada."

"He's lying, Salim."

"You had waited a long time, Abdullah," Faroun went on. "But why did you choose this moment to exact your revenge? You found out what Vera was really doing with your brother, didn't you?"

"Yes," cried Abdullah, seeing his way out. "She was spying on us, Brother. She was spying for the infidels. They are trying to link me to the resistance. They are out to destroy me. Do you want to see your brother hanged too, Salim? That Tamiri woman was helping them. Using you to betray your own brother. That's true."

The two brothers eyed each other as if from across an immense chasm.

Abdullah pulled out a small revolver from a stack of papers on his desk just as Salim leapt on him. The two grappled until the revolver went off. Then another gunshot from the other side of the room. Abdullah clutched his stomach and dropped to his knees with a groan. Salim grabbed his brother's collar, holding up his head. In the other hand, he held a stiletto pointed at Abdullah's throat.

Faroun swung his gun to the other side of the room. Ihab Kabir stood in the doorway that led to the accounting office, a smoking machine pistol in his hand. Faroun turned back to the brothers. "Salim—I want you to stay calm. Just put down the knife and we will work all of this out."

Salim's eyes were flooded with tears. "Why? Give me one reason. Just answer me that."

Abdullah looked down at his hand gripping his belly, blood seeping through the fingers. But there was no reply from Salim's brother.

Faroun barely saw the movement of Salim's hand as the knife glinted and slid across Abdullah's throat. Salim leaped from behind the collapsing body of his brother and went for the inspector, knife raised over his head. There was another shot from the doorway, and another, but Salim's momentum knocked Faroun over. When the policeman opened his eyes, Salim was on the floor beside him, a woeful, orphaned look on his face. Sad, driven Salim. Faroun wondered, fleetingly, what Salim al Quassi had seen in his last second. Had he gained a final glimpse of the woman he had loved before he had fallen away from her forever? Or was his woe because Abdullah was waiting for him on the other side, ready to bedevil him in death as he had in life? Then Faroun was looking at a fretful countenance hovering above him. Wearily, Faroun accepted Ihab's hand as he got to his feet.

From below, cries and clamor. Al-Quassi workers, drawn by the gunfire, clattered up the stairs.

29

I tried to wound him," said Ihab Kabir, a soul in search of consolation. The killings of the al Quassi brothers did not sit easily
on him.

"You did as you thought best, Sergeant Kabir. Since he was
about to slit my throat too, I'm not about to complain."

The sergeant shrugged, but secretly he was pleased to hear
these words. His boss owed him a large favor.

The two men stood on the knoll in the park once dedicated to
King Faisal of Syria. It had been a long night's vigil, and now that the
dawn was coming in the east, the extent of the devastation was becoming revealed. The Citadel looked like a sundered furnace, a
smoking ruin molten red and orange at its core. The fires in the surrounding Al Amara district seemed under control. The sound of
gunfire was tapering off as the screams of fire engines and ambulance

235

sirens rose in lamentation. The night-shrouded city of Damascus was shaking itself free of the evil dream it had witnessed so many times before. And as before, the dream's hold would be hard to break.

"The Syrian militias," said Ihab. "They have done a night's work."

"It's just what Colonel Bremond has been waiting for. I'll bet he has wheeled around his troops and saved the city. But something tells me he has overplayed his hand this time." Faroun then thought of the hotel and Umar's man, Scarface, dead in the corridor. "He's not the only one."

"So where does that leave the rest of us, sir?"

"The living will try and patch up things with the ghosts."

The corners of Ihab Kabir's taut mouth turned up at the grim joke. "About Abdullah—how did you know that he killed Vera?"

"I didn't. Not until Salim went on his rampage, at least. Then everything was leading Salim back to his brother like the current of a dark river. Abdullah had a double motive. He loved his brother, but he also had an old score to settle." Faroun explained the origin of the al Quassi and Tamiri enmity. There were darker currents yet, but Faroun decided to keep silent about these, at least until he had confronted Umar Tamiri one more time.

"Old scores," said Ihab.

"Wounds that never heal," said Faroun.

"That's what's wrong with this place," said Ihab sadly. "Damascus people never forget and they never forgive."

"Not until Judgment Day. If then." Faroun pointed out movement on Maidan Boulevard, a column of four army trucks, preceded by an armored car. "There's our ride, Sergeant. We go to the ministry first for I need to know if Rebecca has made it in this morning. Then see if you can't find a car for us. I will want to make my report to the delegate."

"You're alive!" Rebecca came around from her desk with basket of baklava and a frantic look in her eyes. Faroun decided to be gracious about the baklava; besides, he was hungry. She then took him by the arm and marched him to the inner office. The room was quite airy, for two of his windows had been blown out by the Citadel explosion. He wasn't surprised, as he had walked over a carpet of glass while making his way across the ministry court-yard. He suspected that for most of the civil servants in the build-ing it was the first breath of fresh air they had experienced in years. A new file was on his desk. When he saw that it was stamped with the red imprimatur of the Legal Department, he nearly cast reserve to the wind and hugged Rebecca.

"I just obtained these endorsements from the lawyers." To-gether they spread the documents on his desk and examined them.

Faroun was stunned. "If this means what I think it does, then all the transactions were illegal."

"More than that," said Rebecca. "They never carried the force of law in the first place. At least that's what the legal affairs attor-ney told me."

"So Faisal's confiscations, the creation of the Royal Land Trust, the transfer and the administration of these lands, none of it holds."

"That's right."

"Wonderful!" exclaimed Faroun, clapping his hands and rub-bing them together. "Someone is in for a very rude surprise. Re-becca, you are a genius!"

"Well, I did have a little help. That young man from the Intel-ligence Division?" she asked diffidently in reply to her boss's fur-rowed brow.

"The one who has been sending around flowers?"

She looked at him a bit coyly, an unusual expression for Re-becca. "Justin Latrobe. That is his name. We both worked on get-ting the documents in order and identifying the pertinent ones. There was quite a stack to sort out. We finished just before you arrived."

"You stayed up working all night?"

"We watched the Citadel in flames for a while. Compelling. And of course," she hastened to add, "a terrible tragedy."

"Then you never went to your aunt's in Arnous?"

"There was too much to do. Then came the attack. So where could we go?"

Faroun looked at her skeptically. "Do you mean to tell me that the two of you stayed up all night in the Ministry Building to work on these papers?"

"There were almonds to eat. And Justin had a small flask of cognac."

For the first time, he noticed that her red hair was in disarray and the blue ribbon that bound it had hastily been retied. "Here in the office, drinking cognac and eating almonds?"

Rebecca tossed her snarled curls. "For all we knew, it might have been our last meal. Now, what do you want me to do with the papers?"

"I'll take them with me to Palace of Justice. Thank you, Rebecca, and when you see him, thank . . ."

"Justin Latrobe."

"Yes, Monsieur Latrobe."

By the time Faroun was able to make his way through the army checkpoints to the Palace of Justice, it was late morning and the sun was beaming with unseemly cheer. Sandbagged machine-gun emplacements guarded the front gate, and snipers looked down their scopes from the roof. The incendiaries had not gotten close enough to the administration buildings to do any damage, but that did not lessen the feeling of a state of siege. The soldiers at the entrance gate let him through, but one of the Legionnaires spat on the pavement after he had passed. French pride had been singed, and revenge against the Arabs was not only in the air, but Faroun suspected, also written out in the order of the day.

The mood was no less forbidding when the inspector was ushered into the delegate's office. A deathly pale Montcalm tried to control himself while Colonel Bremond made excuses. He was not to be blamed. He had been deceived and betrayed by fifth columnists. Even now they were loose in the city. He would impose martial law, the colonel proclaimed. The Old City would be cordoned off and house-to-house searches initiated. Suspects would be held in detention camps outside the city until they were interrogated. Those who resisted would be shot. The process would then be extended south to the Maidan district and into the northern suburbs as well.

"I have listened to you," the delegate said in a steely voice. "And what is the result, Colonel? I have only to look out the window to see the result."

Bremond displayed a touch of injured pride, but he was not as sure of his ground since the last time Faroun had seen him. "Do not let your eyes deceive you, Delegate," the colonel said, trying to hide a tremor in his right hand. "We shall build a new Citadel, new barracks, new prisons. As for the rest, acceptable losses. Luckily I had two thousand men at my disposal to keep the lid on."

"You left us undefended!" cried Montcalm. "Three city districts have been leveled. Hundreds of dead and wounded. What is acceptable, Colonel, tell me that?"

"You exaggerate, Montcalm. The old gives way to the new." The officer shook his riding crop across the wall map of Syria as if to tame it. "In five years, you'll see. A model city. A modern city to rival anything in Europe."

"After you destroy, Colonel, then you build. One would almost think you had something more to gain than glory."

"What do you mean by that, Delegate?" Bremond turned on the heel of his polished boot as if he might dress down a subordinate.

Montcalm rounded on him first. "Your soldiering days in Damascus are over, Colonel. I've already spoken to the high commissioner. You are relieved of your command until an official inquiry is completed. General Vincennes is flying in this afternoon to handle security arrangements."

"I believe we can add charges of corruption and conspiracy," said Faroun. "You are right, Delegate. The colonel had more at stake than glory."

The colonel tried to assume a look of injured pride. With a curt bow, the stricken soldier withdrew.

"I suppose I should congratulate myself for having stolen a march on that martinet," the delegate sighed as his glance fell on Faroun. "Brace yourself for the next storm, Inspector. At least General Vincennes won't militarize my staff and the secretarial pool." He offered a sardonic grin. "Or the Prefecture." His face clouded again. "But those worries are not going to be mine for much longer. I'm being recalled. Tomorrow morning, I'll make a damage assessment of the city, then head for Beirut in a week or two. My wife will be happy at least. She always wanted us away from this place."

"What is going to happen, sir?"

"To me?" The sharp tone of acrimony the delegate had used with Bremond had given way to self-doubt and recrimination. "I can't say I'll be in mourning over my career. Why waste time with a cadaver? We've had good years, my wife and I—consulates in North Africa and Indochina. I've held three or four ministerial posts too, not all that unimpressive, so . . . You might say I'm lucky to be leaving now, before someone produces evidence, real or imagined, to bring me down. That's what happens in this line of work, Faroun. Someone is bound to bring you down. Someone is always thinning the herd. However, I would have preferred to go out with a decoration instead of standing amidst a pile of rubble." Then his eyes fell to his desk. He shuffled through a few papers on his desk as if they were incomprehensible artifacts. "I've been a right fool, haven't I, Inspector? An old fool who gave his ear to unscrupulous men—not the least of them a man whom I counted as a friend. The city was left wide-open for last night's attack, as you told me it would be. I should have listened to you. I lost my way." An awkward silence followed this admission. "I wonder now if Umar Tamiri had something to gain by his advice. More to the point, has Umar Tamiri done anything but for gain?"

"You shouldn't be so hard on yourself, sir. Not all has been lost. I hope you will hear me out."

"What brings you here anyway?" The clock on the desk chimed eleven. "Vera's case, isn't it?"

"Yes, Delegate. I wanted to make my report before noon."

"You are good at meeting deadlines, Faroun. Perhaps I should put that in your next performance appraisal. More than that, I will make a commendation. I'll do that before I leave. But let's not dwell on that outcome. What do you have for me? Can we at last find some justice for Vera Tamiri?"

Faroun took the papers from the file Rebecca had provided. He placed them one by one on the delegate's desk.

"Justice for Vera, sir, and an order for a criminal inquiry against the man who betrayed you."

The delegate looked at him wonderingly.

"We cannot prove everything I am about to explain to you, sir, but there is no doubt about Umar and what he had to gain by last night's debacle. He has committed treason against the state. He has been involved in a criminal conspiracy to murder. And here are the weapons with which we begin to bring him down. We can strike him where it most hurts until the evidence bubbles to the surface, as it will. If you will provide me with the order for a criminal inquiry against Monsieur Tamiri before I leave, I shall set everything in motion. And never rest until I have settled these charges against him."

Montcalm's skepticism turned to resolve as Faroun presented his case. At length, the delegate reached across his desk for his pen. It was the most decisive move Faroun had seen him make in a long time.

Faroun left the delegate's office heavy of heart even though he had Montcalm's written order in hand. The two men had not found common ground until it was too late. The policeman had not been able to save Montcalm from his folly, but he could bring some measure of vindication to his defense. An image of the Bourbons once more came to mind. On his way to the guillotine, Louis XVI had lamented that if only people had left him alone, he would have made a fine watchmaker. Montcalm had been out of his element too and now was about to lose his head, at least figuratively, because he had trusted too well.

All the more reason he was glad to grant Faroun's request as the best way to strike back at the man who had so thoroughly deceived him. It was one bright possibility in a day of ruined prospects, Faroun was thinking, when he encountered Agent Philomel Durac hobbling up the stairs of the Palace of Justice. This was the very spot where Durac and he had had their first altercation. The bully had gone out of Durac, however; in fact, with a bloodstained bandage wrapped around his head, he nearly provoked sympathy. The inspector remembered the ceiling as it came crashing down at the pilgrims' inn.

"So you made your report to the delegate," said the agent with a grunt of pain.

"I have, and it seems you'll have to release Captain Martel after all."

"Sorry to disappoint you, Faroun, but our guest is missing, along with many other prisoners in the Citadel. Possibly incinerated, for all we know. On Martel's level, though, the force of the explosion blew open some doors. The men vanished, most of them anyway. Perhaps Martel was one of them; we can't be sure."

"It's a pity—now that the Tamiri case is closed."

Durac squinted at him until understanding came into his eyes. "Abdullah's dead, isn't he?"

"My sergeant and I were there. Abdullah al Quassi's body is waiting to be picked up at his office in the Maidan. Throat slit by his brother, Salim al Quassi, whose body will have to be picked up too. It was, among other things, an old family feud. But Abdullah was onto your game and said so before he died—the game in which you used Vera Tamiri as an informant. I know you were hoping she would help nail him for you. No doubt she proved an able spy, but she died before she could make her final report. The delegate bought me some time because he suspected your motives. He knew you had fingered Captain Martel."

Faroun took his measure of the wounded man. If anything, he had become more forlorn. "As for Vera . . . You should have looked more deeply into the family connections of this town before you put her out on a limb. By hiring her to do your dirty work, you signed her death warrant. You lost the man you were trying to trap. What did you gain?"

"It went wrong," Durac admitted grudgingly. "All I wanted Vera to do was to use Salim to get at Abdullah."

"Abdullah was playing for far higher stakes than Vera, no doubt. You'll have to tell me about that sometime."

"That's right, we'll have another round of drinks at Le Chat Rouge. I'll explain to you how you compromised over a year of investigative work on al Quassi. Don't forget to bring that notebook you were telling me about. Maybe we can make another deal."

"Good. I'll bring an extra clip for my Walther too," said the policeman. "As insurance."

"You're a son of a bitch, Faroun."

"You must be feeling better, Durac."

Durac groaned as he mounted another step, leaning heavily on the balustrade. "In case you were wondering, I would have shot you at that fleabag hotel," said the agent. "I would have enjoyed it. I would have enjoyed seeing you roll around the floor while I pumped lead into your heart. Then the damn ceiling fell in. End of comedy."

Faroun smiled like a satisfied cat as he descended the staircase. "Nothing comic about it, Philomel. It's pure melodrama. Better luck next time."

30

Sergeant Ihab Kabir drove Faroun south of the Old City wall, along the Maidan Road to its intersection with Boulevard Ibn Assaker, about a half mile farther and just south of the Haret Al Yahoud, the Jewish quarter of the Old City.

"It is odd," said the sergeant. "There was no funeral for Madam Tamiri. It is troubling and a little sad."

"Odd and sad," Faroun repeated pensively. "That says something about Vera Tamiri. I would add *brave* as an adjective. She tried to face down her demons. She even tried to take on the mightiest dragon of them all, but he proved far too clever for her."

"Abdullah al Quassi is a dead dragon now. We took care of him, sir."

"I wasn't talking about Abdullah al Quassi."

"There was another?"

Ihab turned off Assaker and down the poplar-lined road that led to the entrance of the cemetery. A long, low iron fence marked the perimeter between the dead and the living. The Renault passed under the iron-wrought arch depicting St. George the Trophy Bearer striking down a serpent. It was a pleasant place, at least pleasant as these places go. For centuries, Damascus Christians had been buried here, though the area was small, a hectare or two enclosed by tall plane trees and Roman pines. Some fifty yards down the gravel road, Faroun nodded to his subaltern and stepped out of the car. Ihab was to wait for him at the south gate of the cemetery.

Despite the bright face of a spring day, Faroun could not dispel a sense of oppression as he hurried down the narrow lane that led to a tree-shaded knoll. Monuments towered on either side, topped by avenging angels and dour saints, for the Christian churches of the East, having survived for centuries as suspect minorities in Muslim lands, preached a tougher creed than their Western counterparts. Most of these Eastern churches were represented in this plot of earth, the Greek Uniates, the Nestorian or Assyrian Christians, and even a few Maronites. Some decades ago, the churches had reached an accord that permitted the dead to put aside their doctrinal disputes and be buried together. The accord did not extend so far as the Protestant faiths, however, so no Calvinists found rest here, or Anglicans either.

At the end of the lane, Faroun found a fountain devoted to Mary of the Immaculate Conception. Water bubbled from her cupped hands and spilled through her fingers into a blue pool at her alabaster feet. Faroun dipped his hand in the pool, dabbed some cool water on his forehead, and hurried on. Mounting the incline of a grassy hillock, partially hidden by a crowd of young alders, he spied the remaining dragon.

A somberly dressed Umar Tamiri stood over an earth grave bearing a simple headstone. He held a posy of blue, crocuses, and he was not pleased at the interruption and particularly not pleased to see Nikolai Faroun. Not pleased and rather surprised.

"You will pardon me, Monsieur Tamiri. I stopped by your house and your servant told me where to find you. If the time is inopportune, then I will go away, but I thought you might like to know that you are no longer under suspicion. Your sister's killer has been brought to justice."

Umar masked his skepticism with a supercilious smile. "You have decided to accept the confession of that French officer."

"No, no," said Faroun, frowning. "Captain Martel is now quite in the clear."

"You found another murderer, Inspector?" Umar was nearly jovial. "Perhaps you should just present me with a list and let me choose."

"One name. Two, actually. Since I have to distinguish between the killer and the murderer."

"What kind of riddle is this?"

"Abdullah al Quassi is the killer. He confessed last night to the crime before his brother, Salim, killed him." Faroun stopped when he faced Umar from the other side of Vera's grave. On the recently turned earth, a light dusting of ash from the conflagration of the night before. "No need to feign surprise, monsieur. Actually, it all worked out splendidly for you. Mustapha Ni'mat, the Bek brothers, Salim and Abdullah—and the young woman in this grave—they are all gone. There's no trail of evidence to lead to your door. I must applaud you; it seems as if you have even manipulated fate to stand on your side."

"You have some kind of evidence to back up this insinuation?" Umar asked quietly. He looked down at the crocuses in bereavement. "They were Vera's favorite."

"That's the beauty of it!" Faroun exclaimed. "I can nab the killer but not the murderer. Yet I know one as surely as the other. There's just the two of us here, Umar, so why not unburden yourself? Give yourself something to really gloat over. You can tell me how you worked out your crime and I won't be able to do anything about it."

Umar seemed willing to humor Faroun. "Well, I must say you

have me interested, Inspector. Let's hear what kind of preposterous plan you've concocted. I'll let you know how far you are off the mark."

"Your love for your sister was always compounded with hate. You ruled over her and cheated her of the money your father had left her. However, she had always been an unruly subject. Somehow, you could not yoke her entirely. But things became hideous when she finally broke from your tyranny to try to make a life of her own. For Umar Tamiri, this was insufferable. The bond of love, whatever bond survived, was sundered. So you became spiteful and burned down the Women's Clinic. But this did not bring her back. She simply became more defiant and more of a smear on the family name. Then you discovered—I suspect via Colonel Bremond, with whom you had a discreet and lucrative business arrangement at government expense—that Vera was not only a sybarite, but a traitor to the clans—a paid agent for the Sûreté."

"So—and so," Umar said, cocking his head to one side. He pulled one of the flowers from the posy and dropped it on the grave.

"There was a side I couldn't see at first, but my inquiries kept coming back to the same ground. It is one of these things that everybody knows and doesn't talk about—the power of the old families, the power of the Twelve. 'Invisible and indivisible,' I believe that is how one of my colleagues put it. Vera had crossed the one line that no one of her station can cross, she had turned against her own, and she must be dealt with."

Umar raised his eyebrows. "You have been industrious, Inspector. But what does that tell you?"

"Like every other social arrangement in this town, it is not what it appears. The al Quassi were outcasts, thanks to your father, who coveted their lands. No matter, this is Damascus and the al Quassi were still Old Family, still among the Twelve. Actually, you and your fellow elites found the al Quassi clan useful, because they could do dirty work when it was needed, for they were dirty already. So the serpent hissed in Mustapha's ear, who hissed in turn into Abdullah's."

"A colorful allusion, Inspector." Umar pulled another crocus from the bunch and dropped it on the wet earth. "Abdullah al Quassi did not need much hissing."

"Of course not," said Faroun, feeling himself growing into the theme. "It was mutual convenience all around. Your sister was making a fool of his baby brother and using him to spy on the al Quassi connections with the resistance! Besides, there was that old score to settle, your father's betrayal of his father. You made a hideous bargain with Abdullah. By agreeing to let him kill Vera, you allowed Abdullah to even the score and get rid of a traitor too. Justice for all concerned—except for Vera, of course. Nevertheless, Abdullah got his final kick by carving the sign of the cross into your sister's flesh, carving it on her body as a sign of his contempt for you and all infidels, Old Family or not."

"He did that to my sister!" Umar's eyes flashed with anger. "Then he will suffer all the torments in hell. I'm not sorry the bastard is dead. Killed by his brother, you say?"

"Salim tracked him down via Mustapha and the Beks, leaving bodies in his wake."

"He was always a bit off-center, Salim," Umar said reflectively. "Assuming, hypothetically, part of your theory is true, why should you think I was involved?"

"The signs were there for me to trace, but I wasn't entirely sure until your assassin, that fellow with the scar, caught up with me last night at the Ras Algetta Hotel. That's why I hinted at my suspicions the last time we met. To let you know I had felt the tug of the undercurrent. To see if you would rise to the bait. I suspected you had been kept informed by your agents of Salim's hideout. Actually, Salim's vengeful murder spree fit into your plans perfectly. All that remained was a little cleanup. I suspect Scarface had orders to eliminate both Salim and the galling policeman

Faroun. Since I told you I was closing in on Mustapha Ni'mat's killer, you knew where to send your man. Bad luck that he failed the job. You were genuinely surprised to see me this morning."

Umar pulled out another crocus and sniffed it before dropping it on the grave with the others. "They don't have much of an aroma, these flowers. Your theory, on the other hand, is overripe. And unproven, as you yourself admit." Umar dropped the rest of the flowers on the earth and dusted off his white-gloved hands. "Actually I'm glad to see you still seated as chief of the Prefecture. I like my government officials incompetent. If not corrupt."

Faroun offered the businessman a ghastly smile. "I'm pleased to make you happy, Umar. That makes presenting this document all the easier."

Umar did not bother to take the envelope Faroun held out to him but rather slipped a gold case from his pocket, looked over the cigarettes, and took one. "Why don't you give me the gist of it, Faroun? Now that I've paid my respects to Vera, I've got business to attend to. I hate to confess this to a French official, but the building contracts flower after every civil disturbance. Since this was a particularly bad one, it seems I'll be very busy for some time to come."

"Yes, I'm sure all the Twelve Families prosper from French folly. For this reason, you won the delegate's ear. You urged him to support Colonel Bremond's march into the countryside. This set the stage for an attack on the Citadel with the aid of Abdullah's friends in the resistance. As you say, new building contracts grow out of the ashes, and you were poised for a windfall. That's what it's about, isn't it?"

"What is?" asked Umar.

"Prospering," said Faroun opening the envelope. "Prospering regardless of who gets hurt. Even your fellow Syrians. You may find your affairs inconvenienced, however, since it seems you will be spending a lot of time, and money, defending yourself in court."

"What are you talking about?" Umar snapped. He grabbed for the document but Faroun pulled it away.

"History does have a way of catching up with us, Umar. Here, then, is the *gist*. The charges in this warrant go back to your father's assumption of al Quassi lands after King Faisal awarded them to him through the Royal Land Trust. The Trust, administered by your father, was Faisal's cover for offering the spoils to his most loyal supporters. The Trust took on a life of its own, especially after you became the chief executive on your father's death. You struck a deal with the heads of the other Damascus families to keep the Tamiri clan at the helm and assume any risk, in exchange for a split of the profits. Faisal had set up a bequest which you disguised as a corporation and folded in with your other enterprises, so it did not attract the scrutiny of French authorities—however, legally, the Trust had a gaping hole in it. You see, Faisal was an illegitimate sovereign in 1919, when the properties were transferred. The Versailles Treaty had just concluded and named Syria as a French mandate of the new League of Nations. Accordingly, Faisal had no authority to hand over the properties to your family. Legally, they still belong to the al Quassi. But Nayef al Quassi is long gone and now, his sons, so there is legal precedent for the lands reverting to the state. Until a court decision some years hence, the funds of the trust are frozen and the lands fall into state receivership. Naturally, since you are under investigation for administering an illegal trust, you will be disqualified from bidding on any state building contracts. A pity, Umar, but you are about to become a very poor man." Faroun leaned over Vera's grave, grabbed Umar by the lapel, and slipped the envelope inside his coat. "The man whose friendship you betrayed and whose career you have ruined—Delegate Montcalm—has the last word it seems. You'll find his signature on this list of charges."

"You won't get anywhere with this!" Umar fumed as Faroun took the gently rolling slope down to where Ihab had parked the Renault.

"Consider it an offering," Faroun called back. "For the soul of Vera Tamiri."

Although it was the day after a shuddering upheaval of the city, Maxim's on the Nile was packed with merrymakers by the time Faroun arrived in the late afternoon. The inspector had invited his sergeant in for a drink, and Ihab could do little but frown at the provocatively clad foreign women, their swank escorts, and their dissolute companions. Their high, giddy laughter chimed in with the clink of glasses and the feverish music of the band. Garishly painted mummy cases peeked out from the corners, the lighted death masks of pharaohs looked down from the walls, canopic jars that had once bore the remains of cats and ibises now served as the repositories of cigarette butts and cigar ends. And along the bar, the servants of this festive mausoleum bumped each other's elbows, rapping their glasses for more champagne and zombies and French 75s, while the little lateen-rigged Nile boats feverishly plied their trade down the center of the bar.

"Meet the Dandies, Faroun," Maxim shouted in his ear over the din. "I once read that during the Black Plague, people just danced themselves to death. It was better to go out hoofing it than wait for sores to break out all over your body and turn you into a sorry bubonic wreck." He waved one hand about as he poured the detective a generous dose of arak. "Witness how history repeats itself, *mon ami*." As if in reply, the Syrian Jazz Clique brought their song to a wailing crescendo, and French officers whistled and cheered on Shammara. The voluptuous dancer's feet whirled over a carpet of banknotes.

"What will your sergeant have?" asked Maxim, taking in Ihab's dismay. "He looks like he prefers lemon juice. Maybe one for you too, *mon ami*. You two look like you've been to a funeral. Then again you must have been busy last night."

"Both," said Faroun. "A soda water for the sergeant."

"I watched the business last night from the roof of the club," said Maxim, pouring Ihab's drink. "The word out on the street was that something was about to happen, so I hired a dozen stout lads, gave them weapons, and we kept vigil. But the thing didn't boil over into the northern suburbs, so we just watched the show. Colonel Bremond must have a gleam in his eye about now. The insurgents set fire to the seat of his pants. Caught him napping, I think."

"Then again, maybe it was just what the colonel ordered."

"Come again?" Maxim handed Ihab his drink wrapped in a paper napkin.

"A good night to stay indoors," said Faroun. "Or pour drinks."

"It's always like this after a riot," said Maxim. "Business triples. A few more civil disturbances and I can buy Shammara that diamond she's always demanding. She'll get it too, because I'm nothing but a fool." He threw up his hands in exasperation and ran a bottle of vodka to the other server at the end of the bar.

Ihab sniffed at the drink and nervously accepted a toast. A platinum blonde with tightly permed hair bumped into the sergeant, spilling some of her drink on his uniform, and glared at him. She then leered at Faroun until her disheveled escort, one shirt flap hanging below his cummerbund, caught her by the elbow and took her into a niche at the corner of the bar. He let her know he didn't like girls who flirted, but when she burst into laughter, he decided to paw her instead. They lurched into a darker recess of the room. Faroun's eyes roved about the bar until he caught a glimpse of a beautiful woman in a black dress with a string of pearls. His felt his heart drop. She smiled at him over her martini glass as one smiles at a lover from long ago, her deep eyes tinged with melancholy. Lifting her glass, she offered a toast before vanishing in the chattering throng.

"What did you see out there?" asked Ihab Kabir. "Some girl you know?"

"I was mistaken," said Faroun with a secretive smile, realizing it was not Vera Tamiri he had seen, but someone who resembled her.

"They have no sense of *kayf*, these people," said Ihab Kabir.

"And why do you say that, Sergeant?"

"It is my observation. About us and them. Arabs have an inner sense of what is right, or at least we know how to find it. That is our *kayf*. These Westerners, though, they flit about from thing to thing. They have no sense of inner peace. They do not know what it is to reflect on anything. They just do things, and then they wring their hands and don't know what's wrong with them. I think most of the Europeans are godless."

"Well, I wouldn't judge too harshly by what you see here. They've had a bad scare last night and they are blowing off steam."

"If you will excuse me, Chief, it might be said they brought the scare on themselves. They are out of sorts here, aren't they? This is not their place."

Faroun held up his glass, took measure of the colorless liquid, and let the arak slide down his throat. "Perhaps we are all out of sorts and out of place. You know, there are some Arabs who bewail this idea of *kayf*. It is not inner peace, at all, but a delicious languor and excuse for doing nothing. So while the Arab sits in his garden puffing on his hookah beneath a date palm, the European is out being busy and taking charge of the garden. What good is *kayf* if you lose your land?"

If Ihab made a reply, Faroun did not hear it, for a waitress was suddenly shouting in his ear, trying to get Maxim's attention. "I need a bottle of Clicquot!" she cried out to Maxim. Faroun had seen her once or twice before, a pert little Egyptian girl with a coil of jet-black curls.

"What was that?" asked Maxim, leaning over the bar close enough to nibble her ear.

"Clicquot! Clicquot!"

He popped open a bottle and put it on her tray. "You have the beauty of the little black ermine tonight, Esmé."

"And you have the words of a man who wants to get into my pants," she tossed back. "And why not?" she added, winking at him. "You're the boss."

"Women! How can a man not love them?" Maxim exclaimed, as she walked off to a table of boisterous French soldiers. He winked at Faroun just as the telephone behind the bar began jangling.

Faroun turned to Ihab Kabir, but his sergeant had gone. Instead, a paper was on the bar. Opening it, he scanned through the petition for promotion. In a neat, upright hand, Sergeant Ihab Kabir listed his recent services to the state, his adept undercover work, which he begged Faroun to credit him, and the occasions of his saving the life of his superior, two occasions to be precise: at the Al-Quassi Shipping Depot and earlier the same night when he had sent Agent Durac, with an anonymous tip, to the pilgrims' hostel. A claim of dubious merit, thought Faroun, especially since two men had come close to putting a bullet in him. Three, if one counted Durac. Faroun folded the petition and slipped it into a pocket. He would write a note of appreciation for his sergeant's performance file. But he would not recommend the presumptuous Sergeant Kabir for promotion. The sergeant would bear watching for a while. The man was in a hurry to scurry up the ladder. Too much of a hurry.

"That call was for you," said Maxim, tapping Faroun on the arm, "but she rang off. She said there was some kind of trouble at your house in Mohajirene."

31

Perhaps he had seen the blue sports car speed by as he climbed out of the cab and paid his fare. His mind had been elsewhere, not least on the end of a long chase for Vera's killer and his encounter with Umar Tamiri in the cemetery. However, the wide-open front door and the broom leaning on the front step told him something was amiss at the Villa Artemis, the lovely stucco house with the red tiles and the garden his father had purchased in 1903.

New curtains were hanging over the kitchen window, a stepladder in front of the sink. The last of Gert was gone. The new regime was diaphanous, ivory, and suitable for letting light into the bare, although now remarkably clean, kitchen. He didn't have to wonder who had put them up for there was a note from her on the kitchen table, standing up against a basket of fruit bearing a red ribbon. A bottle of the finest Turkish arak had been included, so Faroun took down a newly cleaned glass from the cupboard and poured.

"Madame Montcalm called to tell me you have found justice for Vera," the letter began in the familiar petite script. "She wanted me to express her congratulations and her gratitude for all you've done, for being, as she put it, 'a friend to the delegate.' But there is news both sad and wonderful, Nikolai. The Montcalms will be leaving Damascus but Madame M. has contributed a generous sum to start a charitable fund for Vera Tamiri. And I will administer it! Henri can like it or lump it. . . . The first thing we are going to do is reopen the clinic. It will be the Vera Tamiri Memorial Women's Clinic. The important thing is that the work she started will be continued. It is the best testament, I think. . . ."

The letter continued in this vein for a few sentences before she came to the "personal matter between them," as she put it, a bit fatuously, Faroun thought. There was no longer going to be a personal matter between them, she proclaimed. Consider the curtains a farewell gift from a friend who will always admire you. Consider it your good fortune that I am going. . . . There were some words about her new responsibilities and her love for her children.

He went out to the garden wall with his glass of expensive arak. Though the fires were out, houses still smouldered in the north of the Old City. The shell of the Citadel exhaled black vapors as if from the lair of a sleeping dragon. Movement in the streets . . . troops on patrol, people cleaning up and salvaging what they could, lights coming on against the encroaching darkness. Normalcy was slowly returning, but for Damascus that meant going back to the uneasy balance that had always been, the same balance that had prevailed since the first mud huts had sprung up in the verdant valley three millennia ago. It was the curse of a crossroads.

And Eugenie? Farewell . . . and just as well.

His life was a forest of complications anyway. He didn't need another. He did not need an affair with a married woman. And certainly, Eugenie Poquelin didn't need the complication, either. They had met, touched for a moment, then let go. Naturally, he felt a little sad about that, but he valued the quiet, decorous good-bye. They had both been spared the recriminations and wounded leave-takings experience had taught him to expect.

He was pleased to learn that Vera's clinic would reopen its doors, to learn that she would be remembered in this way. He thought back for a moment about all that had taken place in the past few days since he had first discovered the dead woman in the Barada. How many people had he spoken to about Vera Tamiri? What had he learned?

He had been considering a theory, perhaps *intuition* would be the better word, that explained Vera's plunge into the maelstrom. Most puzzling was her connection with Durac. Mutual need had brought them together at first, for she needed money to support her philanthropy as well as her gambling and Durac required in-formation. It had grown into something else again, this curious partnership. But Faroun thought it was more than money that had drawn her in so deeply.

The Hand of Maisalun had done that—Durac had no doubt un-covered some garbled information on this secret body of Faisal supporters and, suspecting a resistance connection, had put Vera to work finding out about it. After all, she had the contacts among the Damascus elite. The Maisalun story soon became a very per-sonal bit of espionage for Vera. And so she had discovered how her father had betrayed the head of one of the Old Families for his own gain. Had Nayef al Quassi, a man who had ridden with Faisal, been a traitor? Vera must have wondered about this, for there was no denying that the fall of the al Quassi had marked the rise of a powerful Tamiri clan. She must have concluded, as Faroun had, that Umar's wealth was built on a foundation of deceit.

To her sadness, she already knew that her manipulative brother had betrayed his own country by climbing into bed with the French. He needed the French to broker the big government construction contracts. Vera had been driven to get at the truth of the matter. With Maisalun, she had something to use against Umar— Umar the tyrant, Umar the deceiver, Umar the brother who had shamed the family far more than she.

And then there was the wonderful instrument of Salim al Quassi, but with Salim, things had become complicated. Surely, Vera couldn't have been blind to the irony that by working for the French to gain information on the resistance, she had become a traitor too. Following this line of thought, Faroun suspected this knowledge had turned her to despair and led to her downward spiral. Her only lifeline became Salim. He was handsome and wild, and though he was weak, they had endured the same trials and humiliations at the hands of despotic brothers. She had fallen in love with him, redeeming herself through her passion for Umar's enemy even as she used him to bring down Abdullah. It was a game played too close to the edge, and one that could have had no happy end.

There was more to Vera's story than guilt and guile, for in his summation, Faroun perceived her as a woman who was trying to break free of the cage and could not find the right key among the few she held in her hands. At least not in time. Umar had worked too dark and deadly a poison, one that had brought ruin to two families. More than one life had been lost when Vera was tied in a burlap sack and tossed into a river that, legend told, once flowed from the earthly paradise.

Perhaps a monstrous self-hate had driven Umar too, but of this Faroun was not so sure.

He recalled his visit with the blind Sufi, Azad al Abila, in the village of Maraba. They had spoken of the *Arabian Nights* and Azad had reminded him of the story whose title he could not recall—the story about the evil prince who sets about destroying two brothers. Well, that story had found its ending in the cemetery with Umar Tamiri, hadn't it? In this fable, there was no explanation of the evil

that drove the prince to ruin the lives of others. There are n
tives for evil in the old stories. It needs no explanation. Ch
recognize it instantly, as did Toni Moulmenian when he trem
before the Afreet. Evil is impenetrable to the core. And that is
we have amulets like the hand of Fatima. And pray they work.

Faroun looked down in the rocky defile below for a moveme
had suddenly caught his eye. A ghostly, silvery shadow move
among the rocks and thornbushes. The long, thin head of th
hunter peered around a rock and seemed to be looking right at him.
Outlined in the dying sunlight, the saluki was poised to leap and
then bounded off, chasing a furry ball, a hare that had skittered into
the brambles. Of course, it couldn't have been the same hound that
had led him to Faisal's park when the streets of the Old City were
ablaze. There were many stray dogs, after all, and many salukis.

The slamming of the front door ended his meditation.

He must have left it open. A gust of evening wind had closed it,
for the mountain currents picked up this time of day. Still, it
might just be a visitor from past or present, someone who had left
something behind, or unfinished, at this lonely villa overlooking
the ancient city of Damascus.